The *Reluctant* BACHELORETTE

The *Reluctant* BACHELORETTE

Rachael Anderson

HEA Publishing, LLC

ISBN-13: 978-1479269679
ISBN-10: 1479269670

Published by HEA Publishing

For my Taycee Lynne.
Your smile makes me happy.

Other books by Rachael Anderson

Novels
Working it Out
Divinely Designed
Luck of the Draw
Minor Adjustments

Anthologies
All I Want: Three Christmas Romances
*The Timeless Romance Anthology: Summer Wedding
Collection*

One

$\mathcal{F}$lowers everywhere.

Literally everywhere. Five vases spanned the wall of Pat's diminutive, enclosed patio, another sat atop a small table, and a dozen more covered the brick floor. Roses, lilies, daisies, car-nations—a floral menagerie of pink, yellow, purple, red, blue, and white. And if that wasn't enough, rose petals dotted the ground. Thank goodness the patio wasn't large, or Pat would have emptied his entire savings filling the space.

"Wow." What else could Taycee say? As a florist, she loved flowers—breathed them in and used them in creations every day. But this display was something else. Something else entirely.

"Do you like it?" There was apprehension in Pat's voice, the desire to please. "I know you love flowers, so I thought I'd get you some of everything."

And he had. Even sunflowers. Yikes.

"It looks like my shop," Taycee managed.

Pat grinned, showing his two dimples. "Exactly what I was going for. I'm glad you noticed. I wanted it to feel like home."

But she didn't live at her shop. She worked there. And at the end of the day, Taycee only brought home a small bouquet, and for good reason. There can be too much of a good thing. Way too much. The proof surrounded her.

Although it was sweet of Pat to go to all of this trouble, dates with him were becoming increasingly romantic and extravagant, which wasn't okay. Taycee didn't want him thinking they were serious or spending this kind of money on her. "Pat, I, uh . . . don't know what to say."

"Say you'll marry me." Pat knelt in front of her, mashing a few red rose petals under his knee.

Taycee froze. Oh no. Not this. Not now. How did she not see this coming? If she had, she'd have ended the relationship weeks ago—before Pat had gone to all this effort. Before she'd have to tell him no.

Taycee shook her head back and forth in slow motion. How could she tell such a nice guy that she didn't feel the same way? That she never would. This was exactly why Taycee had always ended relationships before they reached this point. To avoid moments like this.

"Taycee, I love everything about you—from your love of flowers and the outdoors, to your kindness, your beauty, and your smile. You are everything I've wanted to find in a wife. Please say yes."

Taycee bit her lip. She should have said something before he launched into the obviously prepared speech. Now it would be even worse.

"Pat." Taycee pulled him to his feet. His hands tried to circle her waist, but she held on to them, keeping space between them. "Listen. I think you're a great guy. One of the best, actually. But—"

"Don't say but," Pat said, freeing his hands so they could frame her face, with his thumb resting against her lips, shushing her. "*Please* don't say but."

"I'm sorry," she whispered against his thumb.

The light faded from blue eyes that always glowed with happiness. Because that's who Pat was. Ever and always happy, with a ready smile and dimples that appeared often. But now only sorrow remained—a sorrow that bored a hole into Taycee's heart and made her want to run away. "I'm so, so sorry."

A slight nod and he took a step back, his eyes pleading with her to stop him. Another step and he was gone, leaving Taycee alone on his back patio. The front screen door slammed shut, and a car engine rumbled in his driveway. As the sound faded off down the street, Taycee sighed and located a pad and pen on his kitchen counter.

> *Pat, I hope you'll find a girl sometime soon who's worthy of you and these beautiful flowers. I'm so flattered that you thought that person was me, but it's not. Trust me, there's someone better for you out there. I will always think the world of you.*

Leaving the note on the patio, Taycee walked through the empty apartment and out the front door to her white Toyota Camry. She would miss Pat and his quick, boyish smile—but not enough. It was never enough. Not when a vivid image of dark brown eyes still frequented her dreams.

For crying out loud, it's been ten years! Forget him already! He's gone and won't be coming back. He lied to you. Broke his promise. Deal with it and move on.

But at the back of her mind, Taycee worried that he'd ruined her. That no matter how nice, how smart, or how handsome a guy was, he wouldn't be able to erase the memory of Luke Carney—someone who'd left their small Colorado town nearly a decade ago, took her heart with him, and had never come back. Sometimes Taycee felt like hunting him down just so she could punch him hard in the face. More than once, like one of those scenes in a movie.

3

That's for leaving and never coming back. That's for breaking your promise. And that's for breaking my heart!

Lately, dating had become an almost frenzied quest to find a guy who could free her from the shackles of Luke's memory—someone who could make her feel something stronger than respect and like. Someone who could make her *want* to say "yes."

But it was no use. Taycee only ended up hurting unsuspecting guys. Guys who didn't deserve to be hurt. Like Pat.

Well, no more. It had gone too far this time, and Taycee was through. Through with flirting. Through with dating. Through with trying. Maybe if she moved on with the rest of her life, Luke's memory would move on, too.

Two

The Bloom boutique, a refurbished cottage on Main Street, charmed Shelter Springs with its flower lined walkway and yellow siding with white trim. It exuded cozy, and the moment it hit the market three years earlier, Taycee had been first in line to make an offer. Now, it was hers.

The bells on the front door jingled.

"Be right there!" Taycee called from the back.

"No need," a light, breezy voice announced. Jessa McCray waltzed through to the back room and hopped up on the counter next to Taycee, swinging her strappy sandaled feet and showing off her pedicure. Always dressed to impress, with her short, highlighted blonde hair, she never looked anything less than stunning.

Taycee pushed one last sunflower into the green foam and stepped back to study the arrangement. Perfect.

"It's gorgeous. Who's it for?" Jessa asked.

"Mr. Benion."

"Our old biology teacher?"

"One and the same."

"Why?" Jessa's perfectly tweezed arched eyebrows drew together. "Unless . . . wait. Don't tell me he's actually dating someone."

A laugh escaped Taycee's mouth. Jessa sounded so shocked, as if no one in their right mind would ever go out with poor Mr. Benion. "You didn't hear it from me, but when he ordered the arrangement, he asked if I knew what Maris's favorite flowers are."

Jessa's jaw dropped, as well as her voice. "Shut up. Are you serious? Mr. Benion and Maris?"

Taycee shrugged. "Who knows? I just do as my customers ask."

"You never do as *I* ask."

"I meant my paying customers."

Jessa let out an exaggerated sigh. "And you call yourself a friend."

"Your *best* friend, and don't you forget it," Taycee said as she pushed in the plastic card holder and slid the white envelope into place.

"Um, yeah . . ." Jessa hedged. "Funny you should mention that."

"Why?" Taycee said, wary. It had been awhile since Jessa had played the "best friend" card, and it wasn't a good thing when she did. Her favors were never small.

"I'm actually here to call in a little favor." Jessa bit down on her lower lip, moving it back and forth between her teeth.

"What's up?"

Jessa hopped down from the counter and focused her light brown eyes on Taycee. "Remember in high school when you snuck out past curfew to meet David at the movies?"

"Uh . . . yeah." Oh no, not this. Not the favor of all favors. Taycee had secretly hoped it had joined the archives of forgotten memories. If only she could be that lucky.

Jessa stepped closer. "And remember how your parents called my house, and I lied for you and told them you were studying with me?"

"Maybe."

"And remember how you promised me you'd do anything to pay me back?"

"That part's a little hazy." Why oh why had she ever made such a promise? Especially knowing full well Jessa would never forget and it would come back to haunt her one day. Today, as it turned out.

Jessa picked up a discarded sunflower and plucked the petals one by one. "Hazy or not, I'm calling in that promise, best friend of mine."

Taycee grabbed the sunflower from Jessa, saving the remaining petals. "Sorry, but I think there's a clause somewhere that states all promises are null and void after seven years."

"Not a chance." Jessa smirked. "Those kinds of promises never expire. Besides, it's too late anyway."

Oh no. What did Jessa do now? "Too late for what?"

"To say no." Jessa shrugged as if it were no big deal. "You're already committed."

"Committed to what? Jessa! You can't commit me to anything without asking first. Even you should know that." Not that it really came as a shock. Jessa always did whatever she wanted, because if Jessa thought something was a good idea, then of course it was.

With a sweep of her hand, Jessa brushed her layered bangs to the side. "So how did your date go with Pat last night?"

"Not so fast. I want to know what this favor is first."

"And I want to know about your date with Pat."

Taycee's fingers itched to strangle her friend, but Jessa was nothing if not resilient. Going up against her took Taycee back to her sixth grade spelling bee, when she'd made it to the final round where she'd faced off against Daphne—the school know-it-all. Taycee had been determined to win, but after going back and forth and back and forth for over four hours—yes, four—Taycee finally misspelled a word on purpose just to put an end to it. Pure torture. That's what it had been.

Just like trying to win an argument with Jessa.

"So . . . how did it go?" Jessa repeated.

Taycee sighed. "It didn't. We broke up." She left it at that. If Jessa ever found out that Pat had actually proposed—especially how he'd done it—the poor guy would become the subject of one too many jokes. He was too nice for that.

Jessa examined her nails. "And another one bites the dust."

"A little harsh, don't you think?" Pat hadn't tried to call or stop by, and probably never would again. Which was fine. But Taycee didn't like the way things had ended—so unfinished. As if she'd broken something, and then left without repairing it.

"Harsh, but true," Jessa said. "How many guys have you been through this year? Three so far, right? And it's not even May yet."

Taycee frowned as she fiddled with the sunflowers in the finished bouquet. Jessa was right, but that part of her life was over now. She'd always wanted to get more into the wedding business with her flower shop, and it was time to focus on that instead.

"Hey, you heard Luke Carney's back in town, right?"

A sunflower stem broke between Taycee's fingers, and the flower landed with a small thud on the countertop at the same time her heart thudded to the floor. She stared at the fallen flower, feeling a creepy-crawly sensation move over her body. Like a million tiny somethings had landed on her and were now picking away at her skin. She wanted to shake the feeling off. Start jumping up and down and bat it all away.

Luke? Back? Impossible.

"You know, Caleb's old friend?" Jessa said. "The guy you used to be secretly in love with?"

Taycee turned to Jessa as if she'd said the most outrageous thing. Something that couldn't possibly be true even though it was. "I was never in love with him."

"Please," Jessa said. "If I had a nickel for every story you told me about him, I'd be rich enough to save Shelter. I feel like I know the guy, and I've never even met him."

Taycee swallowed, fighting back that creepy-crawly feeling again. Ten years and the mere mention of his name brought on a panic attack. Pathetic. Deep breath in. Deep breath out. In. Out.

"Is he here to visit?" Taycee managed. Please let it only be a temporary thing.

"Nope. For good," Jessa said. "Or so the rumor mill says. According to the mayor, Luke bought the old McCann place and is planning to set up a veterinary practice here."

It were as if the room suddenly drained of oxygen. Taycee couldn't breathe. For good? Why? Why Shelter? Why now? His parents had moved away years ago, so why come back here? Why not find some other small town to post his sign and open for business?

No. He couldn't come back. He'd already done enough damage, and besides, Shelter Springs was already taken.

By her.

"Earth to Taycee," Jessa cooed.

Taycee's hand shook as she reached for another sunflower to replace the broken one. "Sorry, what did you say?"

"Nothing important." Jessa pushed away from the counter and stole an Andes mint from the candy jar. "But about that favor . . . you're good for it?"

"Yeah, sure, whatever." Who cared about some stupid favor? Taycee had bigger things to worry about.

"Ta ta." Seconds later, the bells rang again, and the door fell closed behind Jessa.

Taycee slumped against the counter, needing the support it offered. A reoccurring nightmare had just become reality. Luke was back. In town. For good.

Heaven help her.

Three

Taycee breezed into the diner and held back a groan. Fabulous. Liza was working today—Liza Woolrich, president of the Taycee Emerson Not-a-Fan Club. It had all started back in high school, when Liza's boyfriend dumped her and asked Taycee to the prom. Taycee had been paying for it ever since. Even more so now that Liza worked at Maris's Diner—the *only* diner in town, and therefore Taycee's only option on days like today when she didn't have the time or the inclination to drive home for lunch.

Not that coming here would be any faster now.

Taycee glanced at a clock. Only thirty minutes until she needed to be back at her shop. Was it enough? The diner was practically empty, so there was at least a chance. Stupid high school grudges. Why couldn't Liza get over it already?

A deep breath, and Taycee stepped up to the counter.

"Well, if it isn't Taycee Emerson." Liza's smile was as fake as her hot pink nails and current peroxide-blonde hair color.

"Hey, Liza, how's it going?"

"Just peachy. What can I get ya?"

Did she really have to ask? It was the same every time. "I'll have a chicken salad on wheat with some curly fries on the side. Just like always." Taycee's fingers drummed on the marble counter as she eyed the clock once more. "I actually have to leave in about twenty minutes. Do you think it will be ready by then?"

Liza flashed another smile and flipped through her pad. "There are several orders in front of yours so I can't say for sure. I guess you'll just have to wait your turn like everyone else."

Everyone else? Only two other people sat in the diner, both of whom had their lunch already. The bell on the door jingled, and someone shuffled in behind Taycee. "Are you talking about orders for pick-up?" Taycee asked.

"What?" Liza blinked at her through mascara-caked eyelashes.

Taycee spoke slowly. "You said there are several orders ahead of mine, and since Will and Kris already have their lunch, I'm wondering if the others are call-ins."

The pencil tapped against the pad. "Uh, yeah. Of course."

"Whose?"

"Whose what?" Liza frowned.

Once again, Taycee slowed her speech. "Whose. Orders. Are they?" No way was Liza getting away with this. Not today. Not after the sleepless night Taycee had spent agonizing over seeing Luke again. Liza had picked the wrong day to mess with her.

Liza's eyes narrowed. "I'm sorry, but that's really none of your business. It's, uh . . . classified."

Classified? That was the excuse she chose? Taycee almost laughed out loud. "So relieved to know you keep everyone's orders private." She leaned across the table and whispered loudly, "Because I'd *die* if anyone found out I'd ordered a chicken salad sandwich with curly fries."

"I'll pretend I didn't hear that then," a deep voice spoke from behind. "I'd hate to see you die before we have a chance to catch up."

Taycee froze even as her heart pounded. No. Not now. Not here. Not when she was wearing her oldest jeans and rattiest T-shirt and arguing with none other than Liza Woolrich. It wasn't right.

Slowly, Taycee twisted around, and then clenched her jaw to keep it from dropping. It was like watching the Captain America movie where the scrawny guy goes into the machine and comes out looking . . . well, everything but scrawny. Not that Luke could have ever been called scrawny before. Skinny, maybe, but that was about it. Now, he looked toned. Robust. Solid. And drop-dead gorgeous. His dark, wavy hair was shorter now, but his eyes—those amazing, beautiful eyes—were still that rich coffee color that used to melt her heart.

Used to. *Used to, Taycee! Get a grip. It's been ten years for Pete's sake.*

Luke flashed a disarming smile—the same smile pictured in several of the photos she kept stashed in a scrapbook at the bottom of her pajama drawer. "Wow, look at you, all grown up and everything," he said.

For some reason the comment made Taycee feel like a little girl playing dress-up with adult clothes. He only remembered her as the gangly fourteen-year-old with braces and a rat's nest for hair. Taycee forced a smile that strained her cheeks. "Luke? Wow. What's it been? Five years?"

"More like ten, but who's counting?"

Who indeed. "So . . . what are you doing back in town?"

His arms folded, and he cocked his head toward the street outside. "I'm leasing the McCann place just outside of town. Thinking of setting up a veterinary practice here."

Leasing—*not* buying. Jessa needed to get her facts straight. Taycee gave him three months before he was gone again. "That's . . . uh . . . great. So . . . *so* great."

The register slammed shut, and Taycee twisted back around, grateful for Liza's interruption. "I'll let you know when your order's ready," Liza said with a touch too much sweetness. "You're welcome to wait at the bar."

"Thanks." Stomach rumbling, Taycee stepped away and slid onto a barstool.

"Wow. Luke Carney, is that really you?" Liza's squeal made Taycee wince.

"In the flesh." Luke planted his hands on the counter as he studied the menu.

"I heard you were back in town. I hope this means we'll see you around the diner often."

"Thanks, uh . . ." Luke eyed her nametag. "Liza. I'm sure I'll be here often enough, especially if the food tastes as good as it used to."

"Oh, it does. You can trust me on that. What can I get you?"

Taycee forced her attention to some daytime talk show playing on the TV. Her fingers played in her lap as she fought the desire to peek at him again. Why hadn't she put on her cute jeans that morning? Dabbed on a little more makeup? Actually styled her hair instead of pulling it back?

Taycee shifted in her seat. What she needed was an excuse. A reason to leave and come back later—*after* Luke had gone. Her shop. Yeah, that would work. And it wouldn't be a complete lie since she really did have to be back, just not this second.

Perfect. It's settled. Now leave.

But Luke had already pulled up a stool next to her, and now he sat with his elbow on the counter, facing her with that lopsided smile she used to love. A day or two's worth of growth framed his face, and Taycee felt the urge to reach out and run her fingers along the scruff. He looked really good. Taycee should have run when she had the chance.

"So, how've you been?" he asked.

"Good."

Luke's head shook as he studied her. "It's crazy how the town looks pretty much the same and yet everyone has changed so much. Is Caleb still around? I can't believe we didn't stay in touch."

And whose fault is that? Taycee wanted to ask. "He's in Phoenix now, but he should be back in a few weeks. He wants to set up a practice somewhere near here."

"Practice?"

"Law." How pathetic Luke didn't know that.

"Really? Caleb went to law school?" Luke chuckled. "He always did love a good argument, didn't he?"

"Still does." Which he would know if he'd bothered to keep in touch.

"And he's coming back to Shelter? Awesome. It'll be just like old times."

"Yeah . . . totally." Not. Taycee shifted in her seat, willing Liza to hurry for once in her life. The creepy-crawly panicky feeling was back, making her antsy to leave.

Luke's hand dropped to the counter and tapped out a rhythm. "Your parents still around?"

Good. Neutral topic. Taycee could handle neutral. "No. They retired and moved to Florida a few years ago. Warmer climate and all that."

"But you're still here," Luke pointed out. "I would have thought you'd be long gone by now. What kept you here?"

So much for neutral. A quick glance at the clock and Taycee pushed the barstool back. "Believe it or not, I actually like it here," she said with an edge to her voice. Before she made a complete fool of herself, she added, "Sorry, but I've got to go. Great seeing you though, and good luck with your practice."

Taycee started past him, but a hand on her arm stopped her. His touch felt like a warm jolt—uncomfortable yet nice at the same time.

"Hey, are you free for dinner tonight?" Luke asked.

Her eyes flew to his. Did he just ask her out? "Uh, d-dinner?"

His hand still on her arm, Luke nodded. "Yeah. You know that meal you eat in the evening? Between lunch and dessert? What do you say? I'd love to catch up."

A traitorous thrill shot through Taycee. Not good. She couldn't say yes. Wouldn't. "Um, sure, that'd be great." Stupid, stupid, stupid.

Luke's hand fell from her arm as he reached for his cell. "What's your number? I've got a few things to do this afternoon, but I'll call you later when I know what time I'll be done."

Taycee rattled off her number as Liza approached, flashing Luke a smile. Before she could say anything, Taycee asked, "Hey, Liza, any idea how long it will be? I really need to get back."

Liza shot an annoyed look her way. "Not sure, but you know what they say, 'Good things come to those who wait.'"

If by good, Liza meant a warm and soggy chicken salad sandwich, then Taycee would have to take her word for it. "Can I pick it up in an hour or so?"

"Sure, whatever." Liza turned her attention back to Luke. "So, you're setting up a vet clinic?"

Taycee offered Luke a quick nod and nearly bolted for the door, leaving him in Liza's obviously capable and collected hands. So not fair that Liza could remain so composed while Taycee could barely utter a coherent sentence. What she needed was air. Fresh air. Air that didn't smell like Luke and make her do idiotic things.

The first meeting is always the hardest. It's all downhill from here.

16

Taycee breathed in deeply. The further from the diner she got, the calmer she felt. Maybe it was actually good that Luke was back. Maybe now she could learn to see him as a regular guy, just like everyone else. Maybe she could finally get over him. And maybe, just maybe, when he left again— which he would, she was sure of it—he would take all of those memories with him.

Taycee waved goodbye to Mr. Benion, who left with yet another sunflower arrangement, and then made her way to the back of the shop. One rose bouquet to go and she could return to the diner for her lunch. Her *cold* lunch. Taycee frowned.

Her fingers ran across the shelf of vases, finally pulling down a clear, square one. Perfect. Different enough to make the unoriginal red rose bouquet look a little more original. Red roses might symbolize love, but in Taycee's mind, different was always better. Much, much better. Which was why she always kept a stash of flowers like Jean Giono's on hand for those blessed customers who said, "Surprise me."

They were never disappointed.

Taycee hunted through the floral refrigerator for the best roses and baby's breath. Minutes later, two dozen long-stemmed roses dropped to the counter next to the clear glass vase. Time to create—her favorite part of owning a floral shop.

Bells jingled, and someone stepped into the store. Taycee leaned sideways to get a better look, only to immediately duck back out of the way. Luke. Here. In her shop. Why? Taking another step sideways, Taycee's elbow caught the vase and sent it shattering to the floor. She groaned inwardly. So much for staying hidden.

"Taycee? That you? Everything okay?" Luke's voice called out.

Taycee eyed the storage closet longingly, wanting nothing more than to disappear inside and hide like a coward. Instead, she sank to the floor to pick up the bigger pieces. "I'm fine. Be right there."

Footsteps approached, and a pair of sneakers came to a stop beside the broken glass. "What happened?"

Taycee's eyes travelled up his body. Toned calves, plaid shorts, dark T-shirt, beautiful eyes. Why did he have to look so good? Why couldn't he have hair growing from his nose? Nasty warts covering his face? Why couldn't he smell like the animals he took care of?

Luke set a Styrofoam box that he'd been holding on the counter. "Here, let me help you with that. Do you have a broom?"

The spicy, fried aroma of curly fries wafted through the room. Glass shards forgotten, Taycee rose slowly, staring at the white take-out box. "You brought me my lunch?" *No, don't be nice. Please don't be nice.*

"Just call me your own private delivery boy."

"Liza actually let you?" If only Taycee could have been a fly on the wall for that conversation.

"It took some coercion, and I had to sign a waiver that I wouldn't tell anyone else what you ordered, since, you know, it's classified info." He grinned. "She also made me promise not to eat any, which I tried really hard not to do."

Taycee laughed. "Liza probably laced them with something and didn't want you to suffer the consequences."

"She loves you that much?"

"And then some."

Luke shoved his hands in his pockets and leaned against the counter. "I did eat a couple on my way here. But I feel fine, so they must be safe."

"Wow, how kind of you to risk your life for me."

"I'm thoughtful like that."

As if. Thoughtful people didn't just disappear. Taycee opened the take-out box and stuffed a fry into her mouth to keep from saying as much.

Luke glanced around. "Where's that broom?"

"Broom?"

He pointed to the floor. "Broken glass?"

"Oh, right. Just a sec." Taycee retrieved the broom from a storage closet and started sweeping up the mess.

"I can do that. You should eat. I could hear your stomach growling from the diner." Luke took the broom from her hands and started sweeping.

Taycee frowned as she shoved another fry in her mouth, chewing slowly. Luke wasn't supposed to be the kind of guy who would sweep her floor so she could eat. He was supposed to be thoughtless, annoying, and forgetful. He was supposed to be a jerk.

Hmm . . . maybe he could be a jerk for *not* being a jerk. Yeah, that might work.

Luke dumped the glass into the trash and nodded toward the food. "You're not eating."

Probably because she was staring. At him. Her cheeks burned as she forced her gaze away and picked up another fry.

The broom went back in the closet, and Luke scanned the shop. "Nice place you got here. I'd never have pegged you for a florist."

The fry turned bitter as she swallowed it. Wow. Did Luke really not remember? The goodbye present? Her strange fascination with flowers that he used to tease her about? She'd relived those memories over and over and over again. Every word, every look, every smile. But had Luke? Apparently not. Taycee suddenly felt as memorable as a blade of grass.

"Flowers have always been a hobby of mine," she said. "I opened the shop three years ago."

"Looks like business is good."

"It's hit and miss, but most days I stay busy enough. I'm really hoping to get involved with more weddings at some point. I've done a few for some local families, but they couldn't afford much, so we kept it small. I'd love to do something bigger though—something fun and extravagant, with a little more earning potential."

Luke nodded. "Hopefully I'll stay busy enough with my practice." He leaned against the counter and folded his arms. "I have to admit, I'm a little worried. The town seems . . . slower somehow. But it could just be that I've lived in a larger city for the past decade."

"It's not you." Taycee twisted a curly fry between her fingers. "Shelter's kind of floundering right now. Because of increased competition with commercial farms, the independents aren't able to sell their crops for as much as they used to and can't pay off their loans. The banks, of course, are now refusing to loan them any more money, which is why so many farms have gone under, and why more will continue to do so. If things don't start picking up soon, there won't be enough people around to keep the few businesses left afloat. In fact, the only reason I've been able to keep my shop open is because most of my business comes from neighboring towns."

Luke's expression turned pensive, possibly even worried. "I was actually shocked to see the McCann farm on the market. Never thought they'd move."

"They had no choice."

"That's too bad."

"Yeah, it is," said Taycee. "But there is some light at the end of the tunnel. My friend, Jessa, came up with an idea to hopefully turn things around. She's convinced that if the farmers will pool their resources and start their own farmers market chain, they can sell their crops locally and get a much higher return than they would get through wholesalers."

Luke nodded slowly, as if considering it. "That's going to take some major work and money to get going. Not to mention the fact that it will put a lot of extra strain on the farmers to do their own selling."

"I know, but it's their only shot right now." And pretty

much the main topic of conversation around town these days. What will the farmers do if they're forced into foreclosure? What will become of Shelter Springs? A pit formed in Taycee's stomach every time she thought about it. "A few months ago, the mayor even hired Jessa to come up with some fund-raising ideas. Supposedly she has something in the works, but she hasn't said what that is yet. Whatever it is, I hope it will be successful because the farms will be ready to start selling mid-June, which means we have to come up with 50K by then."

Luke whistled. "50K in two months. She's got her work cut out for her, doesn't she?"

"Yeah, but she's pretty motivated," Taycee said. "When she was fifteen, her aunt and uncle—Sue and Martin McCray—took her in. They even helped pay for her college, and now she's determined to use her newly acquired business skills to help them back. If she doesn't, the McCray's will be forced to foreclose on their farm when the loan comes due this fall."

Luke shook his head. "Here's hoping it works and she can pull together that much money. I'd hate to see this town die, not when I've only just come back."

Only then did Taycee realize that she'd given Luke a reason to think his vet clinic could survive here also, if Jessa's plan worked. What was she thinking? She should have kept that info to herself and told him it was only a matter of time before the town went kaput, so he should really get out while he still could.

Luke pushed away from the counter and flicked her under her chin. "Well, it's nice to that you're still around. Enjoy your lunch."

Taycee's eyes followed him as he left. Seriously? Chin-flicking? Granted, ratty jeans and an old T-shirt didn't exactly scream sophistication, but Taycee was no longer fourteen. Nor was she the little girl who used to follow him and Caleb around like a lost puppy.

She'd grown up and had a mind of her own now—a mind that was smart enough to know that if she wasn't careful, Luke would break her heart all over again.

Four

hree days and not a word from Luke. No promised phone call, no dinner, not even a text to cancel. Nothing. It was like he'd already packed up and left town. So pathetic that Taycee had kept her phone nearby the entire time, willing it to ring.

Luke really hadn't changed. Ten years and he was the same old, unreliable, undependable Luke. Out of sight, out of mind. That was his mantra. If only Taycee could adopt it as her own and stop thinking about him.

She sighed and turned her phone to vibrate before walking in the back door of the crowded town hall. Wow. Were all town meetings as packed as this one? There wasn't an empty chair in sight.

"Why, Taycee," said Lexie, her crochet needles pausing, "how nice to see you here, supporting the town. I can't remember you ever coming before."

Probably because Taycee had always avoided town meetings. Long, depressing discussions about the town's troubles wasn't her type of thing. In fact, she wouldn't be here now if Jessa would just call her back. "Hey, have you seen Jessa anywhere?"

Lexie's finger pointed toward the front of the room. Sure enough, on the second row in an aisle seat sat Jessa. Even in the florescent lighting, her gorgeous highlights shone. Was it possible for Jessa to have a bad hair day? So unfair. Taycee grabbed a folding metal chair from the back and carted it up the aisle, setting it up beside her friend. "Hey, Jess."

Startled blue eyes glanced Taycee's way. "What are you doing here? You never come to the town meetings. And you can't sit there."

"Why not?"

"Because that's the aisle."

Taycee plopped down in the chair and gestured toward the space between her and the next chair. "There's still room for people to get around me."

"What are you doing here anyway? You hate town meetings."

"You left a message saying you needed a couple bouquets made for something tomorrow night, but you didn't give me any details. Since you never called me back, I couldn't put in the order. Now I have to drive to Colorado Springs in the morning to pick up whatever it is you need. Which is what, by the way?" Jessa was notorious for doing stuff like this. She seemed to think Taycee was a mind reader and would know exactly what to create based on "I need two bouquets for a town function tomorrow night. You don't mind, do you? Thanks, you're the best!" End call.

"I would have given you more details if it mattered," Jessa said. "It's only the mayor's annual appreciation dinner. No big deal. Throw some blue daisies in a vase and call it good. Simple."

"There's nothing simple about blue daisies, Jess. They need to be dyed."

Jessa rolled her eyes. "Then throw some white daisies in a vase."

White daisies? Was she serious? Those were something you'd give to a teacher or a friend in the hospital, not something you'd use to accent the mayor's annual appreciation dinner. "Are you sure that's what you want? White daisies?"

"I'm saying I don't care," Jessa hissed. "Do whatever you want."

"Fine. How big do I need to make them?"

"I'll say this one more time. I. Don't. Care."

Taycee settled back in her chair and folded her arms against the chilly air coming through the a/c vent. "Sheesh, someone's a little testy tonight."

"Sorry, I've just got more important stuff to worry about than a couple of flower bouquets."

"Like what?"

The mayor stood and started the meeting. Instead of answering, Jessa bit her lip and fingers tapped staccato-like on her knees. Wow, she really was anxious about something. Taycee was about to ask what when the mayor called out Jessa's name and said the floor was hers.

Ah, Taycee should have known. Jessa hated presenting because of all the opinionated people in Shelter who had no problem voicing their thoughts. For the past five months, ever since Jessa had started working for the town, Taycee had heard all about it. Meetings that dragged on and on and on and made Taycee even more determined to stay away from them.

Jessa faced the crowd and clasped her fingers together before clearing her throat. "Several months ago, I introduced the idea of forming a co-op and starting a small chain of farmers markets. Many of you were opposed at first because of the risk and investment involved, but after several weeks of debates, the majority of you all agreed to give it a try if we were able to come up with the $50,000 needed. I'm here tonight to tell you that I think I've found a way."

Jessa lifted a poster from behind the desk and set it on an easel. It pictured Main Street with the words, "Help Save Shelter!" blazoned across the clear blue sky. "Now, many of you know how popular The Bachelor and The Bachelorette shows are on TV right now, so I figured we'd capitalize on that fame. What I've proposed to the council is this: That we create our own show, similar in nature, called *Shelter's Bachelorette.*"

Whispered voices seemed to surround Taycee as she sat in her aisle seat apart from everyone else. Not quite seeing Jessa's vision, Taycee bit her lip as she rubbed at a non-existent spot on her khaki capris. Of all the fundraising ideas out there, this is what Jessa had come up with? A bachelorette show? How in the world was that supposed to raise $50,000?

Jessa forged on, speaking above the murmurs. "Believe it or not, it's already proven to be successful. I came up with this idea months ago, and it's already in the works. A website has been launched, prominent newspapers have advertised it in their papers across the country, and hundreds of bachelors have already emailed us application videos. We even have them narrowed down to the final twenty."

Jessa held out a staying hand to the growing voices. "Please keep in mind that these bachelors understand this is a charity event. They will pay their way here and will cover all expenses related to their dates with the bachelorette. Although we hope the bachelorette will find true love, this show is about funding a co-op to help save the farming community in Shelter."

"How's a stupid polygamist show going to fund anything?" A deep voice boomed from the back of the room, voicing the thoughts of probably everyone present. Taycee included. The question opened the floodgates of even more questions because it suddenly seemed like everyone had something to say. Taycee kept her thoughts to herself, more interested in hearing how it had already proven to be successful.

The mayor's gavel struck his desk a few times, restoring order. "Zip it, folks. I'm going to ask you to please listen to the rest of Miss McCray's presentation before shooting anymore questions her way. I think you'll find she'll answer most of them if you'll just listen."

The room quieted, but the murmuring continued on a more subdued level. Taycee wasn't sure what to think about it all. As much as she wanted to support Jessa, who would be interested in watching a dating show set in Shelter Springs, Colorado?

Her head held high, Jessa continued, "We set up a donation account on our site a few months back and have already received some donation money. In addition, because our website is getting a lot of traffic, we're also bringing in some advertising revenue. So far we've made a couple thousand dollars, and the show hasn't even officially started."

"Are you jerkin' my chain?" a man called out. "There's people out there donatin' to our town?"

"That's right," Jessa said. "And as the word continues to get out, more people will contribute, I'm sure of it. I've interviewed my aunt and uncle, in addition to a couple of others in this room and have posted those interviews on the site. Believe it or not, there are a lot of people out there who don't want to see the independent farms go under. In addition, the local viewers that we draw to the show will also be potential customers. So this is not only a fundraising opportunity, but a great way to get the word out about the market you will open in a couple months."

More murmurs swept through the room as Taycee shifted in her seat. Although Jessa had made some good points and had obviously put a lot of thought and planning into this, Taycee still wasn't sold on the idea. A few thousand in advertising revenue and donations wouldn't make a dent in the amount of money that needed to be raised.

Jessa lifted another poster and placed it on the easel. The schedule. "As you can see, the show will run for six weeks. We'll be doing things a little differently than the real show. In *Shelter's Bachelorette*, our bachelorette won't be choosing the bachelors. That will be up to the viewers, who will vote at the end of each round of dating. I like to think of it as The Bachelorette meets American Idol."

"Polygamy *and* matchmaking?" a man said from the back. "What century are we living in anyway?"

Laughter sounded throughout the room, Taycee's included, only she muffled hers behind her hand. If every town meeting was this entertaining, she'd have to come more often. No wonder Jessa wasn't a fan. She hated being challenged.

Jessa leveled a look at the man. "You're missing the point. By giving the viewers the power to choose, we're giving them what they really want—control over which bachelor wins. Plus, we'll be able to charge them a dollar a vote and potentially earn way more than we ever could through advertising and donations."

That seemed to quiet everyone. Or at least shock them into momentary silence.

Although Taycee still couldn't imagine this becoming popular enough to bring in that kind of money, Jessa's confidence made her believe in the possibility. Besides, it was better than sitting around and doing nothing.

"Burt and Megan, who recently returned home for the summer, have agreed to volunteer their time and talents to film and edit the show. They have a lot of experience and will do a great job," Jessa said. "Each date will be filmed, rapidly edited, and then posted on our site. The voting will open for two days and the winners announced at a rose ceremony similar to what they do on the real show. Only in ours, the bachelorette will be just as surprised as the bachelors. Granted, this won't be nearly as professional as

NBC's show, but it *will* be good and the viewers are going to eat it up."

"You're sayin' we can watch it on our computer?" a woman spoke up.

"If you have an internet, then yes." Jessa drew in a deep breath and scanned the crowd. "I can only imagine what you all must be thinking, but I want to reiterate that this is about saving our town. I'm sick of seeing farms go under and good people being forced to leave Shelter. Starting right now, we're going to put a stop to that. We're going to earn enough money, we're going to start that co-op, and we're going to keep you all in business. And if, for whatever reason, this doesn't work, then I'll think of something else."

Jessa's hand slapped the podium beside her. "I refuse to give up."

A hush fell over the crowd, and Taycee swallowed, feeling suddenly close to tears. Jessa's words seemed to open up people's minds and pave the way to acceptance. No one had anymore arguments—at least none they verbalized.

"Who's the bachelorette?" a girl from the front row asked.

Jessa smiled—her first real smile all night. "If you want to know that, you can check out our site tonight when you get home. Increased traffic looks good to potential advertisers, so this is my way of forcing you to get on our site and drive up that traffic."

"What's the URL?" A man held up his phone. "I'll look it up right now."

"Sorry, but you'll have to wait until the end of the meeting for that info. For now, rest assured that we've found the perfect bachelorette. She's ready and excited to do this."

Taycee glanced around the room, wondering who it could be. Marie? Stephanie? Or—heaven forbid—Liza? Whoever it was, at least they were excited about it. Taycee certainly wouldn't be.

A woman raised her voice above the noise of the crowd.

"Is one of the bachelors from Shelter?"

"No," said Jessa. "We've kept everything quiet around town until we got the ball rolling, so before tonight only a few people even knew about it. Besides, it would be an unfair advantage to have a bachelor from the same town as the bachelorette, don't you think? All the finalists are from various states around the country."

A woman's voice called out above the chatter. "I think it's only fittin' to have a representative from Shelter be one of the bachelors. This is a charity event for us, after all."

A murmur of approval swept through the room, and Jessa nodded slowly, as if considering it. Finally, she shrugged. "All right, if that's what it takes to make you happy, let's do it. We can always start off with twenty-one bachelors instead. Any suggestions?"

"What about Mike?"

"James would be good."

"Stan gets my vote!"

Jessa laughed. "Remember the bachelorette is under thirty. Let's not rob the cradle, people."

A collective chuckle filled the room.

Taycee smiled and folded her arms. Too bad no one suggested Luke. He'd be perfect. In fact—more than perfect. Taycee's smile widened as she pictured him having to compete with twenty other guys for the attention of one girl. It would serve him right. A covert glance around the room, and Taycee assured herself that Luke was absent.

"I vote Luke Carney," Taycee blurted before she lost her nerve.

"Oh yes, Luke would be perfect!" someone agreed.

"If Luke's a bachelor, can I be the bachelorette?" an older woman asked, making everyone laugh.

"Oooh, me too!" another woman called out.

From the back of the room, a deep voice cut through the noise of the crowd. "Don't you think I should be the one to decide whether or not I participate?"

Five

Luke stepped from the shadows. His dark eyes captured Taycee's for a moment before they shifted to Jessa.

Taycee twisted forward and sunk low in her seat—the seat that was smack dab in the middle of the aisle. Oh joy. Why couldn't she have kept her mouth shut? Seriously, was she the only one who never came to these meetings? How did Luke even know about it?

"Consider it a welcome home gift, Luke," Jessa said, smiling. "I think it's a great suggestion, especially since you only just moved back to town. That way, no one can accuse you of having the advantage. Let's put it to vote. Who thinks Luke should be the bachelor to represent Shelter?"

Dozens of hands flew into the air, along with squeals and cheers.

"I don't think so," Luke's voice rose above the noise. "I've got a lot going on right now and don't have the time."

Taycee rolled her eyes. No shocker there. Especially since he couldn't even take the time to make a promised phone call.

"You'll be letting down a lot of people if you don't say yes," Jessa said. "A lot of *potential customers*." Heads bobbed up and down.

"Tell me who the bachelorette is, and I'll consider it," said Luke.

Taycee's mouth dropped open. Of all the self-absorbed, cocky, egotistical—she twisted around to face him. "Oh c'mon, Luke, where's your sense of adventure?"

Calls of, "You'll be great, Luke!" "You're the perfect choice!" and "Do Shelter proud and win that contest!" were heard throughout the room.

Luke leveled a look at Taycee before he shrugged. "You're right. Fine, count me in."

Taycee turned back, a satisfied smile on her face. Revenge complete. She couldn't wait to pop a large batch of popcorn and watch it all play out.

"Fabulous," said Jessa. "It looks like we'll now have twenty-one bachelors at the opening event. What will our bachelorette say to that, I wonder?"

When the meeting dispersed, people flocked to the door, anxiously grabbing flyers on their way out. Taycee lingered in her seat, waiting for Jessa to finish answering a few last questions.

Two brown shoes stepped around her feet, and Luke planted his tall, muscular frame in the seat next to her. Taycee reached for her purse, ready to make a run for it, but Luke's hand on her arm kept her in her seat.

"I don't think so," he said.

"But aren't you anxious to get home and see who you'll be dating in a few weeks?"

"It'll wait." Luke withdrew his hand and crossed his arms. "I couldn't leave without thanking you for the nomination. Really, how thoughtful of you to think of me."

"I only meant it as a joke," Taycee defended, not about to explain why she'd really done it. "And it's not like you had to agree to it."

He watched her. "I'd like to see you say no when over a hundred faces are waiting for you to say yes—especially when you're being accused of having no sense of adventure." He shot her a pointed look. "I couldn't stand by and take that."

"I didn't think peer pressure worked on people after high school."

"Apparently I haven't matured as much as you."

"Apparently." Again, Taycee wished she'd kept her mouth shut. It was only a matter of time before someone else had suggested Luke's name anyway. Why did she have to be the one to do it?

Luke leaned forward, resting his elbows on his knees. "Seriously, what did I ever do to you? Was bringing you lunch the wrong thing to do? Do you like soggy sandwiches or something?"

No, what she didn't like was being stood up—not that Taycee was about to remind him of that. Or of any of the other reasons she'd done it. Her flip flops tap-danced against the hard, wooden floor as she tried not to squirm.

"I don't know," she said finally. "There aren't many guys in this town under thirty. Besides, you never know, maybe I just matched you up with your future bride. You should be thanking me."

"Let's hope not. I'm not ready to get married."

"You can make it a really long engagement."

Luke's lips twitched as he slouched back, resting his arm casually on the back of Taycee's chair. An unwanted shiver ran down her back.

"It's really not a big deal," he said. "I'll just be as uncharming as possible and get voted off right away. One opening social and I'm out."

Taycee frowned. It better not be that easy. "Um, yeah, great plan."

Luke smiled and leaned close, his arm brushing up against her. "I know it's been ten years, but you should still know me well enough to know that I *will* get you back for this, Taycee Lynne." With a wink, he stood and left.

Taycee froze, blinking at nothing in particular. All her life, her parents, brother, and close friends had all shortened her name to Tace. But not Luke. From the day he'd discovered her middle name, she'd always been Taycee Lynne to him. At one time, it had given her warm fuzzies inside. But ten years was a long time ago, and that name should have long since lost its power. Yet here she was, fighting those same warm fuzzies that wanted to make her believe he'd just singled her out.

Good heavens.

It was only a nickname. Only a nickname.

Jessa's heels clacked against the marble as she waltzed back into the room. A surprised, almost worried glance shot Taycee's way. "You're still here?"

"Just waiting for you."

"Why?" It sounded a little too bright for nine o'clock at night. Or maybe Taycee was just in a bad mood.

She stood and walked over to Jessa. "What do you mean, why? So I can congratulate you on a great presentation. I still have no idea how you convinced all those people that hosting a bachelorette show would be a good idea, but you did. That has to be some sort of Guinness World record."

"That's because it *is* a good idea." Jessa moved forward, collecting the posters and collapsing the easel. Another poster rested behind the podium, so Taycee reached for it.

"Oh, I don't need that one." Jessa rushed forward to grab it, but Taycee held it up to get a better look, and then immediately wished she hadn't. The words "Meet Shelter's bachelorette, Taycee Lynne Emerson" were scribbled across the top, practically glowing in a white font against the background of Taycee's dark hair—hair that had been ridiculously glamorized at some studio in Denver months earlier. Jessa had planned a girls' day out and had insisted on

34

it. After some coercion, Taycee had grudgingly gone along with it, but only after Jessa had promised that no one—not even Taycee's mother—would ever be allowed to see the pictures.

But now, here was one of them, blown up to ten times its original size and smiling back as if to say, "Ha ha. Joke's on you!"

Taycee's hands shook as her fingers tightened, digging into the edges of the poster. It had to be a joke. It *had* to be. Even Jessa wasn't capable of something like this.

"You weren't supposed to see that yet," Jessa said quietly.

"Yet?" Taycee glared. "When, exactly, were you planning on showing it to me?"

Blue eyes shifted away. "I was hoping you'd gone home to see it on the internet like everyone else. Then I planned to avoid you for a few days until you'd calmed down."

Taycee shoved the poster forward, right in front of Jessa's face. "You were going to show the town this tonight, weren't you? Because you thought I wouldn't be here."

Jessa took the poster and stacked it on top all the others. "You're perfect for the role, Taycee. Do you know how many application videos came flooding in when we advertised that face?"

"It's not even me!"

"Yes, it is."

"I don't look like that every day, Jessa. See this?" Taycee tugged on her pony tail. "This is me! And these"—Taycee pointed to her jeans and flip flops—"so is this. This"—A finger jabbed at the poster—"is *not* me. I am *not* a bachelorette, nor do I want to be. You'd better fix this, Jessa! Right now! There's no way I'm going on that show."

"I can't." Jessa cringed. "In four weeks, twenty guys will be arriving from around the nation to date *you*—not me, not another girl from Shelter—*you*."

"No." Head shaking, Taycee took a step back. "How could you do this? You're supposed to be my best friend."

Jessa's eyes filled with worry. "Tace, don't be mad—*please?* I knew you'd never go for it, which is why I didn't ask you outright, but I *did* ask. Remember? The favor? You said you were good for it."

Taycee's head pounded. "Are you insane!"

"You're the only one who can pull it off."

"Don't give me that."

Jessa tucked the posters under her arm. "You are. Whether you like it or not, or try to hide behind jeans and T-shirts, you're gorgeous, talented, smart, kind, and fun."

Taycee jabbed a finger at Jessa's chest. "Don't you dare try to smooth this over with flattery," she yelled. "I don't even know what to say to you. This isn't some funny little prank. This is my *life!*"

"You're right," Jessa said, her voice rising. "It is your life. And it will still be your life after the contest. You've spent the last eight years dating guys who never really interested you, so why should another six weeks matter? Especially when it's my aunt and uncle and the rest of the town we're talking about."

"How dare you."

"C'mon, Taycee, be reasonable and think about it. It's not like I had a lot of options to go with. Could you imagine Liza as the bachelorette? People would stop watching after the first week. And Marie? Way too shy. Steph? Cute, but way too ditzy."

"You could have picked yourself, since you're apparently better than everyone else in this town."

"That's just it, don't you see?" Jessa said. "I'd come across as egotistical and vain. Not a good choice either."

"Don't forget conniving and manipulative."

"Exactly," Jessa said, though hurt reflected in her eyes.

Well, good. She deserved it. Jessa, who thought she

knew everything and could go around messing with people's lives just because she thought it was a good idea.

Taycee dropped the poster on the floor as angry tears threatened to spill. She spun on her heel and ran from the room, increasing her speed when her feet hit the sidewalk. How could Jessa do something like this? How could she make Taycee the butt of some bad joke, plastering a Photoshopped, fake face all over the internet and in how many newspapers? Regardless of the needs of the town, it was wrong on so many counts.

For six weeks, Taycee would be forced to turn her life upside down, and to prance in front of cameras, acting happy about being made to date guys she had no interest in dating. She'd be questioned, filmed, and broadcasted across the internet to who knows how many people. She'd be demoralized.

All because of Jessa.

Taycee had seen the show and the schedule on the chart. Six short weeks and you find your true love? Ha. Talk about a joke. Sure, the guys grappled around the girl, romanced her, sought out her attention. Why? Not because they were genuinely interested, not because they cared. How could they? How could anyone say they were in love after a few meager dates? It wasn't real, it was a competition. Each guy wanted to win, and they'd do whatever it took to do that, even fool themselves into thinking they might care.

But they didn't. The large number of breakups after the fact testified it wasn't real. Rather, it was an exploitation of dating, romance, and love.

And now Taycee would be the one exploited.

She stormed into her apartment and slammed the door, shutting out the town and everyone in it who was probably now snickering at her expense. Especially Luke.

Luke.

Oh no. Taycee let out a groan as she sunk to the floor

and buried her face in her hands. What was it she'd said to him? Something about the possibility of matching him up with his future bride?

No, no, no, no, NO!

She'd have to move. Far, far, far away. It was her only choice.

Six

Literally overnight, Taycee became the town celebrity. As she walked down Main Street people clapped her on the back and told her how excited they were for the show to start. How grateful they were that she was willing to do this. How she and Jessa had given the town hope.

Patsy's finger wiggled at her in passing. "I knew it would be you. I just knew it!"

"You've always been such a dear," came from Linda.

A bear hug from Tom.

Taycee mumbled a quick thanks to everyone, and then darted across the street and into the diner. What she needed was curly fries. Lots of curly fries.

"Well, well, if it isn't the famous bachelorette," cooed Liza from behind the counter.

Taycee bit back a groan. Seriously, was she not allowed at least one break? "You seem to be here a lot lately. Are you full time now?"

"As of two weeks ago."

"Oh. How nice." Maybe Taycee should have opened a diner instead of a flower shop for no other reason than to give people another option.

"The fact that you're now the bachelorette doesn't mean you're going to start expecting special treatment, does it?" said Liza, straightening her apron. "Because you still have to wait your turn just like everyone else."

If by "turn," she meant being continuously pushed to the back of the line for at least thirty minutes, then yeah, Taycee already knew that. "Don't worry. I would never let it go to my head."

"Right." Liza rolled her eyes, implying that it already had.

A part of Taycee snapped inside. Who was Liza to judge her anyway? She didn't know anything about anything. She just jumped to whatever conclusions she wanted to make for whatever reasons she wanted to make them. Fine. Whatever. If Liza chose to think Taycee was that conceited, then so be it.

Taycee picked up one of the take-out menus and held it up. "While I'm here, would you like something autographed? A menu maybe? Or would you rather take one of the leftover bachelors? I'd be happy to steer one or two your way once they get voted off."

"You mean like Luke?" Liza baited. "Or are you planning to keep him around for a while?"

Play it cool. She's only trying to get a rise out of you. "Oh, weren't you listening last night? That decision isn't mine to make."

"You only wish it was."

"No. I really don't."

Liza glared. "Then why did you agree to it?"

I didn't, you brat! But Liza already thought the worse of Taycee, so why bother? It's not like throwing Jessa's name under the bus would change anything. She shrugged. "Something to cross off my bucket list, I guess."

40

"Wanting to be a bachelorette on a reality show is on your bucket list?"

"Heavens no," Taycee deadpanned. "Dating twenty guys at the same time is."

"Figures." Liza glowered as she punched buttons on the register. "Let me guess. Curly fries and a chicken salad sandwich."

"Actually, I'll take two orders of curly fries today, thanks."

Liza's finger stilled, and one of her drawn-on eyebrows raised a notch. "You do know the camera adds ten pounds, don't you?"

"Make that three orders."

"Fine." More hard punches. "That'll be a few minutes."

"Shocker." Taycee turned toward the tables. It wasn't too crowded, but her favorite booth was already occupied by the one person Taycee never wanted to see again. Of course it would be Luke. And of course he'd be sitting within hearing distance of her conversation with Liza. Why hadn't she expected it? Prepared for it, even?

Taycee should have stayed home. Closed her shop. Powered off her phone. Sat on the couch and watched TV all day. Maybe that would have put a stop to this Murphy's Law of a week.

She sank down in the nearest empty seat with her back facing Luke. More than ever, she needed those curly fries. All three orders of them. Her fingertips tapped on the counter, beating out an uneven rhythm.

The chair next to Taycee's slid out with a screech, and Luke sat down, dropping his lunch on the table in front of him. "I didn't know you had a bucket list."

"Eavesdropper," she muttered.

"What else is on it?"

"Oh, you know, the usual," Taycee said. "Swim with penguins in Antarctica. Become an American Gladiator. Invent meatloaf flavored ice cream."

Luke's lips twitched. "Dating twenty guys should be a breeze, then."

"Yep. Easy peasy." But really she was dying inside, as evidenced by her burning face. It didn't help that Luke watched her over the rim of his glass as he sipped his drink, making her feel like he could read her mind. Taycee resisted the urge to squirm.

The glass clinked back on the counter, and a teasing glint appeared in his eyes. "You know, if you wanted to date me, you could have just asked me out."

He was taunting her, just like he used to do when they were kids. Still, Taycee stiffened. "Excuse me?"

"I probably would have said yes—at least before you dragged me into your little show."

Could this day get any worse? Why hadn't Taycee left last night? Fled the town, the state, the country like she'd planned? "It's not *my* show."

"You're the bachelorette, of course it's your show." His elbow came to rest on the table as Luke leaned forward, still teasing her with his eyes. "Tell me, is this usually how you get guys to date you?"

Taycee's fingers clenched around her napkin encased utensils. She'd had enough—of everyone. The gratitude. The expectations. The accusations. The taunting. Not even curly fries were worth this. She shoved her chair back and stood. "You know what, Luke? You're just as cocky as you were back in high school. And for the record, you're the last person in the world I'd ever want to date. As far as I'm concerned, the sooner you get voted off, the better."

With that, Taycee turned on her heel and ran straight into a guy carrying a plate of ketchup coated French fries.

Taycee's fist banged against the wooden apartment door.

"Jessa McCray! Open up!" she yelled.

A moment later the door cracked open and two blue eyes blinked at Taycee. "Is it safe?"

"Now!"

"Okay, okay." Jessa unlatched the door and swung it wide, allowing Taycee to brush past her. "Are you here to yell at me again?"

"What do you think?"

Jessa sighed. "That you're here to yell at me again. Hey, what happened to your shirt? Is that ketchup?"

"Yes, it's ketchup! Do you have a problem with that?"

The door clicked closed. "Wow, somebody's in a good mood today."

Taycee glared.

"Okay, okay, fine. Yell away. But then can we please get past this? It's only been one day, and I can't stand you being mad at me." With tentative steps, Jessa stepped around Taycee with her pink and green striped socks. Dressed in matching green sweats, Jessa was obviously working from home today—not that posting Taycee's picture all over the internet could be categorized as work.

Taycee followed. "I want Luke off the show."

"What? Why?"

"Why? Because I do, that's why. I never would have suggested him if I'd known I was the bachelorette."

A jug of apple juice sat on the kitchen table. Jessa poured two glasses and handed one to Taycee. "But I thought you liked him."

"Used to!" Taycee practically shouted, setting her glass on the table with a clunk, sloshing some of the juice over the side. "As in past tense. Back when he was actually nice and not cocky, conceited, and . . . and . . . "

"Gorgeous?"

Taycee glowered. "It's the least you can do after what you've done to me."

In her graceful way, Jessa sank down on a burgundy chair and criss-crossed her legs. With the cup clutched between both hands, she sipped her juice, and then watched Taycee over the rim. "Put yourself in my place, will you? The town all voted Luke in. He agreed. And last night, I added his name and profile to the website as Bachelor #21. Discussions have already started about how dreamy the 21st bachelor is, and how people can't wait to see him on the show. Do you really think I can change that now?"

Taycee groaned and flopped down on the sofa. How had she gotten herself into this mess? How had everything gotten so out of control so quickly? In only a matter of days, she'd gone from being normal, nice, and sane, to the complete opposite—running around like a crazed, immature lunatic. It wasn't her. She was the flower girl of the town—the happy, independent creator of bouquets.

It was all Luke's fault. Jessa's too, of course, but it had begun with him. Before he came back to Shelter Springs, Taycee's life had been good. Controlled. Predictable. Just the way she liked it. But now everything had changed. Luke's arrival had been like a catalyst, catapulting Taycee into a world of emotional turmoil.

"I'm sorry," Jessa said. It sounded sincere, and an apology from Jessa came about as often as a lunar eclipse.

"You do realize you just apologized, right?"

"I know, I know. But you're my best friend, and I don't want this to mess that up."

Taycee sighed. The truth was, neither did she. As domineering as Jessa could be, Taycee really had no better friend in the world. "I'm sorry, too. I shouldn't have yelled at you yesterday, even though you deserved it."

Jessa took another sip of her drink. "If you're really that upset about Luke, we can always change things around and give the choice back to you. I'm sure I can come up with another way to raise the additional funds. Maybe we could hold some auctions instead. I'm sure we could get some businesses to donate stuff."

For a second, Taycee actually considered it. If she were the one to give Luke the ax, he wouldn't be able to accuse her of wanting to date him anymore. Then maybe this whole embarrassment would go away. Maybe he'd go away. Maybe he'd even stop calling her Taycee Lynne.

But the image of Pat's dejected face came to mind as well. The hurt in his eyes. The way he'd run out on her, and the guilt she'd felt at being the cause of it all. It was still too fresh, and Taycee couldn't be the one to say "I like you and you, but not-so-much you or you. Sorry." Besides, maybe Luke really would follow through with his plan to be uncharming and get himself voted off. If so, problem solved.

She shook her head. "No, let's stick with your way. I don't want to be the one who decides."

"You sure?"

"Positive. But I do have one request." Taycee shot Jessa a pointed look. "And you and I both know I'm in a place where I can demand *something*."

Jessa's bright blue glittered fingernails tapped against the armrest. "What is it?"

"No rose ceremonies."

"But—"

Taycee's hand shot up. "I mean it. I refuse to give a flower to any guy in any sort of formal ceremony. It's horribly cheesy and would be an embarrassment to us all. We're going to announce the winners on the blog and that's that. No ceremonies. No roses. And no saying goodbye in person. Got it?" Taycee had given a guy a rose only one time in her entire life—a Jean Giono to Luke the night before he left for college. To this day, she could still see the what-in-the-world-am-I-supposed-to-do-with-this look on Luke's face and hear his "Uh, thanks, just what I always wanted" response. No way would she go through that experience ever again.

Jessa gnawed on her lip for a short time before finally nodding. "That's actually not a bad idea. Not only would it simplify things for Burt and Megan, but you're right. It would be much less cheesy that way." She paused. "If I agree to this, am I forgiven?"

As if Jessa could get off that easy. As *if*. "I don't think so. You're going to have to work a lot harder for that."

"What's it going to take?"

"I'll let you know," Taycee said. "In the meantime, just know that you owe me big-time. We're talking a go-to-jail-for-me sort of favor."

Jessa swirled what was left of her juice. "Are you thinking of doing something drastic that would land yourself in jail?"

"Maybe." The idea had merit. Taycee couldn't be the bachelorette if she were in jail.

"All right, fine." Jessa set her juice aside. "So long as it's not a life sentence. I can only wear those orange jump suits for so long."

"You're impossible." Taycee fought back a smile. That was Jessa. Dictatorial, overly confident, prideful, yes, but also forthright and funny. There was no one else who could make Taycee laugh at her current situation. Only Jessa—the one person who'd put her there in the first place. Go figure.

"So really, why do you want Luke off?" A slow grin spread across Jessa's face. "Methinks you still like him."

"No way." Never, ever, EVER would Taycee admit that to Jessa. Not in this lifetime.

"It's the only reason I can think why you'd feel so strongly about it."

"If I liked him, why would I want him off?"

A knowing look appeared in Jessa's eyes. "Because you're afraid of getting your heart broken again. Admit it."

Again, not in this lifetime. "Please. I was fourteen when he left. You can't have your heart broken at fourteen."

"You did," Jessa said, her expression pensive. "And you've never really gotten over it. That's why you haven't been able to seriously date anyone since then, isn't it?"

The couch suddenly felt uncomfortable. Taycee shifted positions, mentally adding "too perceptive" to Jessa's list of faults. "You're wrong."

"Am I?"

"Believe it or not, Jessa McCray, sometimes even you can be wrong."

Jessa swung her feet to the ground and clasped her fingers together. "Okay, fine, so you don't want to talk about Luke. I get it."

Wow, this was a day for the record books. Not only had Jessa apologized, but she'd even listened and obeyed. She really must be sorry.

Jessa set her empty glass down with a clink. "So, since Luke is off limits, want to tell me where that ketchup came from now?"

Seven

*L*uke weaved his cart through the narrow aisle of the grocery store, dreading the long night of work still ahead of him. People had made it sound so easy. You graduate, pass the state boards, and then set up a practice of your own. No sweat, right?

Wrong.

Business classes weren't part of the veterinary program, so Luke's only experience with that aspect of a practice were the two years he'd spent completing a residency in Ohio. Problem was, he'd focused more on the medical side of things and less on the business side.

Maybe he should have taken the partnership offer. It would have been so much easier to walk into an established practice with established clients and an established billing and filing system. Instead, Luke had turned it down. Not because he didn't like his boss—the man was amazing—but because he decided to move back to Shelter Springs, with its soaring population of 1,000 and a welcoming sign that read:

Welcome to Shelter Springs, Colorado!
(And you thought you were lost.)

Luke shook his head. He honestly didn't know what had prompted him to make this move. Maybe he was running away or maybe he was looking for something he'd once had but lost. Either way, he'd made his decision. He passed the Colorado state boards and now here he was, back in Shelter Springs and wondering what in the world he'd been thinking.

He picked up a can of chili and examined it, and then put it back on the shelf as his mother's words echoed through his mind. "Always cook fresh, you hear me? Always, always, always!" Oh, Luke had heard all right. But it wasn't about the health so much as the taste. His mom had been such a good cook that he was now trained to think canned chili tasted nasty. Which was all well and good, but how many times had he been too busy to cook and wanted to open a can of soup or throw in a frozen lasagna for dinner? Too many.

Thanks to his mom, easy cuisine was now ruined for him.

Luke frowned, and then forced his tired body toward the produce section. He rounded the corner and stopped when he saw Taycee with her back to him, examining some grapes. Her long, dark hair was pulled into a ponytail that swished a little as she moved.

When Luke had first bumped into her, it was like a "welcome home" banner. Taycee Lynne Emerson still lived in Shelter. Who would have thought? Her being here had given him hope that things really could be like old times. Romping around in the summer. Snowball fights in the winter. The slow, easy-going life he'd come to crave so much the past couple of years.

Unfortunately, Taycee had changed. Or Luke had. Either way, things were different. The brother/sister relationship they used to have was gone, replaced by a whole lot of something else. Awkward tension mixed with an unexpected attraction. Taycee had always been cute, with her wild dark hair and hazel eyes, but now she was way beyond that. It caught him off guard—as did the way she kept him at a distance. Add to that the fact that she'd volunteered him to date her on some stupid show, only to tell him he was the last guy she'd ever want to date, and he was more confused than ever.

Taycee opened a bag of green grapes and popped one into her mouth. In a frantic movement, her hand waved in front of her face as she looked around for who knows what. "Blech!" she finally said before pushing the bag of grapes aside and moving on to the apples.

A woman nearby dropped a package of strawberries in her cart and headed for the grapes, reaching for a bag.

"Unless you like your grapes on the extreme side of sour, I'd keep on walking," Taycee told her.

"Oh, thank you."

"No problem." The woman moved on as Taycee examined an apple, and then dropped it into a sack.

Luke gave a wry smile and pushed his cart forward. "Aren't you going to try the apple too? How do you know they're not sour? Speaking of which, I didn't realize we could sample the produce before we buy."

Taycee stiffened as she slowly turned to face him. "Clive knows I hate sour grapes and told me I could try them whenever I wanted."

Luke leaned over to inspect the bananas. They looked ripe, so he tossed a couple into his cart. "Interesting."

"What's that supposed to mean?" Taycee's bright blue T-shirt made her eyes look almost blue today. It was something he'd always found fascinating about her. When he stood close, her eyes were a variegated hazel but back away several feet and they seemed to lighten or darken depending on what color she wore or what mood she was in.

Luke shrugged. "It means I find you interesting. But now that I think about it, it makes sense. You like to sample things first—whether it's fruit or twenty-one guys, right? A quick date with each of them and then what? You'll pick the best looking? Richest? Smartest? Strongest?"

He rested his arms casually across the cart's handle. "How exactly do you like your men anyway?" He'd meant to goad her a little, but he found that he was pretty interested in her answer. What kind of guys did the grown-up Taycee Lynne go for?

Her eyes widened initially, but then the corners of her mouth lifted slightly. "I like them sweet, like my fruit." With a hand on her cart, she pushed it away from him. A few steps later, she stopped to look over her shoulder. "You should try the grapes. I bet you'd love them."

Luke chuckled. He couldn't help it. For all her oddities and confusing ways, Taycee Lynne was always good for a laugh. "Hey. One more question before you run off again."

Her expression turned wary.

Luke nodded toward the grapes. "How do you know that grape you tried tasted like all the others? Maybe you just picked a bad one."

She hesitated, as if seriously considering the question. Finally, she said, "Well, it wouldn't be the first time I've done that. Night, Luke." With that, she steered her cart toward the checkout counter.

Luke watched her go, feeling like she'd just told him something important. Something he should be able to decipher and somehow understand. But whether he was too tired or just plain clueless, he had no idea what she was talking about.

Eight

"Jessa, I have enough clothes. Please no more. Not today. I'm begging you," Taycee complained as Jessa dragged her down a bustling Denver street. Her stomach had been growling for the past hour, but did Jessa care? No. When it came to hunger and shopping, shopping took first priority. Every time.

"Only one more, and then we can get dinner. You're going to love this place. Totally random and eclectic, but oh the finds I've discovered here. It would be a sin to come this close without taking a peek." Jessa stopped in front of a small shop called Talia's Treasures and examined a few shirts and skirts that hung from hooks suctioned to the inside of the windows. She gave a satisfied smile, and then yanked the door open and tugged Taycee inside.

Taycee looked around the dimly lit room. Eclectic was right. Besides several racks of clothing, jewelry hung from stands and plaques from the walls. There were pictures, books, hair accessories—even chocolate covered strawberries—all packed into one tiny space that couldn't be more than 200 square feet. Cinnamon and vanilla scents wafted through the air, making Taycee's stomach grumble yet again.

"Hey, Jess, haven't seen you around for a few weeks," said a girl from behind the register. Her skin was a beautiful rich brown and her black hair had a wild look to it, with tight natural curls that splayed around her face.

Jessa brightened. "Hey, Talia, got anything new for me?"

Talia's head bobbed and she held up her index finger. "One sec." She disappeared into a back room. A moment later she returned, carrying a floral shirt with cap sleeves and rows of ruffles zigzagging down the front. Some earrings dangled from a card in her other hand. "Only the most perfect pair of earrings and a shirt that totally screams your name. I knew you'd want first look."

"Oooh, I love it!" Jessa took the shirt and shoved it in Taycee's arms. "Go try it on."

"But this shirt screams *your* name, not mine." It wasn't Taycee's style at all. Much too frilly and chic.

"Oh, I think it's screaming your name now." Jessa looked in a small mirror resting on the counter and raised the earrings next to her face. "Go, go."

"Fine," said Taycee. "But if I do this—again—you're paying for dinner."

"Done."

Taycee followed Talia to a fitting room and pulled the flimsy black curtain closed with a sigh. It wasn't that she didn't like shopping or buying the occasional new thing, but Jessa had dragged her out nearly every night during the past two weeks for one reason or another. Shopping, hair appointments, makeup lessons, manicures—it was . . . well, exhausting. Taycee's once plain wardrobe now consisted of new spring dresses, designer jeans, shorts, blouses, swimwear, and several new pairs of shoes. Enough was enough. Especially with the opening event only two days away.

Taycee pulled the "screaming" shirt over her head and studied her reflection. Okay, wow, not at all what she'd expected. It fit her well and even tapered in at the waist in a flattering way. Sort of a dressed up casual look.

Sold.

Now for the "I told you so."

"Well, how is it? Let me see," Jessa's voice floated through the curtain.

Sliding it open, Taycee placed her hands on her hips as she walked from the room, model-like. Or at least as model-like as she could pull off.

"I was right," Jessa said, clapping her hands together. "That is *so* you. You're definitely getting that one. Talia, you're brilliant."

Taycee smiled. "No argument here. Thanks, Talia."

With a wink, Talia leaned against the counter. "Anything for Jessa. I haven't been open for very long and can't afford to do much advertising, but so far, Jessa's word of mouth is all I need."

"Well, you now have one more fan," said Taycee, knowing she'd be back—once she recuperated from shopping jetlag, that is.

Jessa purchased the earrings and a few additional items for herself before allowing Taycee to drag her to a nearby café for some much needed food. They sat in a corner booth with sandwiches and a shared order of curly fries.

"We're done shopping now, right?" Taycee said.

"You only wish."

"C'mon, Jess. I'm starting to feel like a dress-up doll. What more do I need?"

"I was thinking maybe one more dress. A long, flowing one would look fabulous with those new wedge sandals we got you."

Taycee jabbed a fry toward Jessa. "No way, we're done. My bank account can't take anymore." She popped the fry into her mouth and chewed hard.

"Fine," Jessa mumbled as she nibbled on her sandwich.

Some of the stress seeped out of Taycee's body as she relaxed against her seat. If only she could put her feet up, they ached so badly. "Hey, how about a girls' night tomorrow?" Taycee suggested. "We can rent a movie and do nothing at all." It sounded heavenly.

Jessa's dangling earrings glinted in the light as her head shook. "Can't. We have to film your first interview tomorrow."

"Interview? What interview?" Jessa had never mentioned anything about an interview.

"Oh, didn't I tell you? We decided to ask you a few questions and get your thoughts before the big event. The viewers will love it."

A pit settled in Taycee's stomach, and suddenly even the curly fries didn't look so good. She'd mentally prepared to start the entire ordeal on Monday night, not Sunday night. Sacrificing her last night of freedom wasn't something she was willing to do. "No. No way. If you want to do an interview, you can do it Monday night before all the bachelors show up. Sunday night is mine."

"But it's better to get as much done beforehand as we can."

"I don't care." Taycee pushed the plate of fries away. "I'm not doing it. I'm *not*."

Jessa eyed the plate before she shrugged and stuffed another fry in her mouth. "Okay, okay, you win. We'll do a girls' night instead."

Taycee's eyes narrowed. That was easy. Too easy. What did Jessa have up her sleeve? "Come to think of it, I'd rather have a quiet night at home alone, if that's all right with you."

"What, you think I'm planning to invite Burt and Megan and their cameras along?"

"That's exactly what I'm thinking."

Jessa swirled a fry through the ketchup before biting into it. "You wound me with your lack of trust."

"And you wound me with your inability to earn that trust."

"Touché."

By Sunday night, all the bachelors had arrived. The town's one inn was completely packed, along with a few others in neighboring towns. While new, handsome faces were probably causing quite a stir around town, Taycee remained safely inside her apartment, hiding behind closed blinds and a locked door.

Only one more day.

A knot formed in her stomach every time she thought about it. Luke. The bachelors. Luke. Being on Camera. Luke. Oddly enough, Taycee felt more nervous about facing him again than all the other bachelors combined. He'd been mysteriously absent during the past couple of weeks, which would normally be a good thing, but it only meant that their next meeting, which was sure to be awkward, would take place in front of cameras and a room full of other bachelors. Luke was bound to goad her into saying something mortifying. Or, more likely, just to be a pest, he'd bring up the fact that she talked in her sleep—not a comment that would go over very well in a room full of potential dates.

But that's exactly why Luke would say it. To torment her. Because heaven forbid he'd ever grow up.

Taycee's forehead dropped to the counter, hitting the town newspaper resting there. She needed some aspirin. She needed some sleep. She needed to stop thinking and worrying and stewing about Luke.

Sigh.

If only there was some way to keep him from showing up. Not only would she be able to get through the night with some sanity still intact, but Luke would be a no-show. A slacker. Someone who obviously didn't take the show seriously and would therefore be one of the first to go. Taycee would be free from having to see him and date him and be goaded by him.

Hmm . . . not a bad idea. It bordered on brilliant, actually. But how to pull it off?

Taycee lifted her head and flipped through the paper. Think, think, think. She paused on the last page when an ad for Carl's Feed and Seed caught her attention. She knew Carl's store well, with his bright red, cursive sign and the putrid smell of fertilizer that drifted through the town on days when the wind blew the wrong way. Whether it was the fact that Carl could use some extra business or the reminder of the smell, inspiration struck.

In the morning Taycee would call Carl, and with any luck, Luke would be MIA tomorrow night.

Nine

Taycee dressed in one of her new flowery summer dresses and slipped on some white strappy sandals. The dark pink pedicure Jessa had insisted on actually looked terrific. A few last curls in her hair, a swipe of lipstick, and she was as ready as she would ever be.

Butterflies swarmed in her stomach as Taycee slid into her white Corolla and headed toward The Barn. On the outskirts of town, The Barn was exactly that—a barn. Or, at least it used to be. After significant renovations years earlier, the painted wood building that had once housed hay and animals now boasted hardwood floors, a log burning fireplace, a cozy leather sectional, rustic stairs and banisters, and a large kitchen. The perfect place for the opening "meet the bachelors" event.

"You're here," Jessa breathed when Taycee walked inside. "Thank goodness. The florist I hired from Colorado Springs is botching the job. Her arrangements are decent, but she's a lousy decorator. She doesn't know where to put them. Would you mind?"

"Gladly." Anything to avoid standing around and letting the butterflies wreak havoc. Taycee scanned the room. Burt and Megan were setting up two cameras while a few others were putting refreshments on a table and rushing around doing who knows what. Then there were the flowers. Jessa was right. The arrangements of lilies were beautiful, but they were bunched together in odd places. On the floor, in the corner where no one would see them, or right next to an old TV—not something that warranted extra focus.

Taycee got to work, side-stepping around people as she moved each bouquet to more flattering locations. Next to the fireplace, on the coffee table, and near the entrance, the flowers soon accented the room.

As Taycee searched for one last place to put an arrangement, Jessa approached. "Since you didn't want to do the interview yesterday, we have to do it now, before the guys start showing up. You ready?"

"No," said Taycee, placing the flowers on the floor next to the couch. She'd never be ready.

"Relax." Jessa dragged her over to a seat where Burt had a camera positioned to start filming. "It'll be easy stuff," said Jessa. "You know, what you're feeling, what you hope to find tonight among the bachelor hopefuls—that sort of thing."

Taycee let out a sigh and sat down in front of the camera. Her hands were clammy and cold. Even shaky. In less than an hour, twenty guys from various parts of the country would walk through that door. She'd have to talk to each of them. Flirt. Get to know them as best she could in the space of a few hours. She'd have to act like she was having fun. Like she wanted to be here.

Yeah, her hands were definitely shaking.

"In three, two, one . . ." Burt gestured for Jessa to begin, and Taycee clasped her fingers together.

"So Taycee," said Jessa, "the night of the big event is finally here. How do you feel?"

"Nervous," she answered. "In a few minutes, a whole bunch of guys will show up who've I've never met before. It feels like I'm getting ready for a blind date on steroids. It's nerve-wracking, especially since I've been on enough blind dates to know that some don't end well." Actually, most of them didn't.

"But all it takes is one, right?"

"True." One guy in billions, that's all. Seriously, how did anyone find their soul mate?

"Now that you've seen all the online videos of the bachelors, is there one guy you're especially excited to meet?"

Jessa was right, Taycee *had* watched the short video clips of each bachelor exactly one time. Two weeks ago. She'd even briefly studied their names and bios only hours before, but now they all seemed to merge together as one long string of faces and introductions. Would she even be able to remember all their names? Not likely.

Taycee shifted in her seat. The truth was, only one face stood out above all the others. But she wasn't at all excited to "meet" Luke and hoped beyond hope that she wouldn't have to.

"They all look like great guys," she finally said, "and I'm looking forward to meeting them. It's just going to be interesting doing it all at once."

"Let's talk about bachelor #21. Luke Carney," Jessa said. "He's also from Shelter Springs, and there's been some talk on the site about the fairness of him being a participant. So I wanted to ask how you feel about that. Do you think he's got an unfair advantage over the others because you already know him?"

More like a disadvantage. "Not at all. Luke's been away from Shelter for so long that I hardly know him anymore. Yes, we knew each other when we were younger, but I was only fourteen when he left, and I'm sure we've both changed a lot since then. Besides that, the viewers will be the ones voting—not me—so it's really them he has to impress. In that respect, he's in the same boat as everyone else."

Jessa smiled before continuing on with a few more questions. When they were done, Taycee had a few minutes to catch her breath before she was directed outside to wait for the first bachelor. Gavin Spencer from Spokane, Washington.

She squared her shoulders and steeled herself for the long night ahead. It would be awkward, that was for sure. But if everything went according to plan, at least she wouldn't have to face Luke.

Luke jogged out to his beat-up gray F150. The wind must have changed directions because the stench of the stables was worse than usual. He jumped in and rolled up his window to block out the worst of the smell.

Not long before, Beatrice had brought by her ancient Cocker Spaniel—a dog that had definitely seen better days. Since she wouldn't hear of her precious Sandy being put under, Luke had loaded her up with what medicines might help, and then answered question after question after question about every what-should-I-do-if scenario Beatrice could think of. "What if Sandy stops breathing, what should I do?" "What if she can't get up in the morning?" "What if she wanders outside and I can't find her?"

Luke had finally given her his cell number. That seemed to pacify her.

A quick shower and a change of clothes later, Luke was late. His foot hit the pedal and he reversed his truck, and then headed down his long winding gravel drive toward the highway. He rounded a bend, and then slammed on his brakes. Directly in front of him, piled high in the middle of the road, were several yards of manure. It spanned the narrow road and blocked his only exit out.

"What the—?" Luke flung his truck into park and jumped out. The putrid smell assaulted him, and he groaned. Carl must have mistakenly delivered it to the wrong farm—today of all days. Talk about rotten timing. With a shake of his head, he glanced at his watch and bit back a curse. How would he get to The Barn now? He wasn't about to saddle up a horse and arrive smelling like one. Maybe Betty or Lyle was home. He could always borrow their car.

Luke yanked his keys from the ignition then took off through the trees for the neighboring farm. Several minutes later, he arrived slightly out of breath and pounded on the front door. Betty answered.

"Luke!" Curlers framed her face, matching the robe and slippers she wore. "What are you doing here? Aren't you supposed to be at that bachelorette thing tonight?"

Luke nodded. "Yeah, which is why I'm here. A load of manure got dropped off in my driveway and I can't get out. Can I borrow one of your cars?"

Betty's eyes grew wide. "Oh, dear me, that's not good. My car's in the shop, and Lyle just left with the truck. All that's left is Lumpy."

"I'll take it."

Ten

"Hey, Jake, it's great to meet you," Taycee said to the blond haired, blue-eyed bachelor wearing a tan sports jacket on a warm spring evening. She gave him ten solid minutes before he did away with it and draped it over the back of a chair.

He looked good in it though. Really good.

"It's nice to be met," Jake said, casting a sidelong glance through the door of The Barn where several other bachelors already stood. His smile turned lopsided as he cocked his head toward the room. "How about we skip this thing and go for a ride instead? I've never been good at sharing."

Taycee smiled. "And I've never been good at dividing myself. So sure, count me in."

Jake laughed. "You don't think I'll get beat up for something like that?"

"I don't know. Maybe. You could take it though, right? Think of it as saving a damsel in distress."

He laughed again, louder this time. "A drive with you is sounding better and better. Here's hoping I can take you up

63

on that sometime." With a wink, he backed toward the open door. "Guess I'll see you inside?"

Taycee nodded and watched him walk away. Suave, collected, charming, good-looking. Yeah, she'd definitely see him inside.

"Taycee? So great to finally meet you in person."

Taycee twisted back and blinked at the tall and lanky redhead with slightly bushy eyebrows. Normally she had a chance to collect her thoughts before another bachelor came. "Uh . . . it's Sterling, right?"

"The one and only." He grinned. "I've been looking forward to this night for a long time."

Taycee suddenly felt like she'd been spritzed with some sort of liquid. Had he really just spit on her? She resisted the urge to wipe a hand across her face. "Me too. I'm so glad you could make it."

"Well, I almost didn't." A few more flecks of saliva landed on her neck, and Taycee took a small step back as he told her about his missed flight and mix up with the rental car company. What seemed like hours later, he finally disappeared inside. Taycee tried not to cringe as she wiped the moisture away with the back of her hand.

Note to self: Stand as far away from Sterling as possible.

Jessa glanced her way and held up five fingers. "Only five left," she mouthed.

It sounded like five hundred to Taycee. Already her feet ached, and she had long since run out of different ways to say, "Hey, nice to meet you" or "So glad you could make it." She snuck a glance inside. There they all were, milling about and waiting to be entertained by her wit and charm.

What wit and charm?

Taycee sighed and looked around. The sounds of a car pulling into the parking lot alerted her that another bachelor would be coming soon. She quickly slipped off her sandals and luxuriated in the feel of the cold, soft grass beneath her feet. Her dress was long so hopefully no one would notice.

Moments later, another guy strutted toward her, his keys whipping around his finger and clinking. He had that over-confident look to him that reminded Taycee of a used car salesman. She accepted his hug and shot Jessa a panicked, I-can't-remember-his-name look over his shoulder.

"Alec," Jessa mouthed.

"Bless you," Taycee mouthed back. She pulled free and smiled. "So great to finally meet you, Alec. I'm excited to get to know you better."

"Likewise," he said, giving her a once-over and making her feel like a shiny new car. Taycee waited until his gaze returned to her face before she lifted an eyebrow. Not cool.

She managed to exchange a few more words with him before he said a quick see you later and disappeared inside. Good riddance. Handsome, yes. Cocky, double yes. No thanks. Hopefully the viewers thought so too.

Three bachelors later and still no sign of Luke. When ten additional minutes came and went, Jessa's foot tapped impatiently. "Is he coming?" Jessa hissed.

There were a lot of things Taycee could have said. Maybe he got into an accident. Maybe he'd been held up by a patient. Maybe there was an emergency and he was now performing surgery. Or maybe, just maybe, ten yards of manure kept him hostage in his driveway.

Taycee settled with, "Maybe he forgot."

That earned the absentee Luke one of Jessa's scathing frowns—the kind that meant she wasn't about to let this slide and there would be some serious ramifications later. Taycee bit back a smile. Luke wouldn't know what hit him.

Just then, a rumbling sound emerged through the trees, growing louder and louder as a huge battered and rusted dump truck puttered into view. It reminded Taycee of *The Little Engine That Could*. "I think I can, I think I can, I think I can," it seemed to say as it approached, finally screeching to a halt almost right in front of her.

She choked on a laugh as she waved the exhaust fumes away.

Luke leapt from the driver's seat and tossed his keys at some poor teenager who'd been recruited to help out. "Be careful with Lumpy," he said. "She's pretty special."

The teenager looked down at the keys with a mixture of confusion and worry, but who could blame him? The prospect of parking "Lumpy" would scare just about anyone.

The camera turned Taycee's way and she tried to keep a straight face, but failed. Where in the world did Luke get that thing? And how could anyone look that good jumping out of a ride like that? It wasn't right. Or fair. Especially since he wasn't supposed to be here at all.

"Nice you could finally make it," Taycee managed to say. "Love the wheels."

Luke eyed the wreck of a dump truck. "She's a beauty all right. That engine sure purrs."

Taycee giggled. She couldn't help it. She should have known this would happen since Luke was never one to give up. But a dump truck? Really? "Maybe I should leave you and Lumpy alone together."

Luke cocked his head toward her. The corners of his eyes crinkled ever so slightly. "Jealous of a dump truck?"

"Nah." Oh great, it was starting already. The goading. The taunting. The let's-see-what-embarrassing-thing-we-can-get-Taycee-to-blurt-out-on-camera game. But Luke wouldn't get away with it tonight. Taycee would stand her ground and keep her distance. It was the only way to keep her pride intact.

"Hey, I brought you something." Luke dug into his pocket and pulled out a little white box tied with a bow, like a ring box only a tad bigger.

A few of the other guys had brought her a flower, but no one had given her an actual present. What was he doing? She eyed it uncertainly. "It's too soon for a ring, isn't it?"

"Oh, I wouldn't get your hopes up."

Taycee flushed. He was a toad, that's all there was to it. The kind that never turned into a prince no matter how many times you kissed him. Not that Taycee was about to try. Or wanted to try. Or even thought about wanting to try. Her flush deepened. "Really, you shouldn't have."

"I know."

An awkward silence descended while Taycee stood there, holding the box. She wasn't about to open it while the camera rolled. Anything could be in it. A rubber snake. A framed picture of her with braces and wild, untamed hair. Or that candy from the novelty store that always turned Taycee's tongue and lips blue.

"You going to open it?" Luke asked, his eyes glinting.

"I'll wait until later. We should go in."

"Oh, c'mon. I promise it's not going to bite."

Taycee shot him a skeptical look before giving the box a quick shake. Nothing happened. In fact, it felt empty. She lifted the corner for a quick peek, and then opened it all the way. Inside was a folded piece of paper. "Oh, how sweet. You wrote me a love sonnet," she joked.

"Sorry, no. Did you want me to write you a love sonnet?"

She wanted to kick him. Shake him. Tell him to knock it off right now or she'd call his mother. Honestly, who says stuff like that on camera? Luke. That's who. And he'd keep doing it. All. Night. Long.

Taycee unfolded the paper, not quite sure what to think. It was a take-out menu for Maris's diner, including a coupon for some free curly fries. At the bottom, Luke had scribbled in Liza's work schedule for the next couple of weeks, along with the words,

If you want to avoid long waits, I suggest you
steer clear of these times. Luke

Taycee's heart thump-bumped in her chest. Why did he have to be so nice and thoughtful at times? It was becoming cyclical. Goad Taycee into despising him. Do something charming to throw her off. Then repeat.

Burt stepped closer with the camera, and Taycee slid her fingers over the handwritten words at the bottom. "Thank you, Luke. Curly fries are my favorite."

Luke gave one of his adorable half smiles. "Maybe we'll bump into each other there sometime."

Taycee's eyes met his in a look that made her forget how to breathe. His expression was almost . . . sincere, as if he actually wanted to bump into her. But no, Luke wouldn't want that or even think about wanting that. This was just his way of discomfiting her. And, to her frustration, it was working.

Taycee broke eye contact and refolded the note, placing it back inside the box. "I guess I'll see you inside?" She needed time to compose herself. To slow her racing heart and convince herself that Luke wasn't worth all this fuss. He was a sour grape. The sourest of the sour.

"Am I the last one?" Luke said.

"You were pretty late."

"It was unavoidable." He held out an arm. "Can I take you in or would that mess with some sort of protocol?"

"Um . . ." So much for composure, not that it really mattered. It wouldn't take long before Luke stripped it away anyway. "Sure." She took a tentative step toward him, and then paused when her bare feet touched the concrete. Oops. Her sandals. She flushed yet again. "Uh . . ."

A smiled tugged at the corner of Luke's mouth as he reached for her hand and placed it in the nook of his arm. "Barefoot works for you. C'mon."

Taycee stumbled and gripped him tighter, needing his support to keep her upright. Just touching him seemed to cause some sort of chemical reaction inside her—the kind that made her want to run for cover.

Jessa gestured for them to stop right outside the door so Burt could move his camera inside.

Taycee took the opportunity to lean in closer. "Whatever happened to being un-charming?" she whispered.

Luke winked and gave her that look again—the serious one that couldn't possibly be serious. "Maybe I changed my mind," he whispered back.

Burt signaled that he was ready, so Luke led her inside, where he promptly left her standing alone in front of a large group of staring guys.

Mama Mia.

With two cameras now trained on her, Taycee hesitated, not quite sure what to do now. Soft music played in the background, and a fire crackled in the fireplace. The room grew warm, and the air around her seemed to thicken as she struggled to fight back a rising panic. What was she doing? She hadn't wanted this spot, and yet somehow here she was, forced to pretend that she was worth all this attention. That she really was searching for Mr. Right.

Without meaning to, her eyes rested on Luke. Off to the side and toward the back, he now leaned against a wooden support post—a reminder that Taycee no longer had his arm to lean on. She swallowed and forced her feet forward, toward a group of men who were all about to compete for a date with her—a girl they didn't even know.

A confident person who actually wanted to be here might say something like "Hey, let's get this party started!" But Taycee felt anything but confident, and what she wanted to do more than anything else was to turn and bolt.

"Hey," she finally said, with a pitiful wave of her hand. Boring, yes. Lame, definitely. But there it was.

The bachelors moved forward, encircling her into a claustrophobic cocoon.

"You finally made it," someone said.

Another passed her a white lily he must have taken from one of the arrangements. "I hear you like flowers."

Still another pushed forward. "Since I was the first to arrive, I get Taycee first." Like she was a popular toy at a black Friday sale.

Within seconds, it was apparent that Taycee would never get to know the guys this way. She laid a hand on the arm nearest to her and blurted, "Want to dance?" then immediately regretted it. Why couldn't she have said, "Hey, see those two chairs over there in the corner? What do you say we go chat for a few minutes?" or "Hey, why don't we go scope out the refreshments?" Instead, her dimwitted mind came up with the one thing that kept her front and center, showing off her non-existent dancing skills.

Evidently she didn't need Luke to goad her into saying or doing something stupid. She managed to do that just fine on her own.

"Yes ma'am," said Miles with his deep southern drawl. He grinned, tipped his black cowboy hat that he wore, and then swept her into his arms and started backing her around the room. Oh heavens. The two-step—a dance several people had tried to teach her, but had failed miserably. Good thing she was barefoot. Not only would her shoes have made her taller than Miles, but she would probably be stepping on his toes a lot.

And she thought things had been awkward before.

"So, Miles, you're in the rodeo circuit, right?" Taycee said in an attempt to forget all the eyes looking their way.

"Yes, ma'am," he said. "Calf roping and bull riding are my specialty. There's nothin' like the rush you get in that arena, I tell ya."

Taycee would have to take his word for it on that one. The only kind of rush she'd get from being thrown from a bull and then charged or gored or trampled by a bull would be the heart-attack, brain aneurysm kind. "How did you get into that?"

He shrugged. "It's in my blood, I guess. My daddy was a bull rider so it's the only life I've known." He leaned in closer and lowered his voice. "Between you and me, I can be a bit shy at times, but drop me somewhere near a rodeo and I come out of my shell like a turtle itchin' to sunbathe."

Taycee laughed. "Then you'll be happy to know that there will be a couple of rodeos going on around here during the next month."

"I know." He winked. "Where do ya think we're going for our first date if I get the chance to take you out?"

Hmm . . . to the rodeo with Miles. Definitely not a bad prospect. He didn't spit when he talked, he made her laugh, and he was actually a decent dance partner. All pluses. The fact that he didn't goad her into saying something she'd regret was just a bonus. Her gaze automatically drifted to Luke, who now stood talking to another guy with his eyes trained on her. He looked amused. As if her obvious discomfort was something to laugh about.

She returned her attention to Miles, with his cowboy hat and boyish smile. Yeah, a date with him would be nice. Fun even.

"Here's hoping you get that chance," she said. "I've always been a sucker for a guy in a cowboy hat."

Miles chuckled and touched the rim of his hat. "Good to know 'cause we're pretty inseparable."

Sterling, the spitter, appeared at Miles's side and tapped him on the shoulder. Then he asked to cut in.

Visions of getting drenched with spit filled Taycee's mind, so when Miles moved aside, Taycee said quickly, "Mind if we sit for a minute instead? My feet could use a break." Without waiting for an answer, she led him to two chairs facing each other and sat as far back as she could.

Sterling leaned forward, closing the gap she'd created. "So, you're a flower girl?" He laughed like he'd just stated the funniest pun ever.

Taycee forced a smile to her lips even as spittle landed on her hands. "That's one way of putting it."

"Well, if you ever need an accountant, I'm your guy." More spittle.

Taycee wedged herself deeper into her chair, folding her arms snug against her body. Maybe that would help. Or at least confine it to her dress rather than her bare skin. "I take it you're a numbers person?"

Sterling nodded, adjusting his glasses. "Always have been, always will be. In fact, back in high school . . ." Taycee tried not to cringe as the shower of spit came her way. Where were the other bachelors? On the real show, some guy was always cutting in, interrupting, or stealing away the bachelorette. Why weren't they doing that now?

A hand rested on her shoulder, and Taycee turned toward it, ready to say yes to anything that was asked of her. She followed the hand up to a handsome face with two blue eyes. Jake, the smooth-talker from California who'd wanted to whisk her away for a drive.

"You don't mind if I steal her for a dance, do you Sterling?" Jake said.

"But we just sat down and her feet hurt," Sterling spluttered.

As much as Taycee wanted to blurt out that she felt better now, she kept her mouth shut. Still, her eyes pleaded with Jake to save her. *Do something. Anything. Pretty please? With a hundred million cherries on top?*

He didn't disappoint. From his pocket he pulled out a deck of cards. "Tell you what, Sylvie. We're each going to draw a card from this stack. Highest card wins."

"Wins what?" Sterling stared at the cards in confusion.

"Taycee, of course."

Oh. Nice. Taycee frowned at the deck. Surely Jake could have thought of a less chancy way of saving her. Fifty-fifty weren't her kind of odds.

"Uh . . ." Sterling hesitated. Evidently he didn't like the odds either.

"C'mon. Draw a card. You can do it," Jake coaxed, fanning out the deck.

With a roll of his eyes, Sterling snatched one from the deck. "How do I know you're not scamming me?" he asked, looking at the card.

"You don't. That's part of the fun." Jake held the deck in front of Taycee. "Would you mind picking my card?"

"Uh . . . sure." Her fingers flitted across the top, finally resting on one. Please be higher than Sterling's. Please, please, please. With a tug, she pulled it free and held it up. "The ten of spades."

"I've got an eight of hearts." Sterling tossed the card at Jake and stood. "Looks like you win."

"You're a good sport, Sylvie." Jake slapped him on the back before shrugging out of his jacket and taking the empty seat across from Taycee.

"Do you always carry a deck of cards in your pocket?" Taycee said.

Jake's eyebrow rose. "What, not even a thanks for saving you?"

A red light glowed in her peripheral vision, reminding Taycee that whatever she said could be broadcasted over the internet in a few days' time. No need for all the viewers to know how she really felt about Sterling's salivary glands. "Saving me from what? Resting?"

A knowing smile played across Jake's tanned face, but he let the subject drop. He leaned forward, still holding the cards. "So, what's it going to be? 52-Card Pickup or a dance with me?"

Hmm . . . dancing or cards. Tough choice. Not. "How about this: If you can beat me in a game of Speed, I'll dance with you. If not, we stay here and talk."

A smile spread across his face. "All right. You're on." He pulled a small table closer, and then dealt the cards. Some of the other bachelors gathered around to watch as Taycee picked up her cards with confidence. This was her game—a game she never lost. She was saved from having to dance again.

They started playing, and within minutes, she slapped her last card on the table. "I won!" she called as cheers and clapping broke out around her.

"Hustler," Jake accused.

"Hey, a bet's a bet. You're not going to be a sore loser, are you?"

Murmurs broke out around Taycee, and a bachelor named Greg stepped forward. Tall and thin, he wore a wrinkled button-down shirt. "Move over, Jake," Greg said. "Give the rest of us a chance to win that dance."

And that's how it began. A game of Speed for a chance to win a dance with Taycee. With a contented smile, she settled into her out-of-the way seat and won game after game after game. Time started to fly. Granted, she wasn't getting to know the bachelors as well as she could of if she'd danced with them, but no matter. For the first time all day, Taycee was able to relax and enjoy the night. If a bachelor had a problem with it or didn't like cards then he wasn't a good fit for her anyway.

Taycee smiled in satisfaction as yet another bachelor vacated the seat in front of her. It was probably time to put an end to this game, but she wasn't quite ready—not when giving back the cards meant a return of the awkwardness. So she picked up the deck and shuffled the cards as another bachelor sank down opposite her.

When she glanced up, a few cards flew out of her hand. Luke smiled at her with a gleam in those confident brown eyes of his.

"Think you can beat me, too?" he said.

"Easy." Her fingers shook as she fumbled with the cards. Luke had been the one to teach her the game. There was a time they'd played it often—mostly because Taycee was determined to beat him at least once. So she kept trying and trying and trying, but she'd never won. Not once.

Luke hunched forward, and Taycee's eyes were drawn to the curve of his shoulders. What would it feel like to bury her face right there, just below his collar bone? To have his arms surround her, pulling her in and keeping her close as they swayed to the slow song now coming through the speakers?

It would feel good. Too good. It would make her feel things, want things, wish for things that would never happen.

She *had* to win this game because dancing with Luke would be a very bad idea.

Taycee took her time dealing the cards. It was ridiculous that Luke could upset her equanimity so easily. Here she was, in a room full of handsome guys that most girls would give anything to go out with. Who cared about Luke?

Not her.

No way.

Never.

"Go," said Luke.

No, no, no. She wasn't ready.

In what seemed like seconds, Luke's pile was gone, leaving her with three cards still in her hand. A wicked smile stretched across his face as he stood and held out his hand. "Looks like I won. Care to dance, Taycee Lynne?"

Of all the things he could have remembered about her, that nickname was the worst. Two words and she was like a puppy, lapping it up and drooling for more. But she didn't want to be like a puppy. She wanted to be strong. Confident. The kind of girl who was in complete ownership of her mind and her heart.

Nervous anticipation rippled through her body as she placed her hand in his. With a gentle tug, he pulled her to her feet and took her in his arms. His hand settled on her waist while another clasped her hand. He smelled clean with a hint of aftershave. She felt warm and good and scared all at once. Everything about him intoxicated her. His eyes, his smile, all the pent up memories she had of him.

Memories. Only memories.

Taycee gazed over his shoulder, avoiding those eyes that seemed to see right through her. Why did he have this effect on her? Why did she *let* him have this effect on her?

"Looks like you're having fun," said Luke, his breath hot on her ear.

"I *am* having fun."

"Even though you're stuck dancing with me right now?"

Taycee made the mistake of looking into his eyes. Those gorgeous, beautiful eyes that reeled her in like a fish that'd happily swallow any hook for a chance to be caught by him. "I was hoping you'd gotten rusty at Speed."

A moment of confusion gave way to a knowing smile. "That's right. We used to play that game all the time, didn't we?"

Pathetic, that's what Taycee was. Completely pathetic. Why? Because Speed had become one of her favorite games *because* of him. And he didn't even remember.

"You look good tonight," said Luke.

"Thanks." Okay, so maybe that redeemed him a tad. A millimeter at most.

"I still can't get over the fact that you're all grown up now. It's so . . . weird."

And like Humpty Dumpty, down he went again. It would never change, would it? No matter what, Luke would always think of her as Caleb's little sister. The nuisance. The girl who liked flowers and curly fries. The girl he could beat in cards.

The spicy smell of his cologne invaded her senses once again.

Please, someone save me.

"How do you feel about sharing, Luke?" asked Jake. "I think I've earned a dance."

Taycee resisted the urge to throw her arms around Jake.

This was twice now he'd come to her rescue, which proved that he was exactly the sort of person she should be paying attention to. And she would. Starting right now.

Luke relinquished his hold on Taycee, and she stepped into Jake's arms. Though not as tall as Luke, Jake was still tall. In fact, he was a good fit. His arms were warm and toned. His gait smooth. "So . . . you're a California boy," Taycee said. "Does that mean you surf?"

"Nope."

"Beach volleyball?"

"Occasionally."

"Red convertible?"

"Never."

Taycee smiled. "Well, you're tan at least."

He laughed. "That's debatable, but I do like the outdoors."

"Me too." She also liked Jake. Not only was he hand-some and charming, but he was comfortable and helped Taycee forget about everything else. The staring eyes. The cameras. The red lights. Luke.

Well, okay, *almost* everything else.

As the night wore on, Jake became her wooden post to lean on. He stayed near her side. He made her laugh. He stood back when she talked to someone else, and then stepped in to cover any awkward pauses. He kept her at a safe distance from Sterling. He stared down Alec when things got uncomfortable. And anytime someone asked her for a dance, he'd pull out his trusty deck of cards.

Luke, on the other hand, didn't approach her the rest of the night.

Eleven

wo days after the opening night, the footage appeared on the website. *Episode One,* Jessa called it. Taycee typed in SheltersBachelorette.com, saw that it was there, and then immediately closed the browser without clicking play. The probability was high that if she ever watched any of the episodes, she'd never go back in front of the camera again. Seeing her picture on the site was bad enough.

Business was slow, so Taycee spent most of her day organizing and de-cluttering. When an order of vases arrived that afternoon, she carried the box to her back room and placed one vase after another on the shelf with robotic-like movements. With nothing else to do, she straightened the rows, making all the vases uniform. There. Her mom would be so proud.

Her fingers drummed on the counter as she looked around. What now? A bridal magazine sat in the corner, so Taycee grabbed it and flipped through it, tearing out a few pages picturing beautiful bouquets that caught her eye. She'd been keeping a scrapbook of all her favorites for years now with the hope that someday she would get the chance to do the flowers for a large, extravagant wedding. But right now, the dream of long flower garlands, boutonnières, center-pieces, and gorgeous bridal bouquets was just that: A dream.

Sure, Taycee had done a few smaller weddings over the years, but nothing beyond a few simple bouquets and centerpieces. Those who could afford more impressive dis-plays always went to the larger, more established floral companies in Denver. Someday, though, she'd make a name for herself in the wedding industry. She would.

Bells jingled and Jessa's voice rang out, "Tace, you here?"

"In the back."

Jessa burst into the room, wearing several bracelets that clinked when she threw her arms around Taycee. "I've been trying to call you all day! Did you watch it yet? You were awesome! Our traffic is through the roof, and we've already earned more on voting sales than even I had anticipated. It's crazy!" Jessa let go and clapped her hands together gleefully. "I knew you'd make the perfect bachelorette. Or I should say 'The Barefoot Cardshark.'"

"The what?"

"It's the nickname people are calling you on the site."

"Oh." Taycee didn't know whether to be flattered or embarrassed by that. It sounded . . . well, ridiculous. She shut the bridal magazine and pushed it back to the corner. "I'm really glad for the sake of the town, but honestly, Jess, I'm so nervous about it all. Going out with ten guys during the next two weeks seems so wrong and awkward to me. Knowing that everything I say and do will eventually be viewed by whoever wants to watch it on the internet makes it even worse."

The bracelets clinked again as Jessa hopped up on the counter. "You spent several hours in the same room with twenty-one guys and now you're worried about ten individual dates? Pshh, you'll be fine."

If only Taycee shared her confidence.

"Speaking of which, who do you want the lucky ten to be?" Jessa said.

"So long as it's not Luke, I really don't care." But that wasn't entirely true. Miles and Jake would probably be her top choices. Greg would be fine also. Sterling and Alec, her last—next to Luke, of course.

"Sorry, girl, but Luke isn't leaving anytime soon. Based on the voting and discussions going on so far, he's one of the favorites. Jake's up there as well. Why do you want him off anyway? You two looked like you got along just fine the other night."

"He was supposed to be un-charming and try to get voted off," Taycee muttered.

"He wasn't."

"I noticed."

Jessa pursed her lips as she studied Taycee. "When you two danced, I'm telling you, sparks flew."

Sparks? As if. Maybe from Taycee, but definitely not from Luke. He was spark-less. For him, the highlight of the night had probably been driving Lumpy to The Barn and back. "It's all an act, Jess. He likes to be contrary. I told him I hoped he'd get voted off, so he's doing everything he can to stay on the show—exactly what he used to do when we were younger. It's like he hasn't matured at all in the last ten years."

"He looked pretty mature to me."

"Trust me," said Taycee. "He doesn't care. He never has. I just . . . want him off."

Jessa's expression turned soft. Sympathetic. Possibly even pitying. "He's an idiot then."

Taycee would have laughed, but it would have sounded fake. The kind of laugh where you tried to pretend you didn't care but really did—one Jessa would see right through. Her friend was right about one thing though. Luke was far too likeable and would most likely remain on the show for a while. Not okay.

It was time to get serious and come up with something better than a few yards of manure to get him voted off. But what?

When the morning sun peeked through the blinds, Taycee's head pounded from thinking and worrying and stressing over how to get Luke off the show. She mashed a pillow over her face and groaned until her cell phone rang. She'd barely said hello when Jessa's voice shouted in her ear, making her wince. What had Jessa said? Something about news or an interview or something?

Taycee held the phone away a couple of inches. "Come again? And not so loud this time?"

Jessa slowed her words, but the volume was just as loud. "Both KDVR and 9NEWS want to do an interview about the show and the charity event behind it!" she squealed. "I can't stop shaking I'm that excited."

It was enough to get Taycee moving. She sat up and scooted back against the headboard. Wow. Less than a week into the show and already Jessa had managed to scrounge up media coverage. How did she do it? "Jess, that's awesome. When do they want to interview you?"

"Me?" Jessa laughed. "No, they want to interview *you*."

"What?" Suddenly the news didn't sound so great after all. In fact, it sounded the opposite of great.

"Why would they want me when they could interview the bachelorette?"

Silence fell as Taycee digested this bit of info. Two news programs wanted to interview her. Not Jessa—Taycee. In front of real, professional cameras on real live TV. There would be no do-overs. No take backs. No "Can I rephrase that?" requests allowed. Granted, the bachelorette show really didn't give her those options either, but this was different somehow. Scarier. Actually, petrifying was a better word.

"Hello? Are you there?" Jessa's voice came again.

Ever so slowly, Taycee lowered the phone, pushed "end call," and set it down. Then she got up and walked into her bathroom. When her phone started to ring once again, she closed the door. It was time to get a new phone, along with a new number.

A number she would never, ever, EVER give to Jessa.

Twelve

The votes have been tallied and the top ten chosen! In no particular order, they are as follows:

Greg Jones, from Greensboro, North Carolina
Jake Sanford, from Sacramento, California
Sterling Montgomery, from Austin, Texas
Jason Sparks, from Tifton, Georgia
Luke Carney, from Shelter Springs, Colorado
Alec Jamison, from Rutherford, New York
Miles Romney, from Blackfoot, Idaho
Rhett Cox, from Gilbert, Arizona
Kent Burton, from Lafayette, Indiana
Gavin Spencer, from Spokane Washington

Congratulations guys! Now let's see what our bachelorette has to say about this news:

Taycee's fingers tapped lightly on the keys as she eyed the list yet again, hoping it had somehow changed, but Luke's name was still there. As were Alec's, Sterling's, and

Gavin's—four people she never would have chosen on her own.

Rats.

Really, she had no one to blame but herself. Jessa had given her the chance to take control and Taycee had turned it down. Why couldn't the viewers read her mind? C'mon, people. Alec? Really? The guy was flat out conceited. And Gavin? He didn't like games, small towns, or nature. Hello! Did they not read the profile Jessa had written about Taycee on the site? Apparently not. Either that or there were a lot of people who took the theory that opposites attract to a whole new level.

Oh well, whatever. Taycee could survive a few bad dates, but Luke was a different story. In fact, she'd happily clip another mic to her shirt and answer whatever additional questions Rachel Snyder from 9NEWS threw her way if it meant avoiding a date with Luke. Just thinking about it made her feel like she'd stepped on an ant hill and only just now realized tiny black bugs crawled all over her skin.

Taycee stared at the monitor, feeling completely uninspired. Just write your thoughts, Jessa had said, as if it would be easy. But it wasn't. Probably because Taycee's real thoughts would go something like: *Playing speed was fun and all, but I'm really not interested in dating anyone right now. And Luke, feel free to head on back to Ohio.*

The screen remained blank. Taycee scratched her head. Gnawed on her lower lip. Started to bite a fingernail until the image of Jessa's glare overrode all else. No biting manicured nails. Fine. Okay. She got it. Taycee sighed and did the only thing left to do. She wrote some truth and combined it with a lot of rubbish.

The ratio of twenty-one guys to one girl is something most girls would be ecstatic about. But not me. The night of the opening event, I was flat-

84

out intimidated and had it pegged for the most uncomfortable night of my life. I've never been great at entertaining, nor have I ever been the life of the party, and I worried I'd flop big-time. But, as it turned out, I had nothing to worry about. Each bachelor accepted me for me, which turned an awkward night into one of the most memorable nights of my life. I couldn't have asked for a better group of people to spend the evening with.

For those bachelors who won't be staying, I had a blast and wish you all the best in whatever comes your way. To you viewers who watched and voted, THANK YOU!!! I am obviously in good hands because you did a fabulous job picking the top ten. Some great guys are in that group. Rhett, with your mad break-dancing skills. Kent, and that hilarious episode with the punch. (So sorry—hope it comes out!) Miles, and your rodeo stories. Greg's trusty pen. Jake, and your cards. Sterling. Jason. Luke. Alec. Gavin. You guys all rock.

I'm so looking forward to fun times ahead!

Taycee scanned through the post and clicked "publish" before she second guessed herself. She closed her laptop and pushed it away. There. One more thing to check off her list. Now all she had to do was figure out a way to make Luke look bad so his name wouldn't appear among the next round of winners.

The answer came in the form of Missy Green, the former town flirt. Missy had left for California five years before, set on becoming a big-time movie star. Now she was back in all her tank-top, short-shorts, flaming red-haired glory, claiming it was only a coincidence that Shelter Springs was receiving media attention.

Missy first appeared in the background of Taycee's date with Sterling. He'd picked her up from The Bloom Boutique on Monday afternoon and drove her to a beautiful lake just outside of town. In a pathetic Hail Mary attempt for attention, Missy swam unnoticed to the center of the lake and called out in desperation for rescue during the middle of their picnic.

It was comical, really, considering Missy had always been a terrific swimmer.

But before Taycee could say anything, off came Sterling's shirt and in he went, executing an impressive freestyle to Missy's side. Who knew the spitting accountant could swim?

By the time he dragged her from the lake, Taycee fought the urge to thank Missy. Her theatrics had worked in everyone's favor. Missy got her two minutes of fame, Sterling proved himself the hero of the hour, and Taycee had a few moments free from a spittle shower.

The cherry on top? Taycee finally figured out how to get Luke voted off. Halle-freaking-lujah.

Later that night, she phoned Missy, got some much needed sleep, went to work, and then mentally geared up for date #2. Alec. Next to Luke, he was the most dreaded of all her dates.

A knock sounded on her apartment door as she swiped some lip gloss across her lips. Bracing herself for a long night ahead, she plodded to her door and pulled it open. Immediately, her gaze moved beyond Alec and to the Razor UTV nestled in the bed of his truck. Okay, so maybe the date wouldn't be as awful as she'd imagined.

"Ready?" In a fitted Tee and some khaki shorts, Alec looked great. Casual. The type of clothes you'd wear when romping on around the mountains in a UTV. Taycee, on the other hand, wore white capris and one of her new dressier shirts. Hmm.

"You didn't tell me to dress for that." Taycee pointed at the Mule. "Let me go and change real quick."

"You look great to me."

Taycee headed toward her room anyway. "I'll just be a sec." Did he have any idea how much this outfit had cost? No way was she about to climb in that thing wearing this. She threw on a dark T-shirt and denim shorts, and then pulled her hair back into her favorite navy Broncos baseball cap.

When she returned, Alec was still on her porch. "*Now* are you ready?" The annoyed way he said it made Taycee want to say "No" and shut the door in his face. It had taken her less than five minutes to change—something she wouldn't have had to do if he'd told her what to wear in the first place. Did he not know anything about tact?

Apparently not, because he gave her an un-impressed once-over. Taycee suddenly wished she'd changed into frumpy sweats instead—which she would have done, had he not turned and headed for his truck. Taycee followed. "Do I get to drive, too?" she asked, pointing to the Razor.

Alec's head shook. "Sorry, but it's my name listed on the rental agreement—not yours." With an insincere apologetic look, he opened the door and jumped in.

Taycee blinked. Wow. She turned in search of the camera. Was Burt getting all of this? She felt like grabbing the camera and saying, "Did you see that people? Not only is Alec NOT a gentleman, but he won't even let me drive the UTV. I don't care how handsome he is, if any of you vote for him again, you're idiots."

Burt had his cameral rolling, so Taycee walked around and opened her own door. Megan was already in back with her camera light on, so Burt climbed in beside her. Alec drove to some nearby mountain trails and backed the Razor off the truck while Burt and Megan set up the cameras. Then Megan stayed on the ground while Burt jumped in the back.

Normally, Taycee would have loved romping around in an awesome UTV, but by the time Alec pulled to a stop, she couldn't wait to get out. Not only did he really not let her drive, but he'd done nothing but talk about himself the entire ride. As far as Taycee was concerned, Alec could catch the nearest plane back to New York—assuming there was room for his enormous ego.

Her head pounded as she climbed from the vehicle and forced a smile. "Great ride."

Alec patted the hood. "Yeah, I think I'll have to get me one of these when I get back to New York. It's not nearly as exciting as motocross, but it's pretty cool."

Yeah, yeah, she got it already. He was a motocross fanatic. He'd also played baseball in high school, preferred to make money rather than get a higher education, was a connoisseur of fine wines (or so he claimed), and thought he was God's gift to women. Okay, so maybe he didn't really say that last bit, but he sure acted like he thought it.

"How about some dessert?" Alec said during the drive back. "We could stop at that diner in town—not that it will have much to offer."

"Actually, Maris's apple pie is amazing."

"I'm sure it is." His voice dripped with condescension, and Taycee fought the urge to tell him to stick it.

"I'm really not that hungry though," she said. If this was a chance to end the date a little early, she'd take it.

Alec tapped his hand against the wheel as they drove back toward town. He glanced lazily around as if bored. "Do you know of any good motocross races nearby? I was thinking we could check one out on our next date."

Taycee bit her tongue. Hard. It was the only way to keep from shouting, "If you think I'd ever go out with you again you're one stick short of a bundle!" Miles had used the expression during one of his rodeo stories, and she'd liked it so much she'd committed it to memory. It fit Alec perfectly right now.

"I don't," she said. "I've never been much for moto-cross."

That's all it took for Alec to start talking about the sport yet again, only this time he focused on all the dangers associated with it—as if she couldn't figure them out on her own. Race a bike around a dirt course riddled with hills, turns, jumps, and several other riders, and what do you get? Lots of opportunities to break bones or kill yourself.

Duh.

When Alec launched into a detailed account of every injury he'd ever received, Taycee tuned him out and made a mental list of the flowers she'd need to pick up tomorrow morning. A rush order had come in right before she'd closed up—too late to call in for the following day's delivery. Oh well. A funeral in a neighboring town was something she'd never say no to.

By the time Alec dropped her off, forty-five minutes ahead of schedule, Taycee gave him a quick hug goodbye and escaped inside her apartment. She sighed in relief. Never had her apartment felt so good.

No cameras. No guys. No noise. Only blessed silence.

How would she keep this up for six more weeks?

Thirteen

Luke stopped by Maris's diner for lunch with Missy Green in tow, clinging to his arm and wearing a bright pink tank top and matching high heels. She was like a yapping dog that had clamped down on his pant leg and wouldn't let go. He wanted to shake her off.

Missy had spent the last hour at his clinic prattling away while Luke examined her mother's cat—a perfectly *healthy* cat, albeit fat and lazy. Missy had snuggled up against him and peered over his shoulder the entire time, asking him to explain every little thing he did. The exam should have taken ten minutes, but Missy wouldn't shut up. The girl had more to say than the anonymous *Shelter's Bachelorette* gossip blog, and that was saying something.

Luke finally explained that he needed to close the clinic for lunch, and what had Missy done? Invited herself along. He could have kicked himself. Why hadn't he said he had another appointment? Needed to meet with his lawyer? Call his mom? Any excuse that would have sent Missy packing.

The customer in front of Luke moved forward, and Luke followed. "What do you feel like, Missy?" Maybe if she looked at the menu, she'd let go of his arm.

"I'll have whatever you're having," she purred.

"So you want a double cheeseburger, curly fries, and a chocolate shake?" Okay, so maybe Luke really didn't want that, but unless Missy had the metabolism of a humming-bird, no way would she order the same—not if she wanted to keep her current rail-thin figure.

She frowned. "Don't they have salads here?"

"I don't know. The menu is over there if you want to check." He pointed to a stack of menus next to the register and let out a relieved sigh when she finally relinquished his arm. Maybe he should make a run for it while he had the chance. Luke eyed the door, sorely tempted.

She came back only seconds later, wrapping her arm through his once more. "I'll take the Caesar salad, with the dressing on the side. They always put way too much when they mix it in on their own."

Luke tried not to roll his eyes as he placed their orders. Then he found a booth, hoping to hide behind the tall seat backs. But once he'd slid in, he realized his mistake. Instead of sitting across from him, Missy scooted right in next to him, forcing him to slide to the end of the booth. Thigh to thigh, knee to knee, she clung to his side.

Would it be wrong to push her on the floor and step over her on his way out? Maybe he could slide under the table and crawl out like a two-year-old. He didn't care at this point, not if it would rid him of Missy Green. The girl was like a giant squid with suction cups for hands.

"Luke, if I'd have known you'd be coming back to Shelter, I never would have left."

He cleared his throat. "When are you headed back to California?"

"Don't you worry." Missy scooted even closer, sand-wiching him against the window. "I'll be here all summer."

Luke turned to tell her exactly where she could put those suction cup hands for the rest of the summer, but once again, wrong move. In warp speed, her fingers wound around his neck, and her lips pressed against his.

What the—

In the middle of the day, in the middle of the diner, Missy Green kissed him. Shock gave way to anger and he shoved her away. Out of the booth and onto the floor, she landed in a bright pink heap. Without so much as a sorry, he stepped over her and headed for the door.

"He wants to meet me somewhere more private," Missy's voice echoed through the now quiet diner.

Several chuckles followed him as he fled, his lunch forgotten. He walked past his truck and headed down Main Street, needing some fresh air. What was Missy's problem anyway? She obviously had marbles for brains if she thought that stunt would really work.

Luke began to feel like he was cursed. Ever since he'd returned to Shelter, there had been nothing but problems. The town was about to go under. He was bachelor #21 on some ridiculous internet reality dating show. His veterinary practice wasn't taking off quite the way he'd imagined. And now, Missy Green.

Was this some sort of sign? A get-out-of-Shelter-before-the-sky-starts-falling warning? Luke's steps slowed. His gaze drifted up toward the clouds, willing them to reform into words. Sentences. Answers. Why did he come back here? Why did it feel like it made sense, that it was the right thing to do?

The stratus clouds continued to float slowly past, a freeform display of nothing at all. No answers. No assurances that he'd made the right decision and that everything would start looking up.

Luke let out a breath and turned to head back, pausing when he caught sight of a painted wooden sign. It was simple. No fancy graphics. No scrolls or decals. Just letters painted in a bold burgundy on a whitewashed background.

The Bloom Boutique.

He stared at it for a moment. Then stared at the store itself, with the handwritten "Be back by 1:00" note taped to the front door. Luke felt the sudden urge to hang out on the inviting front porch steps until Taycee returned, just to see her smile and hear what she'd have to say. She'd make the day look brighter.

A strange "here's your answer" feeling washed over him, but Luke shook it off. It was only a coincidence. That's all.

Over a week of early mornings and late nights had finally brought Taycee past the halfway point of the first two weeks. Her dates with Kent, Miles, and Gavin were now in the past, and Jason—well, almost. Only a doorstep scene to go.

Jason pulled to a stop in front of her apartment. "Stay right there. I'll get your door."

As much as Taycee appreciated a guy who'd open the door, Jason was over-the-top. He'd practically pushed the waiter aside to pull out her chair during dinner, and every time the air conditioning kicked on, he'd ask, "Are you too cold? I can ask the waiter to turn that down if you want."

"Thanks, but no. I'm good."

"You sure?"

"I'm sure."

"Are you hot then?"

"No. Really, I'm good. Promise."

It was a good thing they hadn't come across any puddles, because Jason probably would have stripped off his yellow polo shirt and thrown it down. Either that or scooped her up and carried her across. He was like a gentleman on a mission. And Taycee, well, she was a girl who liked to jump a puddle every once in a while, maybe even splash in one.

Jason helped her out of the car and kept her hand in his as they sauntered up the walk. On the doorstep, he caught her off guard by pulling her into his arms and trying to kiss her.

Palms on his chest, Taycee pushed him back. "Down boy."

A teasing glint sparked in his eyes. "Playing hard to get?"

"No. I just don't kiss on the first date. Never have, never will. Thanks for a fun night." With that, she left him standing on the doorstep without even a hug goodbye. The door closed between them, and she immediately twisted the deadbolt as if it would somehow keep her from ever having to see him again.

Taycee took a long, relaxing hot bath, and then wrapped herself in a soft terry cloth robe, crawled into bed, and opened her laptop. It had been two days since she'd talked with Missy and still no scandalous stories had surfaced on the *Behind-the-Scenes of Shelter's Bachelorette Blog*. Started by an anonymous citizen a few weeks before the show began, the blog was always an entertaining read, especially now that it focused mostly on the new bachelors in town. The writer was skilled in taking a tiny morsel of truth and turning into something outrageous.

Like today.

Taycee's jaw dropped when she read the title of the post: "Can Poly-dating Go Both Ways?" Below the words was a picture of Missy sidled up next to Luke in line at the diner. Taycee clamped a hand over her mouth as a giggle escaped. Holy cow, Missy had done it—she'd actually done it. And with photographic proof, no less. Taycee scrolled down. Missy and Luke all cozy in a secluded booth. Missy and Luke talking. Missy and Luke—*kissing? What?*

Her laptop slammed shut with a snap.

Luke had let Missy kiss him? Kiss him! Why would he do that? He'd never fall for someone like Missy, would he? Taycee shoved her laptop aside, hating that she cared enough to regret ever calling Missy Green. Why couldn't Taycee just let it go? Let him go? Why couldn't she move on?

She slid down in her bed and yanked up the covers to her chin. She needed to get her mind on something else. Anything. Work. Yes, that would do it. A lily arrangement needed to be done first thing in the morning. Five white Calla lilies and whatever else Taycee wanted to add. Maybe she would mix in some dark pink roses. Or better yet, keep it all white with added roses, snapdragons and salal. Yes.

White. Classic. Romantic. Perfect for a young couple in love.

An image of Luke's face popped into Taycee's mind. She grabbed a pillow, mashed it over her face and screamed, long and hard. Then she threw it across the room as the strains of Jessa's ringtone filled the silence.

She grabbed her phone.

"Wow, Luke's sure got those discussion boards zinging," Jessa said. "In one day flat, he's gone from one of the favorites to the bottom of the barrel. Pretty impressive."

This was exactly what Taycee had wanted. It was, it was, it was! But the picture of Missy's lips planted on Luke's wouldn't leave her mind. She felt like screaming again. "I'm sure he and Missy will be very happy together."

"Oh please, like Luke would ever go for someone like her," said Jessa. "I guarantee this was all Missy's doing. Her and her giant need for attention."

"He *let* her kiss him."

Jessa laughed. "Is that jealousy I hear in your voice?"

Ugh. Surely there was a better word for what she was feeling. Frustration? Annoyance? Confusion? Anything that sounded less pathetic than jealousy. "More like relief. Hopefully he'll get voted off now."

"You keep telling yourself that's what you really want if it makes you feel better."

"Believe whatever you want. You always do."

"Sheesh, someone's a little testy tonight," Jessa said. "I wonder why."

"I'm tired, okay? You try getting up early every morning, being on your feet all day long, and then going out with a different guy every night while two cameras follow you around."

"Hey, don't blame me. I told you to take some time off from work." Jessa sounded completely unrepentant. She was probably more concerned about what color of nail polish she should choose to paint her toes.

Taycee sighed. "You know I can't afford to do that. Besides, I like work. It's all the dating I could do without. After this show, I'm taking a long hiatus from all men. Did you know that Jason actually tried to kiss me tonight?"

"Did you punch him?"

"Just about."

Jessa laughed. "I would have."

"I have a little more self-control than you do."

"It's not called self-control," said Jessa. "It's called bottling your emotions. You're like a shaken can of soda ready to erupt. I honestly pity the guy that finally opens you up. Boy is he going to get it."

Taycee rolled her eyes. "Look at you, waxing all metaphoric. Maybe you should write that down before you forget it."

"Maybe I should."

"Great, I'll leave you to it then. Night."

"Night."

Taycee resisted the urge to throw her phone as she flopped back on her bed. Her lamp lit up her room in a dim glow, forming abstract shadows all over the walls. When the silence became too much, she turned up the volume on her clock radio, letting a despondent melody crackle through the speakers as she stared at the ceiling. Was Jessa right? Had she been bottling up her emotions, especially where Luke was concerned?

Or had she been burying them? Deep underneath, to a place that could never be breached by anyone. A place they might eventually fade away.

Fourteen

*D*ates #7 and #8 with Miles and Greg went better than all the other dates combined.

Miles took her to a demolition derby and entertained her with hilarious stories from his youth, and Greg took her miniature golfing, making her laugh at the way he sized up every hole and got frustrated when he didn't make par.

Now Friday loomed before Taycee like her own personal D-day, especially when Jake had an unexpected business emergency and asked to change their date from Thursday night to early Friday afternoon, which meant two dates in one day.

Nothing like finishing up round one with a bang.

It had been a bad day from the get-go. Not only had Taycee mixed up an order and needed to make an extra run to Colorado Springs, but she pricked her fingers at least a dozen times and even missed lunch.

By the time Jake picked her up at The Bloom Boutique, her head pounded and the skies threatened rain—a perfect match to her current mood.

Please, please say that Jake had something low-key planned. Like popcorn and a movie or a scenic drive through the surrounding mountains.

"I thought it would be fun to go hiking," he said, killing her hopes. "I hear there's a great waterfall at the end of a trailhead nearby."

Taycee's feet immediately complained, as did her stomach. "Sounds fun. Mind if we stop off at my place so I can change and get some hiking shoes?"

"Sure."

Back at her place, Jake, Burt, and Megan waited in the car as Taycee slipped on some khaki shorts and a T-shirt. She wolfed down two granola bars as she tied her shoes. When she finally resurfaced, Jake leaned casually against the passenger door of his black Audi, patiently waiting. He smiled and pulled the door open for her.

She hesitated on her doorstep before forcing her feet forward. Honestly, what was wrong with her? She should be giddy at the prospect of a date with Jake Sanford. A normal girl would have left work early. Pampered herself. Dressed carefully. Applied her makeup with care, and then waited impatiently for him to arrive with his adorably mussed hair and light eyes.

"Wow, you deserve an award for the fastest change time ever," Jake said.

"Keeping nice guys waiting isn't my style."

"I seriously doubt anyone would mind waiting for you."

Taycee smiled as she sat down on a tan leather seat. "Nice car."

"Thanks. It comes with the job."

The door shut and Jake walked around to the other side. Taycee did a quick inspection of the car, but it didn't really tell her anything about Jake—other than he was a neat freak. Or maybe he'd just had the car detailed for the date. There wasn't a speck of dust anywhere, no gum wrappers, pens, or even coins in the cup holders. Everything was pristine. Perfect. Like Jake. Maybe a bit too perfect.

Was that the problem?

Jake slid in beside her, started the car, and headed out of town.

"What kind of job gives you a car?" Taycee said.

"The family business kind." He chuckled. "Still impressed?"

"Ah. So you're one of *those* kids."

"Guilty yet grateful," he said. "What sort of kid are you?"

"Average," she said.

Jake shot her a doubtful look, but didn't argue. "What about your parents? Do they live around here?"

"No. They retired to Florida several years ago. They wanted sun and more sun, with no threat of snow ever. That's what they got." She smiled, but it wasn't exactly sincere. In her mind, they'd chosen nice weather over her. It still stung when she thought about it like that.

The car started the climb up the narrow mountain road, next to a grove of Aspen trees that seemed to wave at them. Clustered together like one large family unit with their root system all interconnected, they were a rude reminder of what Taycee no longer had. It had been four years since her parents had left, even longer since her brother had gone, and yet she'd never really reconciled herself to the change. It was like her roots were just hanging out there, floundering around and searching for something new to hold onto.

"What do they think of this bachelorette show?" Jake asked.

Taycee blinked, suddenly remembering why she was with Jake in the first place. Burt and Megan sat quietly behind them while a camera filmed her every move and word. She let out a breath. What had Jake asked? Oh yeah, her parents. The show. "I haven't told them yet. They'd probably freak out and lecture me about how dating more than one guy at the same time is asking for trouble."

Jake unrolled his window. "As long as we're both being honest, my sister signed me up without me knowing. I would never agree to do something like this on purpose."

"Really?" For some reason, that made Taycee like Jake even more. He was here against his will, too. A pawn, like her. It felt good to know she wasn't the only one who could be manipulated—other than Luke, that is.

"Yeah." Jake's elbow hung out the window while his fingers drummed against the top of the car door. "She interferes like that. All the time. I was mad at first, but when my video made it as a finalist, I figured, hey, why not?" He shot her a quick look. "Besides, I've always been a sucker for green-eyed brunettes."

"Ahhh, thanks." Even though her eyes were hazel, not green. It made Taycee doubt his sincerity, like he would have said blue-eyed blondes or brown-eyed redheads if her hair and eyes were a different color. Or maybe Taycee had become too jaded.

Jake pulled to a stop at the trailhead at the same time thunder rattled through the skies. He pulled out a few ponchos to take with them while Burt and Amy worked to waterproof their gear. Then away they all went. A mile later, the skies opened up and rain came pouring down. They quickly donned their ponchos, but it didn't take long for the dirt path to become a muddy mess, attaching to the soles of Taycee's shoes like a thick paste that became heavier with every step.

She was about to suggest they turn back when her foot slipped out of her hiking shoe. She grabbed onto Jake to keep from losing her balance and pointed behind her. "The mud ate my shoe."

"What?" Jake twisted his head back, and then laughed when he saw her shoeless foot dangling behind her. With a firm grip on Taycee's arm, he reached back and tugged hard on the shoe. With a *splack*, the shoe dislodged, pitching Jake backwards. Taycee planted her socked foot in the mud to keep from following him to the ground.

Jake sat in the mud, eyeing the shoe with a so-not-worth-it expression.

"Really, that was above and beyond. It was only a shoe." Taycee tried to swallow the gurgle of laughter in her throat, but it escaped. Followed by more giggles.

His gaze shifted to her as he held out his hand. "Do me a favor and help me up."

She shook her head. "I don't think so. I have an older brother, so I know from experience what will happen if I give you my hand." She paused. "I'd love my shoe back though."

Other than slightly raised eyebrows, his expression remained impassive as he dutifully held out the shoe. Taycee hesitated for a second, and then took it from him. It was on the tip of her tongue to say "Thanks" when he lunged for her hand and dragged her down beside him.

"Oh, I'm sorry," Jake said. "I didn't mean to do that."

"This means war." Taycee grabbed a handful of mud and slapped it in his face. Jake reciprocated, and before long, they were both covered in mud and laughing. They sat there for several minutes before Jake finally pulled her up. Together they trudged the mile back to the car and stood there, looking through the windows at the clean interior.

"So what's the plan?" Taycee asked, nudging him from the side. "Let Burt or Megan drive while we ride on top?"

Jake turned his gaze upward, squinting into the rain. "The way I see it, if we stand here long enough, it will be like taking a shower."

"True." Taycee started rubbing the mud from her arms and body as best she could. Jake followed suit while Burt and Megan ducked inside the car. Taycee then removed her poncho and turned it inside out so she had something semi-dry to sit on while she peeled off her muddy shoes and socks. Once again, Jake followed her lead and soon they were all shut back inside Jake's now only partially immaculate car.

"You obviously have experience with this sort of thing," Jake said.

"My mom's a neat freak too."

"I'm not a neat freak," argued Jake. But the stiff way he sat forward, trying not to touch the back of his seat, told Taycee otherwise. She held back a laugh.

On their way back down the mountain, Jake called for take-out from the diner. They picked it up and took it to Taycee's shop where they ate surrounded by the clutter of flowers, vases, and ribbons. No matter how many times she tried to organize and de-clutter, it never really looked clean—something she became even more aware of now that Jake sat across from her.

They ate and chatted until Taycee finally glanced at the clock. Her eyes went wide when she noticed the time. "Oh shoot, we've got to go." Luke would be at her place any second, and she was a mess. Stringy hair, damp clothes, remnants of mud everywhere. She could already hear Luke's voice: *Did you save some mud for the pigs?* or *Hey, you really didn't need to dress up just for me.* Or, more likely he'd say something loaded with innuendo. *Wow, somebody had a good time. Want me to take off so you two can get back to it?*

Jake helped her clean up before they dashed through the rain and back to his car. By the time they arrived, Luke was already there, waiting in his truck.

Crap.

Taycee leaned over and gave Jake a quick hug. "Thanks for a really fun date." In a matter of a few hours, he'd managed to turn a bad day around for her, making her forget about her aching feet and pounding head—not to mention her upcoming date with Luke.

Well, almost forget.

Jake tugged on a clump of her hair. "Not everyone can pull off this look you know. But somehow, you make mud look good."

Taycee smiled, and then grabbed her shoes and bolted through the rain to her apartment door. She quickly scrubbed herself off in a real shower, yanked her hair back into a damp ponytail, changed into some dry clothes, and threw on her favorite Bronco's baseball cap. After shoving her feet into a pair of blue platform sneakers, she raced back outside.

Her shoe landed in a muddy puddle just outside of Luke's truck. She felt like cursing as she jumped inside and slammed the squeaky door against the downpour.

"Your shoes are muddy," was the first thing Luke said.

Taycee looked pointedly at the faded and cracked upholstery, old radio, and matt-less floor—a stark contrast to Jake's Audi. "They fit right in."

Luke patted the dashboard. "It might be old, but it's clean—well, *was* clean."

"Seriously?" Taycee said, but his gaze remained impassive. "Okay, so what do you want me to do with my shoes?"

He gestured behind him. "Back there would work."

"The backseat?" Burt and Megan were already there, looking squished with their camera gear. Taycee wasn't about to hand her shoes to them.

"The bed," Luke clarified.

Taycee blinked. "Are you kidding me?"

"Nope."

"Unbelievable." With jerky movements, Taycee pulled her shoes off her feet, opened the door, leaned out, and tossed them into the truck bed before slamming the door shut again. "There. Satisfied? Or would you like me to ride in the back with my shoes?"

"Nah, you're fine."

"Gee, thanks."

He grinned as he flung the truck into reverse and backed out. Like Taycee, he wore a baseball hat, only his was red with "OHIO STATE" stitched across the front. She'd forgotten how good he looked in baseball hats.

"Don't worry," Luke said. "We're not going anywhere you'll need shoes."

"Is that supposed to make it okay?"

He shrugged. "It's a win-win. You get to ride shoeless, which I know you prefer, and my truck stays clean. What's wrong with that?"

Taycee stared at him. "The fact that you don't understand what's wrong with that makes it all the more wrong."

"There's an argument for you."

Taycee glared but said nothing more as they passed through town and headed toward the highway. Ten minutes later, he turned down his long, windy driveway.

"We're going to your house?" she asked.

"You're quick."

Taycee shot him a pointed look. At first she figured the shoe thing had been his way of messing with her. But he'd been so quiet during the drive here, which wasn't like him at all. Was he upset with her for some reason? Maybe he'd decided that he didn't really want to be here either. Or maybe he'd been dreading this date as much as she had— only for different reasons.

She frowned as he pulled the truck into the garage and turned off the engine. "Stay here," he said before ducking out. With a bang, he jumped into the bed and fiddled with something above them. What was he doing? She unrolled her window and stuck her head out, trying to get a peek. "Need any help?"

"Nope."

Suddenly, a bright blue rectangle appeared on the gray wall in front of her. A few moments later, blue turned to black as words appeared on the wall of his garage. A movie.

And not just any movie. *Sneakers*—a show she, her brother, and Luke had watched over and over and over when they were younger. The boys used to take off their shoes and put their smelly feet in her face while they teased her about how she initially thought the show would be about shoes. She'd loved every minute of it.

Luke actually remembered.

The door opened, and Luke climbed back inside. In his hands, he held a large bowl of popcorn, along with two cans of Red Cream Soda—her favorite. He unrolled his window, and then passed her a drink and the popcorn.

Taycee's eyes met his even as her heart beat a million times a second. "So the shoes . . ."

"I had you going, didn't I?" Luke grinned and pointed to his own feet, now bare. "Just like old times."

But it wasn't like old times—a realization that made Taycee shift uncomfortably in her seat as she stared at the make-shift drive-in movie screen. This was exactly what she'd wanted for a date tonight: A time to relax and not worry about making conversation. But all of a sudden, everything seemed so much more complicated. As if the past and the present had collided with a colossal bang, tearing at Taycee's heartstrings.

She wanted to believe that they could so easily go back to those days, but they couldn't. "Just like old times" was a lie. A clichéd saying that made people believe they could break open a memory and somehow recreate it and relive it for one blissful moment. But ultimately all it did was turn a once-happy memory into a sorry reminder that things could never be the same. No matter how much she or Luke wanted them to be.

Fifteen

Taycee sat on the leather couch adjacent to the stone fireplace in The Barn. Burt had just finished setting up and they now waited for Jessa, who wanted to do a quick interview about the first ten dates.

It seemed like overkill, since Taycee had already re-capped each date on SheltersBachelorette.com, but Jessa didn't think a few short paragraphs were enough. She wanted more. Always more. Jessa was out to prove she could orchestrate the best bachelorette show ever, and Taycee got to be her pawn.

Lovely.

Jessa breezed into the room, said a few words to Burt, and then plopped down opposite Taycee. Without so much as a "hi," she cued Burt to start filming.

"So, Tace, talk about two crazy busy weeks, huh?" Jessa said, sounding perfectly composed.

"Um yeah, pretty crazy. I'm glad it's behind me."

"After tonight you'll be down to only five bachelors. How do you feel about that?"

Would it be rude to say "The fewer the better?" Probably. "Actually, I'm kind of glad. Don't get me wrong, they're all great guys, but dating ten different bachelors over the course of two weeks kept me a little too busy, if you know what I mean. I'm more of one-guy-at-a-time kind of a girl, so I'm ready to narrow it down some."

Jessa leaned forward, clasping her fingers around her crossed leg. "Now that you've spent some quality time with each of them, is it going to be hard to say goodbye to some?"

As long as Taycee didn't have to do it in person, then no. And if Sterling, Alec, Gavin, and Luke were among the five leaving, Taycee might even throw a celebratory party. "Let's just say that I've enjoyed my time with all of them and hope that life deals them a great hand from here on out."

"How diplomatic of you," said Jessa. "Are there any particular bachelors you'll be sorry to say goodbye to if it comes to that? Anyone you've made a special connection with?"

Special? Not really. Connection? Possibly. Or, at least the hope of a connection. "Oh, I definitely feel like I've connected with some more than the others, but since it's in the viewers' hands, I have to trust that they will make a good choice for me." There, how's that for being diplomatic?

"What about Luke? How do you feel about all the pictures of him and Missy? There's been quite a stir on the message boards and people would love your take on it all."

Taycee should have known this question would be coming. Was this the reason for the impromptu interview?

"I . . . uh . . . don't know," Taycee finally hedged. There were a lot of things she could say. Like how she and Luke hadn't even been out on a date when it happened, how they weren't in a mutually exclusive relationship, or how Luke didn't want to be on the show in the first place. But all of those answers would sound as though Taycee didn't find fault with Luke's actions—which she didn't—but she also didn't want the viewers to know that. She wanted Luke voted off.

"I think however Luke chooses to spend his time off camera is up to him." There. Another diplomatic answer that didn't necessarily help Luke's image, but didn't exactly worsen it either.

"Are you hoping he gets voted off, or would you like him to stay around for a while longer?"

Jessa wouldn't let it go, would she? Taycee shot her a thinly veiled you-are-so-going-to-pay-for-this-later look. "Well, that's the great part about it, isn't it? I don't have to hope or worry because it's in the viewers' hands, not mine. They chose ten great guys this past week, and I'm sure the five they narrow it down to will make for a great week also."

"Very true." Jessa settled back in her seat and looked directly at the camera. "Speaking of the final five, the voting is now officially open, so cast your votes for whoever you think will be a great match for Taycee, and remember that every time you vote, your money is going to a good cause. Thanks so much for your support!"

The camera light finally flickered off. Taycee let out a breath of relief before giving Jessa the glare she deserved.

"Sorry." Jessa patted Taycee's knee in a motherly fashion. "I had to do it. You answered them all brilliantly though."

"This is going to cost you another favor, just so you know."

"Yeah, yeah. Just put it on my tab."

Sixteen

*T*aycee squinted through the peep hole on her front door. A distorted, magnified face stared back with large crossed eyes and cheeks sucked in, making a fish face. She squealed and flung the door wide open, throwing her arms around the stocky guy standing on her front porch.

"Caleb, what the heck? Why didn't you tell me you were coming? Are you back for good?" Her brother had always said that he'd consider moving back near Shelter once some of his bigger cases were all wrapped up. That was over eight months ago. Was it finally happening?

Caleb lifted her off the ground and squeezed the breath out of her before setting her back down. "Sorry, sis. I'm only here for the night. We've brought in a firm from Denver to help out with a marathon case we've been working on, so I'll be spending some time up there for the next several weeks. Which means"—He grinned—"I'll get to drop in on you every once in a while. Awesome right?"

"Yeah. Awesome." It sort of felt like someone had given her a beautiful bouquet of flowers and then taken it away, saying, "Oops, sorry. Wrong recipient." Taycee hadn't seen her brother in months, and with every passing day, she worried more and more that he'd never move back. What would she do if Caleb followed in her parents' footsteps and decided to make a permanent life elsewhere?

She would cry long and hard, that's what.

"You don't mind if I crash here tonight, do you?"

"Of course not." Taycee waved him inside. "I'll take whatever I can get. I was just hoping this would be a longer visit—possibly even long enough to check out a few potential office spaces?"

"I'll be working at least sixteen hour days the rest of the week, so no can do," Caleb said, sliding the strap of his overnight duffle over his head. His light brown hair had grown longer since she'd last seen him, but the new look suited his casual, go-with-the-flow personality.

"Sixteen hour days? Are you serious?"

"Cheer up. I'll most likely be back a few more times before the summer's out, so hopefully one of these trips I can extend my stay a little longer and we can really catch up—not that you'll be able to squeeze me in, what with your busy dating schedule and all."

Taycee slugged him in the arm. "Don't make me regret telling you about that or you'll get the couch tonight instead of the guest bed."

Caleb ran his hand across the back of her micro suede couch. "It actually feels pretty comfortable."

So much for that threat. "C'mon, Caleb. I'm embarrassed enough as it is. I don't need you making it worse."

"Fine. But only because I'm starving and you probably won't feed me if I do." He held up his bag. "Where can I put this?"

Taycee showed him to the guest room, and then left him to get settled while she rummaged through her fridge for something to make for dinner. Leave it to a guy to think a girl always had extra food on hand. She frowned at the contents of her fridge. Only a few pieces of chicken and some vegetables. Mmmm . . . maybe pasta. Yes, basil chicken could work.

Soon chicken was frying on the stove next to a bubbling pot of pasta. Taycee diced broccoli and tomatoes when Caleb wandered back in. He sank down on a nearby bar stool. "I hope it's okay that I invited Luke for dinner. Since I'm only here for the night, I figured we could catch up. It's been forever since I've seen him."

The knife stilled in Taycee's hand. Luke? Coming here? Tonight? She resumed her chopping, slicing through the vegetables with renewed force. Caleb and Luke together? In the same room? With the topic of *Shelter's Bachelorette* hot off the let's-gang-up-on-Taycee press? Ugh. She could think of several things she'd rather put up with. Hanging out with Liza for one.

"Why don't you invite the rest of Shelter while you're at it?" Taycee grumbled. "I'm sure I have enough food lying around."

Caleb grabbed a chunk of raw broccoli and tossed it into his mouth. Between chews, he said, "Sorry. Didn't think about that."

Obviously. "Just don't tell Jessa. I'm not supposed to interact with any of the bachelors off camera."

"Wow, they're really taking this show seriously, aren't they?" A chunk of tomato disappeared in his mouth. "If you're really worried, I can always call him back and un-invite him."

"No, it's fine. He's coming to see you anyway—not me."

Taycee checked the chicken while Caleb ate another piece of broccoli. He wandered over to the stove and took the tongs from her, prodding the chicken as if it would somehow make it cook faster. "I still can't believe you're dating my best friend. That's wrong on so many levels."

"I completely agree." Taycee took the tongs back and pushed him out of the way. "Hovering won't make it cook any faster, you know. Now stop snitching and get some plates from the cupboard."

"So bossy." Still, he opened the cabinet doors in search of plates.

Thirty minutes later, just as Taycee removed the finished pasta, the doorbell chimed. Without waiting for an answer, Luke let himself in. He wore a large cowboy hat and a trench coat with the collar sticking up to hide his face.

"Long time no see." Caleb laughed as he clapped his friend on the back. "What in the heck are you wearing, man? Is there a spring storm coming that we don't know about?"

Luke looked down and examined himself as if his wardrobe was nothing out of the ordinary. "Personally, I think The Mysterious Cowboy is a great look for me. What do you think, Taycee Lynne?" He opened the coat, revealing a button down plaid shirt, khaki shorts, and cowboy boots. Yes, cowboy boots. With shorts.

Taycee choked back a laugh. "Change mysterious to goofy, start chewing on some straw, and you'd have it about right."

Luke shrugged out of the coat and tossed it over the back of the couch, throwing the hat on top. Then he removed the boots, revealing white ankle socks and toned calves. *Really* toned calves. Taycee swallowed and quickly forced her attention back to their dinner.

"In case you couldn't tell, it's a disguise." Luke padded toward her, acting as comfortable in Taycee's apartment as he had in their home growing up. "I swear that gossip blog has eyes and ears all over town. My reputation's already tanked, and I don't want to bring Taycee down with me. I even parked a few blocks away to be safe."

Caleb picked up the cowboy hat, examined it, and then dropped it on his head. "Dude, you're paranoid. You both are."

"Maybe, maybe not." Luke plopped down on a barstool and leaned forward on his elbows. "But have you read those discussion threads? Dang, they're brutal. It's completely okay for Taycee to date twenty guys at once, but if I'm caught on camera with another girl, watch out."

Wait, Luke actually read the discussion boards? Taycee felt a pang of guilt at this. Did he really care what was said? He seemed like such an impenetrable wall of confidence that she'd never worried about how something like that might affect him. "So stop reading them," she said. "I never do. Jessa can keep you up-to-date on all the important stuff."

"Hmm . . . Jessa McCray," Caleb said it slowly, drawing out the name as if Jessa was someone worth considering. "What's she still doing here? She's not exactly the small-town type."

Taycee shoved a pitcher under the faucet and started filling it with water. Of course Jessa was a small-town type. She loved Shelter Springs as much as Taycee did. Well, maybe not quite as much, but enough to keep her here and actively trying to save it. Taycee frowned at Caleb, as if his mentioning it would somehow make Jessa want to up and leave, too. "She loves it here. Not that you'd know that since you barely know her."

"I know enough." Caleb leaned against the counter, folding his arms. "She plastered your face and name all over the internet without your consent—not exactly something a real friend would do. The lawyer in me would tell you to sue."

"Wait." Luke shot Taycee a look. "What do you mean without your consent? You didn't know?"

Taycee set the pitcher on the table and faced Luke. "Do you really think I would have volunteered you if I'd known?"

"Why didn't you tell me?"

"It never came up."

"Really?" Luke arched one of his dark brown eyebrows.

"Because I can think of several times in the past few weeks that it could have definitely come up."

Taycee removed the silverware from the drawer, avoiding eye contact. He was right. She could have easily told him before, but something had always stopped her. Maybe there was a bit of a devil inside her that hoped the longer it took for him to discover the truth, the sorrier he'd be for tormenting her when he finally did find out.

But he didn't look sorry. Only confused.

Yeah, well, join the club. I can't figure me out either. "I guess I was too mad at you for accusing me of wanting to date you," she finally said, and then immediately wished the words back. Great. Now she sounded like a teenager coddling a grudge.

Caleb laughed. "That's my sister for you. You should know better than to get on her bad side. Don't you remember that night we went spelunking without her? She didn't talk to us for weeks."

If only Caleb's memory could be as bad as Luke's. "Yeah well, Luke doesn't remember much of his former life, do you?" she said. When his eyebrows knit together, Taycee quickly turned away, opening the closest cupboard in search of who knew what. She'd said too much, and it had come out less light-hearted than she'd intended, possibly even accusatory.

"Dinner's all ready," she said brightly, closing the cupboard with a loud bang. A really loud bang. She turned to find both Caleb and Luke staring and making her feel like she was a new species under a microscope. Taycee pointed to the door and side-stepped toward it. "Oh, I uh, just remembered something I need to do at the shop real quick. Go ahead and eat, and I'll be back in a few minutes." What she needed was a few minutes to herself—away from Luke. Taycee headed for the front door, only to be stopped by a hand on her wrist. Luke's fingers curled around her sensitive skin, sending a jolt up her arm. Her heartbeat slowed to a loud thud as she met his gaze.

"Whatever it is can wait ten minutes while you eat some dinner," Luke said. "Caleb just got here. Don't you want to catch up first?"

Taycee glanced at Caleb, and then back to Luke again. She sighed. "You're right. I'll go after dinner."

With his hand still holding her captive, Luke smiled. "Good. It'll be fun. Just like old times."

There it was again. Just like old times. If Taycee heard that expression one more time, she would scream. Why was Luke so determined to recreate the past anyway, especially when he didn't even remember half of it? He'd been the first to leave. The first to dispense with the friendship they'd once shared as if it were a piece of lint on his clothes.

Taycee pulled her arm free. "Let's eat."

"About time," Caleb said.

Luke followed Taycee to the table, taking the seat next to her. "You got here just in time, Caleb. The videos of Taycee's last two dates went live today."

Taycee's foot connected with Luke's shin under the table.

"Ouch," he said.

"Tonight?" Caleb shot her a meaningful glance. "You said it was tomorrow."

"Oops. My bad." Taycee glared at Luke. "The next time my brother invites you over, just say no, okay?"

"I don't think so. Being with you two is way more interesting than eating alone." He grinned as he picked up his fork. "This really is just like old times isn't it?"

Taycee picked up her glass and chugged the water, drowning out the expletives threatening to spill out of her mouth.

Seventeen

Luke's eyes followed Taycee as she walked out the front door. She said she needed to take care of something at her shop, but it sounded like an excuse—a way to avoid being around him and Caleb. Or was it just him?

Luke frowned.

Why couldn't Taycee be more like her brother? All it took was a few minutes for Luke and Caleb to be back to the easy friendship they'd once had. But with Taycee, things were different. Harder. Why? From Luke's perspective, their date had gone well and they were finally making some headway. But now things were back to stiff and uncomfortable, as though Taycee purposefully threw up walls to keep him out. It made Luke want to tear them all down and force his way back into her life, but he had no idea how to go about it.

Luke missed the idolizing, relentless little tomboy with her braces and wild hair. The girl who'd been wide open and wall-less, demanding the same from anyone who wanted to be called her friend. What had happened to that girl?

"So, you're dating Tace, huh?" Caleb dropped down on the couch next to Luke. He picked up the remote and flipped on the TV. "Isn't that sort of like dating your sister?"

Luke only wished it was, and then maybe it wouldn't bother him so much. But a brother wouldn't miss his sister as soon as she walked out the door. He wouldn't want to keep her from leaving, sit next to her, or touch her. And he especially wouldn't want to kiss that impassive expression off her face.

Argh, what was he thinking? This was Taycee Lynne they were talking about—his best friend's younger sister. Luke needed to remember that. "Actually, it hasn't been so bad. She's . . . cool." More than cool. She was funny, smart, and intriguing.

"No way." Caleb grinned. "You like her."

Luke grabbed the remote from him. "Of course I like her. I always have. She's fun to hang out with."

"No," said Caleb. "I mean you *like* her."

Luke shook his head. He was in no way ready to admit that out loud, especially not to her brother. "Wrong."

"I'm never wrong."

"You are about this." Luke flipped through the stations, stopping on ESPN. "I've sworn off girls for a while, at least until I get my practice up and running. That's why I like your sister. There's no pressure with her."

Caleb laughed. "No pressure? Are you kidding me? You're in a freaking dating contest with her. How can you call that no pressure?"

"Please." A push of the remote button and another show came on. "I'm only doing it because there's a chance it could help Shelter, and I'm pretty sure Taycee feels the same way."

Caleb leaned back and propped his feet on the coffee table. "I'm actually glad she got suckered in to doing it. It'll be good for her, and with any luck, she'll even find someone to settle down with once and for all." He paused. "Hey, you've met the other guys, right? What are they like? Anyone Taycee might go for?"

"You're seriously asking me that?"

"Sure, why not?" Caleb grinned. "Unless of course, *you're* hoping for that honor."

"Sorry, no." Luke punched the remote button again, this time harder. "And I'm no matchmaker either, so don't ever ask me that again. Besides, your sister is old enough to pick her own dates. How would you feel if she tried to hook you up with Jessa?" It was a defense tactic. A way to keep the subject away from Taycee and the fact that she could fall for one of the other guys, because for whatever reason, Luke didn't like that idea at all.

Caleb made a face. "I'd tell her I've already got me a girl."

"Who? An inflatable in your suitcase?"

"Her name's Jenny." Caleb hesitated. "She's actually uh . . . my fiancée. As of two nights ago."

Luke flipped off the TV and turned to face his friend. "Are you serious, man?"

"Yep."

"Congrats! That's awesome. Does Taycee know?"

"Not exactly." Caleb scratched his head, looking a little sheepish. "That's the tricky part. Before I left for law school, I sort of promised I'd come back to Shelter one day and set up a practice here. Taycee's never let me forget it, and I've never dared to correct her. I guess I thought she'd get used to me being gone and stop asking me about it, but she won't. She's got it in her head that I'll be coming back as soon as I wrap up a few cases at work."

Luke nearly laughed at how ridiculous that sounded. What did Caleb think she'd do? Make a voodoo doll, name it Caleb, and torture him the rest of his life? Actually, she might do exactly that if Caleb kept his engagement from her much longer. "Dude, you've got to tell her. She's going to be ticked if you don't."

"I know, I know. It's one of the reasons I came here. But there hasn't been a good time to bring it up. It's a big deal, you know? To her anyway. She's not going to take it well."

"Are we talking about the same person? Taycee's lived on her own since she graduated from high school. She owns her own shop, makes her own food, and stars in her own internet show. I think you're underestimating her. She's pretty independent."

"I agree," Caleb said. "She is independent. But you weren't there after you left, or when my parents decided to move, or when I spilled the beans that I was headed to Arizona for law school. Total basket case. Why do you think she never left Shelter? She *hates* change."

"Wait—what did my leaving have to do with anything?" Luke said, suddenly very interested in the answer.

Caleb shrugged. "She was miserable for weeks. I think she had a bit of a crush on you back then and took it pretty hard when you dropped off the planet. Then when your parents announced they were moving, she practically shut herself in her room for days."

Luke whistled and settled against the back of the couch. "I had no idea. I guess I'm not the type to stay in touch with people. I just moved on with my life and thought everyone else had too." But if he'd known Taycee would take it that hard, he would have tried a little harder. Especially if he'd known he'd eventually wind up back here.

Caleb made a grab for the remote, stealing it from Luke. The TV flipped back on. "Don't beat yourself up about it. She eventually got over it. As did I—after years of therapy, that is."

Luke chucked a pillow at him. "Shut up."

"You shut up." Caleb scanned the channels once again before turning off the TV. "Nothing's on. I say we find Taycee's laptop and watch the show before she comes back and makes us turn it off."

Luke pointed at the bookcase near the TV where a silver laptop sat on top. "You mean that laptop?"

Caleb retrieved it and immediately pulled up the website. All the dates from the first two weeks were posted. Ten in all. Caleb rubbed his hands together gleefully. "Shall we begin? It's been a long time since I had anything new to tease Taycee about."

"It probably doesn't help that you live a state away."

Caleb clicked "play" on date number one, and they both settled back to watch. The filming was definitely low budget, with terrible lighting and not the best sound quality, but Luke hadn't expected anything different when he saw the inexpensive camera equipment they used. The editing, on the other hand, was more impressive, highlighting the interesting stuff and jumping from scene to scene in a fluid way. Luke chuckled when Taycee refused Jason's kiss, and then laughed when Sterling dove into the lake to save Missy Green.

"She's not worth saving," he said to no one in particular, still bitter about what had happened at the diner.

"You sure about that?" said Caleb. "According to Taycee you two looked pretty cozy."

"Please. Missy wanted her five minutes of fame, and I was just an innocent bystander." But the fact that Taycee had brought it up to Caleb meant something, didn't it? Luke picked at a nonexistent piece of lint on his shirt. "What else did Taycee say?"

The look Caleb shot his way made Luke immediately wish the words back. "Holy crap, you do like her."

"Will you stop reading into things? I do not."

"Do too."

Luke ignored him and moved on to the next date. But when he saw Taycee laughing at something Jake said, a pit of jealousy formed in his stomach. Followed by the reluctant realization that he did like Taycee, probably more than he wanted to admit. He liked her enough to want to get to know her. To see if the girl who used to chase butterflies through meadows or challenge him to see who could leave their feet in the frigid spring runoff water the longest was still buried inside somewhere. He wanted to know if the spontaneous Taycee of the past had merged with the stunning Taycee of the present, because that would be some combination.

It wasn't until Luke watched Date #10—*their* date—that he realized something else. Around all the other bachelors, particularly Jake, there were moments when Taycee became that person Luke wanted her to be. She threw mud at Jake. She laughed and joked with Miles. Her sarcasm emerged with Alec and Gavin. Her kindness with Sterling.

But on her final date with Luke, the walls came flying back up. Although she still laughed and joked, something changed. She acted stiffer. More on guard and less relaxed than any of the other dates. Why? It made him feel cheated somehow. Deprived. As though he'd drawn the short straw and now had to sit back and watch everyone else get to interact with the real Taycee Lynne.

When the video clip ended, Luke pushed the laptop closed with a snap, more determined than ever to break down those walls.

Eighteen

The Results are In!

A massive thanks to all of you who voted and donated to our cause! The people of Shelter Springs thank you for your support and enthusiasm for our show. Bless you all.

Without further ado, the top five winners (in no particular order) are . . .

Jake Sanford
Greg Jones
Miles Romney
Sterling Montgomery
Alec Jamison

Now let's see what our bachelorette has to say.

Taycee stared at the list with mixed feelings. Jake, Greg, and Miles were all people she would have chosen if it had been up to her. But Alec? Really? Did the viewers not have the volume turned up when they watched that episode? Apparently not. As for Sterling, well, if going out with him and his overactive salivary glands saved her from seeing Gavin ever again, then she could deal with that.

It was her reaction to not seeing Luke's name that bothered her the most. It landed her back in the ice cream parlor that Luke and Caleb had taken her to years and years before. With over twenty flavors to choose from, her little ten-year-old mind thought she'd never be able to decide. But then she caught sight of a flavor that reminded her of her favorite rose, and she pointed to that one.

"It's sherbet," Luke had said. "You're not going to like it." Taycee didn't care. To her, it was now rose flavored ice cream and she wanted to taste it more than anything else in the world.

Turned out it tasted like yucky orange sherbet—exactly like Luke said it would.

Taycee felt much the same way now. She'd wanted Luke off the show so badly, and now that it had finally happened, it was like eating orange sherbet once again. It left a bad aftertaste in her mouth.

She'd miss Luke and his shoeless drive-in style type dates. What would he have planned for round two? Most likely something fun. Something she would have filed away in the corner of her mind where only precious memories were kept—most of which had Luke's name on them.

Luke walked out of the hardware store only to stop short, and then slowly take one step back. Followed by another. He nearly made it back inside the safety of the store when Missy looked up from the magazine she read on a nearby bench. Her eyes found his. Luke tensed. Should he make a run for it?

Before he could decide what to do, Missy stood and walked toward him, her red stiletto sandals clacking against the sidewalk. "Hey, Luke. I've been waiting for you."

Luke's gaze flickered past her to his truck. Only twenty feet away and yet so far. He should have called in the order and paid Chuck to deliver it. Avoided town until Missy left for good.

"Oh relax." Missy flashed a too bright smile. "I only wanted to say sorry—and to thank you for being such a good sport."

"A good sport?" Luke took another step back, running into the door of the hardware store. A customer tried to exit, so Luke moved out of the way, side-stepping around Missy.

She tapped him on the shoulder. "This bachelorette show is pretty popular, which is actually great for me since my face is now attached to it. My agent thanks you, and so do I."

An agent? Missy actually had an agent? Who in their right mind would agree to rep someone like her? "So glad my tanked reputation could help advance your career."

"Oh, don't be such a crank," said Missy. "It was more of a favor to an old friend. The fact that I benefitted from it was only a bonus."

"What are you talking about?" Luke side-stepped again, positioning himself so that she was no longer between him and his truck.

Missy sidled up to him, her face inches from his. "Not he—*she.* Someone who wanted you voted off, obviously. I just did my part to help make it happen. But now that you're free, if you want to continue where we left off, I'm all yours. At least until I head back to LA." She looked up and down Main Street then back to him. "Not even someone as cute as you could make me stay in this backcountry town."

Luke studied her. Maybe she really could act because he couldn't tell if she was being serious or not. "What do you mean someone wanted me off?"

Her hand covered her mouth in mock embarrassment. "Oops. I promised not to say anything. My bad." Her hand came to rest on his shoulder, and then trailed down to his bicep where she squeezed. "Oooh, someone's been working out." With a smile, she backed away from him. "Have a great day, Luke."

Then she was gone, the clack of her heels echoing back to where he stood. Luke watched her go with a mixture of confusion and relief. He pulled his keys from his pocket and headed for his truck, but a sign caught his eye. "Carl's Feed and Seed." He paused, re-reading the words.

Maybe Missy's words made him paranoid, but Luke now wondered about that load of manure. Had it really been a mistake? A coincidence that it was dropped off the same night as the opening event and happened to block his driveway completely? Come to think about it, Carl had seemed a bit on edge when Luke asked him about it.

Was Missy right? Did someone want him off the show?

Luke hesitated outside his truck, twisting his keys around his finger as he studied the sign. Then he shoved the keys back in his pocket and headed for Carl's Feed and Seed.

Nineteen

Round two of dating turned out to be nearly as crazy as round one. Alec begged for the Monday night slot because he'd found out about a nearby motocross race going on that night. And by nearby, he meant a two hour drive away, which meant four hours of trying to tune him out while he went on and on and on about himself.

Longest. Night. Ever.

Tuesday, Jake took Taycee to an indoor go cart racing facility in Denver, where she actually got to drive one of the carts herself. She even beat Jake once, probably because he let her win, but still, she'd take it. Wednesday brought a night of skeet shooting with Miles. Also fun, but her sore shoulder protested doing it again anytime soon.

By the time Thursday rolled around, Taycee was ready to fake an illness just to get a night off. At five o'clock sharp, Greg rapped on her door. Dressed in a wrinkled short-sleeved button down shirt, he looked as though he'd wrung out his clothes and left them to dry.

Despite his disheveled appearance, there was something refreshing and honest about Greg. He never tried to be anything but himself. It made Taycee feel like she could wear sweats, eat whatever she wanted—even burp—and he wouldn't care. Or if he did, he'd call her on it. With him, Taycee always knew where she stood.

Unlike someone she didn't want to think about.

Greg drove her straight to the diner for some take-out food, and Megan followed them inside with a camera. Why, Taycee wasn't sure. Standing in line and ordering food would be the most boring footage ever.

Of course, this was before Taycee noticed Liza behind the counter.

"We'd like two specials please," Greg told Liza before glancing at Taycee. "You do like chicken fried steak, right?" The way he said it made Taycee feel like she didn't have a choice. Which was fine. It wouldn't have been her first pick, but it wouldn't have been her last either.

"Uh, sure, that sounds great."

Liza eyed the camera nervously, and then pointed to the whiteboard behind her. "The chicken fried steak is actually the special tomorrow. Tonight, it's beef tenderloin. Would you like that instead?"

Greg planted his hands on the counter and leaned forward. "I was actually hoping we could get the special price on the chicken fried steak today, rather than tomorrow. I don't like red meat."

Taycee's lips twitched. Apparently the "chicken" in the name confused him, which was completely okay because Liza had never looked so flustered. Score one for Greg.

"Chicken fried steak is actually made with cubed steak," Liza finally mustered. "And I'm sorry, but I'm only allowed to give you the special price on the day of the special."

"I see." Greg nodded, and then folded his arms. "Mind if I have a word with your manager?"

Eyes wide, Liza actually looked to Taycee for help—something Liza was sure to regret later since Taycee had no help to offer.

"Uh, Maris won't be here for another hour," Liza finally said, her gaze flickering once more to the camera.

"Do you have a phone number for her?"

"It's only a dollar difference." Liza's fingers trembled as she pointed out the prices on the menu.

"Exactly my point." Greg reached for his wallet as though he knew he'd won. "If it's only a dollar difference, what's the big deal? Whatever happened to customer service?"

"Okay, fine." Liza's hands shook as she rang up their order. Two chicken fried steaks were done in record time. Score another one for Greg.

Taycee allowed herself a small smile as they left the diner behind. Greg ushered her back to his car and soon they were on their way. "You know, Taycee, there's really no set price for anything. It's always negotiable, and I make it a point to get a better deal on everything I buy. If someone's not willing to meet me partway, I always walk away. No matter what."

"Good to know." Although Taycee didn't exactly agree. As a business owner, she knew how difficult it was to make ends meet, especially in a small town. Sure, it was good to be economical, but she also believed in supporting small businesses—Maris's diner included.

"It's why I make such a great buyer," Greg continued. "My company always gets the best deals with me around."

"It's great you like your job so much."

"Yeah, and if you ever need help getting a better deal on flowers, let me know. I'm your man."

"Will do." Not. Taycee already got a great deal on flowers from her wholesaler—someone who'd become a good friend over the years. She wasn't about to jeopardize that relationship by asking for more.

Greg came to an intersection and stopped. Though no other cars were around, he looked both left and right before driving through it at an almost painfully slow pace. "Want to know a secret?" he said.

"What?"

"The best place to get great deals are at yard sales."

"You don't say."

"In fact, just last month I got an awesome push lawn mower for five bucks. They wanted ten, but I talked them down."

Taycee shot him a look. What kind of lawn mower was only worth five bucks? Or ten for that matter? Maybe one of those really old they-don't-make-'em-like-they-used-to models that Greg planned on fixing up. "Does it still run?"

"Run? Oh, no. I'm talking about those mowers that don't have engines, only reels. You just push it around your grass and it cuts your lawn. No gas needed. Money saving *and* eco friendly. Hands down, my best yard sale find this year."

Taycee smiled as she peered out the window. Some might argue that a conversation about push mowers and yard sales would be dull, but somehow Greg made it entertaining. Just like he'd made ordering chicken fried steak entertaining.

No wonder Megan wanted to follow them everywhere with her camera.

Greg pulled to a stop in front of an abandoned building that had been the old hardware store before it downsized. He grabbed their take-out food, slung a backpack on his shoulder, and led Taycee around back to a rickety-looking ladder propped next to the building. He gestured for her to go up first.

She shook the ladder. "Is it safe?"

"You tell me." He chuckled. "Just kidding. Yeah, it's fine. Go on up."

With tentative steps, Taycee climbed to the top where a blanket covered a small portion of the gravel roof. Burt lounged in a lawn chair with his camera affixed to a tripod while Megan followed behind. Taycee breathed in the fresh air and looked around. Although the roof itself was hot and dirty, the surrounding view of the woods at the edge of town made up for it. The trees were like a natural wall, keeping Shelter hidden from the rest of the world. She loved feeling like she lived in her own secret little town.

Taycee settled next to Greg on the blanket, and they ate the warm chicken fried steak. With every bite, she pictured Liza's pale face and tried not to smile. After all these years of dealing with Liza, it was nice to see someone take her down a notch.

When they finished eating, Greg pulled out a few games from his backpack, including Scrabble, Yahtzee, Backgammon, and a deck of cards. "I know you like games so I brought a few choices."

The sun hovered just above the horizon, casting a myriad of warm colors across the sky. Orange, red, yellow, and pink, with some blue and purple here and there. It was like a rainbow that had been flattened and reshaped into a stunning abstract piece of art. And here she was, on the roof of an abandoned building about to play games. Greg couldn't have planned a better date.

It made Taycee wonder what Luke would have planned. Something similar, maybe. Or maybe not at all similar, like spelunking.

Taycee frowned and forced her mind back to the present. She pointed to Backgammon—a game she'd never played with Luke. "You'll have to remind me how to play it. I'm not sure I remember all the rules."

"Backgammon it is." Greg set up the board, gave Taycee a brief run-down of the rules, and then promptly beat her twice in a row. Evidently she didn't provide a big enough challenge, because he pulled out Scrabble next.

As twilight descended, they packed up and climbed back down the rickety latter. During the drive back, "Coming to America" by Neil Diamond came on the radio.

Greg's hand flew to the volume knob, turning it up. He joined in, belting out the lyrics.

Taycee laughed. Wrinkled shirts, yard sales, games, and now Neil Diamond. Greg was a riot.

When the song came to an end, he turned down the volume. "I love Neil Diamond."

"So I noticed."

"He sings Christmas songs too, you know."

"I didn't know."

"Don't you find it strange that a Jewish guy sings Christmas songs?"

Taycee bit her lip to keep from smiling. "Very." Not that she'd ever given it any thought before.

Red and blue flashing lights lit up the dark sky behind them, accompanied by a shrieking siren. Taycee looked over her shoulder and rolled her eyes. The siren? Really Ralph?

"What did I do wrong?" Greg squinted at the speedometer as he slowed to a stop. "I wasn't speeding."

"Don't worry, it's just Ralph," said Taycee. "I've known him forever." Megan jumped from the back of the car to get a better camera angle as several people exited the diner down the street. A live audience. Awesome.

Moments later, Ralph peered through the window, shining a flashlight in the car. "Your license and registration, please."

"Ralph," Taycee said, leaning closer. "What's the problem?"

A bright light zoomed in on her face, blinding her. "Taycee, that you in there?"

Her hand went up, shielding her eyes. "Yeah, it's me. Mind turning that thing off?"

The light faded as Ralph holstered it at his side.

"Greg wasn't speeding, was he?" Taycee said.

"A little. But I was more concerned with the swerving." He nodded at Greg. "I'm going to need your license and registration. Then I'd appreciate it if you would both get out of the vehicle."

"You've got to be joking," said Greg. "I wasn't swerving or speeding."

"Sir, I need you to get out of the vehicle."

Taycee leaned even closer, her eyebrow raised. "C'mon, Ralph. You know me. I never drink and Greg hasn't been drinking either."

"I would never drink and drive," spluttered Greg, as if the implication alone was horrifying. "I am a law-abiding citizen."

"Great, then you won't mind getting out." Ralph opened the driver's door and waited.

Taycee's hand rested on Greg's arm, keeping him in the car. This had gone far enough. Ralph was being ridiculous and she refused to play along. "We've done nothing wrong, Ralph and you know it. Are you sure it isn't you who's drunk?"

Probably not the smartest thing to say because Ralph's expression hardened. His gaze flickered to Megan's camera and then back to Taycee. Evidently he didn't like being accused of drinking while on camera, especially while on duty. Well too bad for him. Taycee didn't like being accused either.

"Unless you'd like me to update your mug shots, Ms. Emerson," Ralph said, "I suggest you get out of the car now."

Taycee's mouth fell open. He did not just bring that up now. It had been over seven years. Seven! She'd been a teenager, for crying out loud. So much for thinking Ralph was a decent person. No Christmas poinsettia for him this year.

"Mug shots?" Greg's horrified eyes turned on Taycee. "What's he talking about?"

"Please. It happened a long time ago." Taycee glared at Ralph. "It's not even on my record anymore."

"Will you two please step out of the car?" Ralph asked again.

"Fine." Taycee shoved open her door and got out, walking around to confront Ralph head on. "Would you like me to walk the line or touch my nose? Or are you planning to use the breathalyzer?"

Greg got out of the car and folded his arms, staring at Taycee with accusing eyes. "How long ago, exactly, and why did they need mug shots?"

"Walking the line should be sufficient," Ralph said.

Taycee started forward, and then stopped. "Wait a minute. Why do I have to do it? I wasn't driving."

"And I'm not drunk!" Greg practically shouted. "Now will someone please explain about the mug shots!"

"Oh for the love of Pete!" Taycee threw up her arms, shooting Ralph another glare. "In high school, I participated in a silly prank, okay? We spelled out the name of our school on a rival's football field with Roundup and got caught."

"You vandalized a school?" Greg looked appalled. "What were you thinking?"

"I wasn't thinking, obviously," said Taycee. "It's called a mistake, Greg. Surely you've made a mistake before."

"Not bad enough to get a police record!"

"Taycee's right," Ralph interrupted. "She doesn't need to walk the line, but you do."

"No way," said Greg. "I'm not about to be humiliated for something I haven't done wrong."

Ralph reached for his belt. "All right. I'll have to cuff you and take you in."

Taycee let out a breath of frustration. "Greg, just walk the dumb line so we can get out of here. And Ralph, I'm warning you . . ."

Greg glared at Taycee before he finally capitulated and walked several steps in a straight line. Then he turned to Ralph and spat, "There. Satisfied?"

"Looks like you two are good to go," said Ralph, scribbling who knows what on his notepad. "Sorry to have troubled you, but I have a responsibility to keep our streets safe. Enjoy the rest of your night." He plodded back to his car.

Without a word, Greg climbed in his car and waited for Taycee to do the same. They drove the last few blocks to her place in silence. When he walked her to her door, Taycee let out a breath and laid a hand on his arm. "Listen, Greg, I'm sorry about Ralph and that whole scene back there. But thank you for today. Up until a few minutes ago, I had a great time."

"No problem." Greg barely even looked at her.

Taycee waited another few seconds. When he said nothing more, she gave up and opened her door. Once inside her apartment, she resisted the urge to slam the door shut and leaned against it instead. How had she let things get so out of control? Why didn't she just get out of the car when asked? Walk the line? Make Greg walk the line? Instead, she had to try and prove that she could talk the local sheriff out of giving them a ticket, like some sort of cliché hick-town girl.

Taycee walked over to her couch and plopped down on it, resting her forehead on her palms. What a night.

A light tap sounded her door.

Taycee groaned. What now? "It's open," she called.

The door swung open and Jessa's voice intruded, "Hey Tace. Ready for your postdate interview?"

Twenty

Luke squinted out the diner window and into the bright morning sunlight. According to Liza, Sterling should have been here by now. His orange juice swirled in one hand while his fingers tapped the table with the other. C'mon, Sterling. Show yourself.

Although Ralph had gone a little overboard and things had gotten out of hand last night—at least according to Ralph—Luke was far from feeling sorry. The whole Missy fiasco aside, he could still smell the stench of manure every time he stepped out his front door. It now seemed to surround his house, and he couldn't open his window at night like he used to.

Yeah, Taycee definitely deserved it. And then some.

One more prank, and he'd call it even. Although Taycee tried to hide it, Luke knew she struggled with Sterling. The opening social and video recaps of their dates made it obvious. The spitting issue. The forced conversation. The fact they seemed to have very little in common. It all

135

combined to make Sterling the perfect choice. Now all Luke needed was a few minutes alone with him.

"Hey, Luke." Liza stood next to his elbow, water pitcher in hand. "Need a refill?"

He eyed his nearly full glass, but nodded anyway. "Sure. Thanks."

"No problem." Her hand rested on his shoulder as she slowly poured the orange juice. "So, how ya been?"

"Good. And you?"

"Fine, thanks." She sank onto the bench across from him and leaned forward, resting her chin in her hands. "My feet are killing me. You don't mind if I rest them for a sec, do you?"

"Sure, go ahead." Luke peered out the window once more, but still no sign of Sterling.

"How's business?"

"It's going okay. Not as busy as I'd like, but things will pick up when I start advertising in neighboring towns." Something he should be working on right now, in fact—if it wasn't for Taycee and his inability to quit thinking and plotting about her.

"I just love animals." Liza smiled. "In fact, I'd love to come and watch you work sometime."

For whatever reason, a mental picture of Missy hovering at his side came to mind—an experience he didn't want to repeat anytime soon. "You're a pet owner?" Luke asked. She didn't strike him as the type.

Liza shook her head. "Not right now, but I had a cat growing up."

"I've always been a dog person myself."

"You have a dog?"

"When I was younger," Luke said. "Maybe once I'm settled I'll consider getting another."

"You're not settled yet?" Liza perked up. "Need any help?"

136

Luke swirled his juice once again, darting another glance out the window. "No, but thanks for the offer. The house doesn't need much work, and what it does need I can get done in my spare time."

"I'm happy to make you curtains if you need them. Or anything like that. I'm actually pretty good at sewing."

Luke's gaze rested on Liza's bright pink fingernail polish, making him think of pink frilly curtains. "Uh, thanks, but I'm more of a wooden blinds kind of a guy. If I think of anything I need though, I'll let you know."

"All right." Liza's fingers fiddled under her chin. After a moment of silence, she blurted, "Would you like to go out some time? With me?"

Luke blinked. Go out with Liza? The thought had never occurred to him, not that he'd had much time to think about dating in general—beyond the bachelorette show and Taycee, that is. But now with Liza sitting across from him and asking him out, Luke still wasn't interested. Not in Liza. Not in Missy. Only in Taycee—the girl who'd arranged for fifteen yards of manure to be dumped in his driveway and had asked Missy Green to make a move on him.

Go figure.

Luke glanced up and caught Liza watching him expectantly. Waiting. Oh right. She wanted to go out. "Um, yeah that would be fun. But I've actually got a lot going on right now. Can I take a rain check?"

Liza nodded and stood just as the diner door opened and Sterling walked in. "Sure, just let me know when."

"Will do."

Liza headed over to Sterling and took his order. When Sterling eyed the room for a place to sit, Luke gestured to the seat across from him. "Want to join me?"

"Uh, okay." Sterling sat down with a wary expression on his face. "Did you need something?" Spittle landed on the table between them.

"Nope." Luke pushed his juice aside, out of range. "It's just that I know you have a date coming up with Taycee in a few days, so I thought I'd offer you the use of my horses if you want them."

"Why?"

Luke shrugged as he reached for his wallet, tossing some bills onto the counter. "She loves to ride. I was planning to take her myself, but now that I'm off the show, I figured why not let someone else do it? But if you already have other plans, I can always see if Jake wants to use them."

It was almost comical the way Sterling's expression changed from wary to eager the moment Luke mentioned Jake. He leaned across the table. "No, no. I mean, I'd love to take her riding. I just don't have a lot of experience with horses. Will that be a problem?"

Luke waved the concern aside. "Not at all. They used to be trail horses and are trained for inexperienced riders. There's even a nice trail through the woods behind my house. All you have to do is point them in that direction, and they'll take you straight to a beautiful meadow."

"Really?"

"Really, really."

Sterling smiled and nodded. "Okay. Yeah, that sounds nice. Let me think about it, and I'll let you know."

"Sure." Luke stood and dropped a business card on the table. "That's my number. Give me a call if you're interested. I can have them saddled and ready to go whenever."

Sterling picked up the card. "Thanks, Luke. That's really nice of you."

"No problem." Luke patted Sterling's shoulder as he left the diner with a smile. Despite the spitting issue, Sterling seemed like a decent guy—someone who was about to get a lucky break in the form of some extra time with Taycee Lynne.

And he'd have Luke to thank for it.

Twenty-one

"We're taking Luke's horses?" Taycee said to Sterling as he pulled his car to a stop. She didn't know why the thought bothered her so much, but it did. That, and the fact they'd be riding in close proximity to Luke's house. It was like she couldn't get away from him. Why offer his horses anyway? Was he rooting for Sterling to win or something?

At least Taycee would be out of Sterling's spitting range during the ride. That fact alone made her grudgingly grateful to Luke.

They walked around the house and found three horses already saddled and tethered to a fence. One for Sterling, one for Taycee, and one for Burt. There was a note affixed to the post:

> *Just fed and watered them, so they're good to go. The dark brown mare is Chaos, the light brown gelding is Pants on Fire, and the brown and white*

one is Flirtatious (yeah, there's a reason he's now a gelding). Have them back whenever.

Taycee bit back a laugh as Sterling studied the animals with a worried expression. "Are you sure these horses are tame? Luke promised they'd be easygoing, but with names like those . . ."

"They'll be fine," Taycee said as they waited for Burt to get the camera set up several yards away. When he signaled he was ready, she unhooked Chaos from the rope, led it away from the others, and mounted easily. "Us females will stick together," she said, patting Chaos's neck.

Sterling didn't respond. He was too busy fiddling with the rope. When he finally managed to free Flirtatious and try to mount, the horse side-stepped away and headed toward a well-worn trail at the back of Luke's house.

Taycee had to muffle her giggles as Sterling tried and failed again. Finally, he managed to throw his stomach over the saddle, grab onto the horn, and swing his body around in an awkward move, but at least it worked.

Taycee looked over to see Burt shoulder the camera and swing up onto Pants on Fire. He trotted to catch up. "I'll wait until we get out a ways, and then dismount to get some steady shots of you guys. That okay? We won't need too much footage."

"Fine by me." A few minutes of camera-free time sounded great to Taycee. She spurred on Chaos—or, at least tried to. Apparently the mare preferred to walk, so Taycee settled back and let the horse meander down the path behind Flirtatious. Not the most thrilling of horseback rides, but at least Sterling was too preoccupied trying to find a comfortable position on the saddle to attempt conversation.

Taycee looked around at the beautiful surroundings, feeling an unwelcome memory tug at her heart. She, Luke, and Caleb used to spend hours and hours riding through these mountains when they were younger. They went camping one weekend, and at some point during the night, Taycee's horse broke free and wandered off. Luke offered to give her a ride, so Taycee hopped up behind him and held on tight. It had been the best ride of her life.

She frowned and tried to spur on Chaos, as if she could outrun the memory and somehow put it behind her. But once again, Chaos refused. "Stubborn horse," Taycee said.

Sterling looked back. "Sorry. Didn't mean to take the lead. Normally, I'm a ladies go first kind of a guy."

Taycee laughed. "Looks like your horse doesn't agree with you."

"I have no idea where I'm going," Sterling called back to her. "Flirtatious won't stop."

"Don't worry. There's a happy little meadow a few miles down this trail. They're probably trained to head there so just sit back and enjoy the ride."

"If you say so."

As they neared the meadow, Burt wanted to take the lead and get some footage, but Flirtatious still refused to stop, which made Taycee smile. Maybe the horse didn't like being on camera either. When they finally arrived at the clearing, the horse finally stopped abruptly, nearly forcing Sterling to topple over his head. Pants on Fire and Chaos followed suit, reaching down to nibble at the grass.

Burt slid from his horse and started setting up the tripod. "I'd like to get some footage of the two of you riding for a bit, if that's okay."

"Sure." Taycee tugged on the reins, but Chaos shook her head and continued to eat. She tried again, with no better luck, so she slid to the ground. "Um, I don't think that's going to happen. These horses obviously have minds of their own."

"Well, how about you both hold the reins while you talk?" Burt made it sound so easy, as if she and Sterling should be bubbling over with topics they couldn't wait to discuss.

"Okay," Taycee hedged. "What do you want to talk about, Sterling?"

"How about how to get these horses to move." He still sat on top of Flirtatious, tugging unsuccessfully at the reigns. When that didn't work, he kicked the horses' flank. "C'mon, move you stubborn animal."

"He wants to eat," Taycee said, trying not to laugh. From the corner of her eye, she caught the light of the camera and searched her mind for something to say. Anything. "So what do you think of the meadow?"

"It's nice."

"There's a waterfall on the other side of that rise over there. Want to see it?"

Sterling looked around. "We need to tie up the horses first. I don't want them running off."

This time Taycee giggled. "I really don't think they're going anywhere."

"Says the girl who won't be held accountable."

"No," Taycee said. "Says the girl who knows trail horses. Now, c'mon. We won't be gone long."

With an uncertain look, Sterling wrapped the reins around the saddle horn and slid awkwardly from the horse. Burt followed behind as Taycee led Sterling up and over a small rise to the river. Only about six feet tall, a small waterfall gushed with the spring runoff, spurring on the narrow river as it wound its way through the meadow. Being small herself, Taycee had always felt a kinship with the little fall. She'd spent hours and hours playing in it, unafraid to stand beneath it like some of the bigger ones. Luke had once even given it a name once: Taycee Lynne Falls.

"This is it?" Sterling said. His hands rested on his hips as he studied the waterfall. "Back in Washington, we have falls that are hundreds of feet tall. This is more like a trickle."

"Maybe to you." To her it was a special treasure. She walked over and placed her hand under the cold rush of water, loving how it splayed up her arm.

Sterling stepped up beside her. He shoved his hands in his pockets and looked around like he was bored. "Hungry?" he finally said. "I brought some food in my backpack."

Taycee wasn't hungry, but the sooner they ate, the sooner they could leave, so she nodded and followed him back to the horses. Sterling spread out a thin blanket before kneeling down, and Taycee sat as far from him as possible, hoping he wouldn't notice. He handed her a slightly smashed sandwich. "I hope you like club."

"Sounds great. Thanks."

"No problem," he said. "I take it you're into horseback riding?"

Taycee leaned back on her palm and stretched her legs out. A gentle breeze trembled through the air, carrying with it a scent of earth and pines. She breathed it in. "Yeah, although it's been awhile. When I was younger we used to go riding all the time."

"We?"

"My brother and I." And Luke, although Taycee kept that part to herself.

Sterling took a big bite and studied the horses while he chewed. Small bits of sandwich flew from his mouth, making Taycee grateful he wasn't facing her. "I didn't know you had a brother."

"Yeah. He graduated from law school awhile ago. Right now he's with a large firm in Phoenix, but he's hoping to move back here and start a practice soon."

"I can't imagine there would be much business in Shelter—especially lately."

Taycee rested her sandwich on her lap, not liking what Sterling implied. "He'll probably look closer to Colorado Springs. But Caleb's the type of guy who will be successful wherever he decides to practice law."

"He really should stay with a big firm for a while and get some experience. At least that's what I'd do."

"Well, Caleb isn't you." Or, at least Taycee hoped he

wasn't. Lately, she was beginning to wonder. And worry.

"He's going to have a hard time of it then," Sterling said. "It's important to get several years of experience with an established firm before you set off on your own."

Taycee leveled him a look. Sterling didn't even know Caleb. Who was he to say how much work experience her brother needed? It hit a nerve. "He's been working sixty to eighty hour work weeks for a couple of years now. If he keeps that up, he's going to forget there's more to life than work. I wouldn't wish that on anyone."

Sterling set down his sandwich and looked straight at her, his face serious. "That's what I'm doing right now. It's called putting in your time. Someday I'll make partner and it will all pay off."

"That's a matter of opinion," said Taycee, knowing she needed to change the subject before she said something she might regret. "By the way, how did you get the time off for this if you're . . . uh . . . still putting in your time?"

"I'm using all the PTO time I've accrued."

"Oh." Taycee immediately wished she hadn't asked the question. She didn't want to hear about the sacrifices these guys made to be here. It made everything too real, too heavy. She preferred to believe that everyone felt the same as her. That this was a silly competition benefitting a good cause—not something worth investing too much money or emotion or PTO time in. Yet deep down, Taycee knew these guys were doing exactly that. The knowledge didn't settle well.

"What about you?" Sterling said, brushing crumbs from his shorts. "Is living in Shelter Springs and arranging flowers something you want to do for the rest of your life?"

"Yes," Taycee said without hesitation. "I'm happy here."

He nodded. "So what happens if you fall for one of us bachelors? What then? Are you planning to ask whoever it is to drop everything and move here?"

Taycee shifted in her seat and picked at a nonexistent

piece of lint. It was a fair question and one she should have been prepared for. But she wasn't. Probably because she never thought a few dates could lead to a discussion like this. Yet here it was, waiting for an answer.

A few blades of grass tickled her palm, and Taycee tugged on them, uprooting them from their home—the same thing Sterling thought she should be willing to do.

"No," she finally said. "I would never expect anyone to pick up and move here for me. But if I do make a lasting connection with someone, I'd hope we'd both be willing to compromise."

Sterling nodded and took another bite of his sandwich. "Fair enough," he said, as if they'd reached their own compromise.

But Taycee didn't feel like they had at all. The fact was, she wasn't falling for any of the bachelors and would never be willing to compromise. She suddenly felt like the type of person who was okay with stringing people along in a game where the stakes had suddenly increased—stakes that were never supposed to get this high.

They continued to eat in relative silence, and as the sun dropped closer to the horizon, Taycee finally said, "It's starting to get dark. We should probably head back."

"Okay."

Sterling repacked the backpack while Taycee folded the blanket. Once Burt had secured his camera equipment, she walked to Chaos's side and swung up on the horse's back. After a gentle prod on the reigns, Chaos lifted her head, only to drop it back down and continue to nibble. A stronger tug produced the same results, only this time Chaos took two steps further into the meadow.

"You've got to be kidding me." Taycee slid to the ground and pulled hard on the reins, trying to lead the horse from the meadow and back toward the trail. Sterling and Burt weren't having any better luck.

Taycee surveyed the scene as an uneasy thought struck.

Trail horses were stubborn, lazy animals. But given enough time to graze, they should be willing to head back. Unless, that is, they were used to following a certain leader and that certain leader wasn't here.

No, Luke wouldn't.

Well, that wasn't entirely true. He *would*—just not without a good reason.

Did he have a good reason? An uneasy thought came to Taycee's mind, accompanied by an uneasy feeling. Luke couldn't possibly know about Missy or the manure, could he? Carl would never say anything, and Missy, well . . . she promised not to either.

The uneasiness magnified.

Luke had to know. It was the only explanation. That's why he offered Sterling the use of his horses. Her eyes drifted shut. Not good. Not good at all.

An eye for an eye.

It was a saying Luke had used often growing up, mostly to rationalize all the pranks he used to play. Was he now hanging out in the comfort of his home, thinking those same words and laughing at her?

Probably.

Burt stepped into Taycee's peripheral vision, a rude reminder that her crazy, messed up life was no longer as private as it used to be. She suddenly felt like stomping her foot and asking everyone to go away and leave her alone. She was beyond sick of it all. Dating. Being filmed. Worrying what she said, how she looked. And now, here she was, stuck in some stupid meadow with a spitter and a camera-happy guy, miles away from any civilization—not that Luke could be called civilized.

Sterling tossed the reins on the ground and strode toward Taycee, throwing his hands in the air. "I give up."

Spittle hit Taycee's cheek and she cringed. If Sterling spit on her one more time, she would throw him into the river he'd called a trickle and hoof it back dateless. Taycee loped Chaos's reigns around a nearby tree. "C'mon, it's getting dark. Let's get going."

Sterling gestured to the horses, looking horrified. "We're just going to leave them here?"

"Unless you want to carry them, yes. Luke will have to come back for them in the morning. It'll serve him right."

"Serve him right? For what? Loaning us horses?"

"Loaning us *trail* horses," Taycee corrected. "I should have seen this coming."

"What are you talking about? Of course they're trail horses. How do you think we found this place so easily?"

"Because they wanted to come here. Problem is, they don't want to go back, and I refuse to spend any more time trying to coax them."

Sterling frowned and glared at the horses. "This is crazy."

"Crazy, but true. Horses can be stubborn when they want to be. Especially trail horses." Taycee squinted through the trees at the lowering sun. It would be dark soon and they didn't have a flashlight. Not good. She headed for the trail. "C'mon, guys. We need to hurry. It'll be a lot harder to find our way in the dark."

Sterling grudgingly followed as Burt tucked his camera back in his bag. Taycee breathed a sigh of relief. It was bad enough being filmed when she was in a good mood.

Dusk settled in as they trudged down the mountain. The sounds of shoes scuffing the ground, crickets creaking, and twigs snapping underfoot filled the silence. As the sky turned from gray to black, Taycee slowed and walked with her hands outstretched to keep from running into something. Sterling's hand rested on her shoulder. It was the blind leading the blind, and Taycee could only hope they were headed in the right direction.

"Burt, doesn't your camera have a light?" Taycee asked.

"Sorry, I left it in the car. Figured we'd be back before it got dark."

Taycee's leg scraped against a painful prickly bush, making her want to curse. Loudly. But she wasn't the swearing type and she wasn't about to let Luke turn her into one.

A loud crunch came from behind, and Sterling's hand ripped from her shoulder as he stumbled and let out a loud groan. She turned to find him lying in a heap on the ground, grabbing onto his ankle.

Taycee squatted beside him. "You okay?"

"No. I twisted my ankle."

"Here. Take my arm." Burt came to Sterling's other side, and together they hefted him to his feet. He hobbled along, and their progress slowed to a turtle's pace. At this rate, they wouldn't be back until morning.

"Sterling, I'm sorry, but it's going to take forever like this." Taycee pulled out her cell phone and squinted at it. No reception. "Can either of you guys get a signal?"

Both Sterling and Burt studied their phones, and then shook their heads.

"Okay." Taycee searched the trees. "Here's what we're going to do. I know this trail well, and I'm sure I can find my way back. So how about I go on ahead, find Luke, and we'll bring a horse back for Sterling to ride on."

"How will you find us again?" Sterling asked. "It's pitch black out here."

"I'm not sure I'm comfortable with you going on alone," Burt added. "I'll come with you."

"And leave me here alone?" Sterling squeaked.

Taycee rolled her eyes. "I'll be fine, Burt, I promise. I can use the light from my phone. And don't worry, Sterling, we'll be able to find you with a flashlight. We can't be that far from his house. I'll be back in a half an hour. Forty-five minutes tops."

Sterling grabbed a hold of her arm and brought her closer. "Are you sure?" A spray of moisture hit her face.

"Positive," she said.

Twenty-two

Luke saddled up a horse in the barn, berating himself for thinking this had been a good idea. The sky had darkened and Taycee still wasn't back. He figured they'd have trouble getting the horses to leave the meadow without Sally, but had they refused outright? Was everyone walking back on foot? Had they gotten lost? Was Taycee okay?

He cinched up the belly strap with a bit too much force and reached for the bridle.

"Luke!" Taycee's voice rang out.

His body stilled as he let out a breath. She was okay. She was fine.

"In here," he called. "It's about time you guys got back."

The barn door flew open, and Taycee stood there in the dim light with a few leaves poking out of her disheveled hair. She looked beautiful. And angry.

"I'm the only one who's here," she said, hooking a thumb behind her. "Sterling's back about a mile with a twisted ankle."

"And the horses?"

"In the meadow." Taycee glared. "How kind of you to send us with your most stubborn trail horses."

Luke smiled as he walked over to her, reaching to pick the leaves from her hair. It was soft and looked silky in the lamplight. He felt the sudden urge to pull her to him, but rested his hand on her shoulder instead. "I figured you'd get along really well with them."

"Very funny." Taycee stepped away, making his hand fall from her shoulder. She pointed to the animal behind him. "Will you please put a bridle on that horse so we can go find Sterling? He and Burt weren't exactly thrilled to be left in the dark."

Luke gave her a lingering look before he reached for the bridle once more.

"Where do you keep your flashlights?" Taycee walked past him and started looking through his gear, pulling open drawers and slamming them closed when she didn't find what she wanted.

"In the bag on the saddle," Luke said as he fit the bridle in place. "I was just about to come looking for you." He led the horse from the barn and double-checked the saddle. Then he mounted and held his hand out to Taycee. "Coming?"

She hesitated, as if touching him was the last thing she wanted to do. Finally, she placed her soft hand in his, stuck her foot in the stirrup, and swung up behind him, immediately relinquishing his hand.

When her arms didn't come around his waist, Luke glanced over his shoulder to see her gripping the back of the saddle instead. He bit back a grin. "I know you're mad, but it'll be a lot safer if you hold on to me."

"No thanks."

"Suit yourself." A quick *tsk*, a kick, and the horse leapt forward. Taycee gasped, and her arms came around Luke in a tight hold as she steadied herself. His grin widened as they started forward, reminding him of other times they'd ridden together like this. Only now it was different. Better.

"You're smiling and thinking 'I told you so,' aren't you?" Taycee accused.

"I wouldn't dare."

"Right." As they settled into an easy pace, her grip around him slackened. Luke resisted the urge to grab her hands and keep her close.

"Thanks for the great date, by the way," she finally said. "It was a real adventure."

"No problem." From the sounds of it, she would never forgive him for this.

"And thanks for the other night as well. That was you too, wasn't it? Ralph sure did a great job. How much did he charge you for that performance? Or was it just a favor to an old friend?"

"No idea what you're talking about."

"Oh please. Ralph's too nice to come up with that idea all on his own."

"And I'm not a nice guy?"

Silence.

"I'll take that as a no," Luke said, shining the light through the darkness as they picked their way along the trail. The crunch and scuffle of the horse's hooves mingled with the creaking of crickets as they moved along. "What about you, Taycee Lynne? Are you a nice girl?"

"Yes."

"I wonder if Carl and Missy would agree. Or me, for that matter."

More silence. Her hands fell from his side, probably gripping the back of the saddle once again. What happened to her anyway? They used to be such great friends. Could time really do that to a friendship? Erode it to nothing?

The fact was, Luke wanted her friendship. Craved it even. Especially since it could be the start of something even better. But Taycee refused to give an inch. It made him want to give her a good, hard shake.

"So tell me this, Taycee Lynne," he finally said. "Why did you do it? Have things really changed that much between us that you couldn't stand the thought of going out with me? I don't get it."

"And I don't get why you wanted to make me look bad on camera—especially since I'm only doing this for Shelter Springs."

He shrugged. "It's called retaliation, something you know all about."

"How would you know?" Taycee accused. "You don't know me anymore. You may not have changed much during the past ten years, but I have."

"Too bad. You were a lot more fun back then." Okay, so maybe he'd gone too far, but it was the truth. Where was the girl who used to hold on tight and urge him to go faster? The girl who used to follow him anywhere and looked up to him. Who'd tease him and talk to him. Made him feel like the older brother he'd never gotten to be—not that he wanted to be her brother anymore.

What happened to that girl?

"What did I ever do to you anyway?" Luke asked. "You've treated me different since I got back, and I don't get it. I've done nothing to you."

"Nothing? You call tonight and Ralph nothing?"

"I'm talking before that. Why the manure in my driveway? Why Missy?"

"I was helping you out. You said you didn't want to be on the show, remember?"

"No," Luke said. "I said that I would get voted off if I wanted to—not that you should take it upon yourself to do it for me."

"Well, excuse me for helping you out. You should be thanking me right now."

"Thanking you? For making me look like a jerk in front of a whole lot of people? Sorry, but forgive me if I don't."

"Please. Since when have you ever cared about people seeing you with different girls? Or is it the fact that it's now all over the internet that bothers you?"

Luke yanked on the reins and twisted around to face her. He felt like he was being accused of a crime he didn't commit, as though Taycee grasped at any excuse she could find to rail on him. "What are you talking about?"

"Will you please keep going? Sterling is probably freaking out."

"Not until you explain."

"Seriously?" Taycee said. "You really need me to point out the fact that you've never had a problem dating a bunch of girls? Back in high school you did it all the time, or is your memory really that bad?"

Luke slid off the horse and pulled Taycee down with him, fighting the urge to shake her senseless. "Who cares if I dated a lot of girls in high school? It was ten years ago, Taycee! Ten years! And since I got back, I haven't had a chance to go out with anyone but you."

Taycee's fingers fisted at her side. "You left, Luke! You promised to call and you didn't. You promised to email and you didn't. You walked away without a backward glance and forgot all about me and Caleb. You don't do that to friends!"

Whoa. Luke shook his head to clear his thoughts. Caleb had said that Taycee had a hard time when he left, but that was so long ago. Was she still hung up on it? "Is that what this is about? Why I've been getting the stiff arm from you since I got back?"

No answer.

A deep breath and Luke tried again. "I don't get it. Caleb doesn't care that I didn't keep in touch, and no one else in town does either. In fact, everyone else has welcomed me back with open arms. Why can't it be the same with you?"

"Because I'm not Caleb or everyone else! I'm Taycee!"

"Duh."

With a stomp of her foot, Taycee spun on her heel to leave, but Luke grabbed her hand and pulled her back. "Oh no you don't. You aren't going anywhere until we finish this. Are you really still blaming me for something I did ten years ago?"

Taycee yanked her hand free. "You did it when you got back, too. You said we should get together for dinner. You said you'd call. But did you? Of course not. Why? Because you really haven't changed. Ten years later, and you're still the same unreliable excuse for a friend."

Her words slammed into him with a brutal force. Luke took a step back, as if distance would somehow lighten the impact. But it had the opposite effect because Taycee's eyes now appeared darker. More condemning. The expression looked so out of place on her. So wrong. And yet somehow, he'd put it there.

Luke suddenly had this insane urge to drag her toward him and kiss her until she stopped looking at him like that. Until she stopped blaming him for something Luke didn't understand or feel like he deserved.

He needed to get away. Somehow figure out where he'd messed up and sort through his mixed up feelings about her. He reached for the reins and jumped back onto the horse, and then pulled an extra flashlight from his bag and tossed it to her. "We're not far from the house. You can wait inside, and I'll go and get Sterling."

With that, he sank his heels into the horse's side and lurched forward, putting as much distance between them as he could.

A sickening pit formed in Taycee's stomach as she watched Luke ride away. She'd gone way too far, unleashing ten years' worth of pent-up frustration. But no matter how much she wanted to take the words back, they were already out. She may as well have said, "I've been in love with you for forever and jealous of every girl you've ever dated!"

Turned out Jessa was right after all. Taycee was a shaken can of soda, and Luke had just opened her up.

It had been a problem she'd been plagued with her entire life. Let things build inside until one day the pressure became too much and everything spurted out. Her mother had always warned her not to let things fester, to say what needed to be said before it reached this point. But Taycee had never quite learned how to do that. Anger had always given her words the wings they needed to fly right out of her mouth.

The problem was that when it reached this point, the words usually came out tainted with a nastiness she didn't really mean. A nastiness that Luke may never forget.

Or worse—forgive.

Twenty-three

Taycee blinked at the bright light sneaking through the blinds. She'd spent most of the night replaying over and over what she'd said to Luke, and with each replay, it got worse. Almost to the point that Taycee didn't deserve to see the sun or bask in its warm glow.

She tossed her covers over her head and burrowed beneath them, keeping the light out. But it was no use. Sleep offered an escape that she really didn't deserve either, so she threw her covers off and headed to her bathroom. What she needed was to get away. Away from Shelter and everyone in it. Away from that cloud of nastiness that hovered over her. Away from everything.

Maybe if she drove fast enough, she could leave it all behind.

She donned her swimming suit, dressed in a T-shirt and shorts, and packed a backpack with water, some snacks, and a towel. Then she hopped in her car and headed west.

Thirty minutes later, she pulled off the side of the road and started the three mile trek through the woods to a place Caleb and Luke had discovered over fifteen years ago: The

Hole. Perfect for swimming and hanging out, The Hole became their secret place of escape. And over the years, Taycee had kept that secret, unwilling to share it with anyone—even Jessa.

She trudged toward it now, ducking under branches and stepping over rocks, heading purposefully toward her own private retreat—a place packed full of the most wonderful memories she had of Luke. Maybe the bittersweet reminder would serve as her penance.

She finally emerged through the trees to find The Hole looking almost exactly as it had all those years before. The same small pond. The same waterfall off to the side. The same boulder to jump from. It was one of the things she loved most about this place. Other than the rope swing that had seen better days, it never changed.

Unlike the people who once spent so much time here.

Taycee dropped her backpack to a flat, grassy spot and quickly stripped down to her swimsuit. Then she waded to her knees and dove into the chilly mountain water. It had been awhile since she'd come. Not since the summer after college. Without Caleb or Luke, it had never been the same.

Taycee swam for a while before spreading a towel across a sunny patch of ground and settling down to soak up the sun and enjoy the sounds and smells of nature. The rustling leaves, the chirping birds, the scent of fresh pine needles. It had an almost hypnotic, soothing effect, and before long, her eyes drifted shut.

"Taycee Lynne." The voice drifted through her muddled brain, wrapping her in a blanket of warmth. How she loved it when Luke called her that.

"Taycee." Fingers gently prodded her arm, nudging her subconscious to fully awaken. Real fingers. On her arm.

157

Taycee popped up quickly, whacking something with her head.

"Ow," she groaned, holding her hand to her forehead as her eyes adjusted to the bright sunlight.

"Ow is right," Luke said, rubbing his own forehead. "Remind me never to wake you up unless I'm in the mood for a headache."

She blinked. Luke. Here. At the swimming hole—*their* swimming hole. "What are you doing here?" She squinted at him.

"Saving you from a nasty sunburn. Although I might be a little late." His fingers brushed against her cheekbone, just below her eye.

Taycee's hands flew to her warm cheeks, unable to tell whether the heat was from a sunburn or the sizzling sensation that came when he touched her. "How long have I been asleep?"

"I don't know." Luke shrugged. "How long have you been here?"

Taycee glanced up. The sun hovered high overhead now, which meant it had probably been a few hours. Great. She grabbed her bag and pulled out some sunscreen. Normally it wouldn't be a big deal, but in a few days she'd be on camera again and didn't want to show up sporting a sunburn. Her last few dates had been embarrassing enough.

She squirted some lotion onto her hand and rubbed it all over her face, arms, and shoulders, before trying to reach her back.

"Want some help?" Luke asked with half a smile.

"No."

He shrugged. "I get it. You want goofy-looking variegated lines covering your back. Like a non-permanent tattoo, right?"

Taycee held out the bottle of sunscreen. "Fine, you win."

He eyed it, not taking it from her. "I didn't hear any magic words."

"Pretty please?"

"Now you're talking." Luke took the bottle and scooted behind her. His warm, lotion-covered hands rubbed slow, methodical circles over the back of her shoulders and between her shoulder blades. Taycee's eyes drifted closed, willing him to keep going. She could sit like this forever, soaking up his touch, his warmth. Him.

"There, all set," he breathed into her ear as he held the bottle in front of her face. Happy shivers sped down her spine, making her cheeks burn even more. It wasn't fair that he had this effect on her.

"Thanks." She shifted away from him and held up the bottle. "You want some?" Part of her hoped he'd say yes and part of her didn't. Her eyes lingered on his broad shoulders and already tanned skin.

"I don't know. Am I allowed to stay?"

Her gaze fell to the ground, and Taycee's finger drew circles through the long blades of grass next to her towel. She owed him an apology. But what could she say without embarrassing herself even more?

"I'm sorry, Luke," the words finally tumbled out. "I didn't mean half of what I said. It's just that . . . well, I'm sorry. You're not a poor excuse for a friend. In fact, there was a time when you were one of my best friends." She looked out over the swimming hole, not wanting him to see the emotion in her eyes or how badly she wished for those days back.

Luke scooted closer until they sat side-by-side with their shoulders lightly touching. "You say that like it's behind us. But we can still be friends, can't we? Even after all these years?"

Friends. As much as Taycee would love to say yes, she didn't think she had it in her to just be friends. Once it had been enough, but now Luke's reappearance in her life had exposed all the feelings she'd tried to bury over the years, making them even more imposing than they'd been before.

"You were right," Luke said when Taycee remained silent. "I should have kept in touch. I guess I got a little self-absorbed and threw myself into college life without really looking back. Then when my parents moved, I figured it was better that I move on. So I graduated from college and vet school. I even did an internship. But after that . . . I don't know. It's like I took a peek into my past and couldn't seem to stop looking back. I missed it. So I made the plunge and moved back to the one place I never thought I'd return to." He paused. "Maybe I made a mistake, though. I never meant to stir up past hurts."

There was a time when Taycee had wanted him to realize that—to leave Shelter and stay far away. But the thought of him disappearing again made her want to throw her arms around him and hold on tight. He'd break her heart all over again if he left now.

Not that it wouldn't break if he stayed, too.

"And I'm sorry for not calling you back that day I first saw you again," Luke continued. "I wanted to, but I figured after showing up at your shop and hanging out for a while, you might think it was overkill. So I didn't. I thought I was saving you, not hurting you."

Taycee wanted to crawl under her towel and hide. Why was everything so much more embarrassing in the light of day? "Can we just call a truce? Or, as Caleb would say, strike yesterday's conversation from the record?"

Luke chuckled. "Consider it stricken."

Taycee offered him a tentative, relieved smile. "For what it's worth, I'm glad you came back, even if it's only temporary." Whether it was because she'd let out all her frustrations yesterday, or because she now understood why he hadn't kept in touch or called, Taycee meant it. She was glad he'd come home. Maybe now she'd finally be able to heal and move on.

His shoulder nudged hers. "Don't kick me out just yet. Maybe *Shelter's Bachelorette* really will be able to help save the town."

Taycee pulled her knees to her chest and wrapped her arms around them. "Last night, Sterling asked if I'd be willing to move if I fell for one of the bachelors. It made me think." She twisted her head to face him. "Don't you think it's kind of ironic that something I'm doing to help the town might be the one thing that finally gets me to leave?"

The waterfall and zipping bees suddenly sounded loud in the silence that followed.

"Are you falling for one of the bachelors?" Luke said.

Not falling—fallen. And yes—the one that got voted off last week. She shrugged. "I don't know. Sterling's starting to grow on me."

His startled eyes shot her way, and then relaxed in a look of relief. "You're joking."

"Maybe." Taycee shrugged, fighting back a smile.

Luke stared down at her, making her lips twitch. He shook his head. "I can't believe I almost fell for that."

"And I can't believe you'd actually think I'd go for someone like him."

Luke nudged her shoulder again, nodding toward the water. "Can you still do a flip off that boulder?"

"I will if you will."

"You're on." He grabbed her hand. It was something he'd done all the time when they were younger—something a big brother would do. But now Taycee couldn't help the goose bumps that broke out across her arms. She wanted it to mean more than brotherly friendship. She wanted it to mean that he liked her the way she liked him.

He dragged her into the frigid spring water, and then relinquished her hand as they swam to the boulder. He scrambled to the top, reaching to help her up behind him. Then he winked, ran forward, and let out a whoop as he threw his body off the boulder, completed a graceful one and a half, and dove neatly into the water. Moments later he surfaced and shook the water from his dripping hair. Taycee could have stared at him all day.

"Show off," she said.

"Impressed?"

"Maybe."

"Admit it. I'm the king of the swimming hole."

"Never!" Taking a few steps back, Taycee rushed forward, leaped into the air, brought her knees to her chest and yelled, "Cannonball!" before landing with a whack right beside him.

She surfaced and wiped the water from her eyes. "I just blew up your kingdom. Now I'm the king of the swimming hole, so there."

"So there? What are we, in second grade?"

"I was trying to speak on your level."

"You are so going down for that one." Luke grabbed her, twisting her so his arms came around her shoulders from behind. "Any final words?" he said into her ear, his breath sending chills down her spine.

"You forgot to say Your Majesty."

With a hand on her head, Luke pushed her under the water, and then pulled her up seconds later. "Now who's the king?"

Taycee blinked the water from her eyes. "You forgot to say Your Majesty again. Honestly, how many times do I have to—"

Down she went again.

When she resurfaced the second time, she laughed. "Fine, you win, but only because I said mean things to you yesterday." She wiped her eyes and pointed a finger at him. "But the day you tell me you'll call me and don't, you become the scum of the earth forever."

Luke's smile widened. "Do you want me to call you?"

"That's not what I said."

"That's what I heard."

"You need to get your hearing checked." She broke free and splashed him in the face. He splashed back, and then lunged for her and pulled her against him, making her heart pound like crazy. Without meaning to, her eyes rested on his mouth. A knowing smile tugged on his lips, making her face burn and her gaze drop to his tan, muscular chest. Her cheeks flushed even hotter.

"My hearing's fine," he said, his voice low and teasing, as if he knew exactly what she was thinking.

Taycee pulled from his grasp and splashed him again. "Man, you're cocky." Then she swam back to her towel where she collapsed on her stomach and buried her face in the soft terry cloth, hoping he couldn't tell how easily he'd gotten to her. A few words, a look, and she was a muddled-up mess.

Luke trudged from the water and dropped down next to her. She kept her face buried while her body shivered from the cool breeze. As the water evaporated from her skin, the warm rays of the sun warmed her, inch by inch. It was like she was fourteen all over again, hanging out with Luke on a gorgeous spring day.

If yelling at him produced this kind of day, maybe she should do it more often.

"What was it that made you start looking back, Luke?" Her voice was muffled, so she twisted her face to the side and clarified, "To Shelter, I mean."

Luke let out a breath and shifted on his towel, squinting up at the sun. "I don't know. Do I need a reason? Why didn't you ever leave?"

Taycee raised her head, tucking her elbows beneath her as she picked at her towel. "I did leave for a few years. I got an Associate in business, and then enrolled in a floral design program for another year. But you're right. I always planned to come back, and I did."

She snuck a peak at him. He watched her with an unreadable expression on his face. Did he think she should've moved away? Found a life outside of Shelter like so many other people had done? Or did he think she figured it out early on that Shelter was a good place to plant roots?

"And yes," she said. "You do need a reason. Everyone has a reason for doing something that doesn't make sense."

"Moving back to Shelter doesn't make sense?"

Taycee shook her head. "Why would it? Your parents don't live here any longer, and you didn't keep in touch with anyone. What prompted you to even consider it?"

Luke shifted again, tucking his hands under his head and squinting at the sky. "After high school, I couldn't wait to get away from this place. I felt stuck here, as if Shelter would keep me from having experiences and living my dreams. So I jumped on the college bandwagon and left town.

"Fast forward ten years, and there I was, finishing my internship and considering a great opportunity to partner with the vet I worked for. He wanted to ease me into the practice before he retired so I could take over. The fact that I also happened to be engaged to his daughter made it a no-brainer."

Taycee's eyes flew to his. Luke had been engaged? The news slammed into her in an uncomfortable way, making her feel so many things. Hurt that he'd loved someone else. Curiosity about what had happened. Jealousy that he'd been able to date and fall for another person without the memory of someone else always getting in the way.

"Then one day a box arrived in the mail. My mom went through a de-cluttering phase and sent me a package of some of my old stuff. My high school yearbooks were in it, along with a bunch of pictures of you, me, and Caleb. As soon as I opened it, everything changed. I had so many amazing memories from this place. It made me start thinking about moving back here instead—to a place I could raise my kids with the kind of lifestyle I once had. This swimming hole, horseback riding, hiking, camping, fishing, sledding, even cow-tipping." He chuckled at that. "I couldn't get the image out of my mind, so I got on the internet and found the McCann place."

"What happened?" Taycee asked, unable to hold the question back any longer. "To your fiancée, I mean."

Luke twisted his head, and his gaze rested on Taycee. "She grew up in Ohio and wanted to stay there, near her family. She wanted me to take over her father's practice and keep living the life she'd always wanted to live." Luke swallowed, making his Adam's apple bob. "I guess the fact that I had a hard time deciding between her and Shelter made me realize that maybe I didn't love her as much as I thought I did. So we broke up."

"Just like that?"

"It was tough, but it felt right, you know? So I went with it. I called the McCanns and asked if they'd consider letting me lease their farm before I committed to buying," he said. "It was my way of doing something that felt right without risking everything."

Taycee flipped onto her back and shaded the sun with her hand. "Wow, I don't even know what to say to that except—wow."

"I know. I thought I would ease right back into my old life with no problem. But then I ran into you and quickly discovered that wasn't going to happen."

Taycee gave him a rueful smile. "I guess I didn't really make it easy on you, did I?"

"Let's just say I learned the hard way that I should have kept in touch."

"You always were a slow learner."

Luke laughed.

The rest of the afternoon, she and Luke caught up, laughed, swam, teased, and applied more sunscreen. It was one of those days that surpassed all the others before it. By the time they hiked back to their cars, Taycee realized that even though things could never be the way they once were, maybe they could be better. Maybe having Luke back as a friend really was enough.

For now.

Twenty-four

The interview at the end of the second round of dating went almost exactly as it had before. Taycee felt like a broken record as she answered Jessa's questions. Great guys, check. Fun times, check. Looking forward to more, check, check, check.

And now here she was, at her flower shop on Monday morning, staring at her laptop screen once again and wondering what to write about the latest winners: Jake, Greg, Miles, and of course—Alec. Evidently there were a lot of people who thought that what Alec had to say about himself was incredibly interesting. Either that, or Burt and Megan did too good of an editing job, which Taycee wouldn't know since she never clicked "play."

Maybe it was time to set all the viewers straight. Right here. Right now. On this blank laptop screen that seemed to mock her with its glowing brightness.

First off, you should all know that Alec is a
self-absorbed motocross fanatic who also happens to

*be the world's worst date! Pick him again and
I'll . . . I'll . . .*

Taycee sighed, highlighting the words and hitting
"delete."

> *The viewers have done it again! I couldn't have
> picked them better myself!*

Delete.

> *So sorry to see you go, Sterling, but . . . well,
> not really.*

Delete.

> *Hey, guess what? I'm secretly in love with Luke
> Carney, and as of today, I'm respectfully stepping
> aside as Shelter's bachelorette. I'm going to be that
> lame girl who makes a fool of herself by chasing
> after a guy who only thinks of her as a sister. TTFN!*

Delete, delete, *delete.*
Argh.
Jessa's ringtone sounded, and Taycee gratefully grabbed
her phone—anything to put off writing this post.
"Please tell me you haven't posted the results yet,"
Jessa's voice blared in her ear.
Taycee bit her lip as she studied the blank screen that
now seemed to glow brighter than ever before. "Um, not
quite yet."
"Whew." Jessa let out a breath. "Okay, so Greg left town
this morning."
"He what?"
"After giving it some serious thought, he decided that
you're not the one for him," Jessa said. "So sorry, Tace," she
added dryly, "I know how much this must devastate you."

"It *does* devastate me." Jessa could joke all she wanted about Greg, but this wasn't good news at all. The show still had over three weeks to go, which meant they'd either have to end it early, an option Jessa would never go for, or—

"Looks like Sterling's back in the lineup," Jessa said, as if it was no big deal that Taycee would be subjected to his spitting and forced conversation for yet another night. "You don't mind changing Greg's name to his, do you?"

"Yes, I do mind. Why can't we just end this thing a week earlier than planned? You did say that we were bringing in more money than you anticipated, right?" It seemed like a reasonable request to Taycee. More than reasonable, in fact.

"Yes, but it hasn't been increasing the way I thought it would. We're going to need every voting opportunity we can get. In fact, I'm wishing we'd gone from ten bachelors to seven, instead of five, so we could have carried this on for a couple weeks longer."

It was a lesson in this-could-always-be-worse-so-be-grateful-you-only-have-one-more-date-with-Sterling. Taycee sighed and deleted Greg's name. She forced her fingers to tap out Sterling's while trying to tell herself that it could be worse. "Okay, it's changed. Anything else?"

"Actually, yes." Jessa hesitated, which was never a good sign. It meant something big was coming. Something Taycee probably wouldn't want to hear.

"I need you to up the romance."

"What!"

"Seriously, Tace. People are starting to comment about it a lot. 'Why hasn't he kissed her?' 'Does she even like these guys?' 'How is she not falling all over Jake?'" Jessa paused. "Would it kill you to show some affection?"

"Yes!" How could Jessa even ask such a thing, especially when she knew full well that Taycee didn't want to be here in the first place? Wasn't it enough that she'd agreed to be the bachelorette? Wasn't it enough that she'd gone along with it all, smiled for the camera, and gotten spit on, told off, and leered at in the process?

"C'mon," Jessa coaxed. "You've done such a good job luring the voters in so far. But what they want now is some good old-fashioned romance."

"Well, too bad for them." No way would Taycee ever kiss Sterling or Alec. No. Way. As for Miles? That would be like kissing a brother. Jake? Well, he'd definitely be a step above brother, but it would still feel wrong.

The simple truth was that none of them gave her that tingly, warm feeling that made her want to wrap her arms around them and hold on tight. None of them goaded her into wanting to silence them with her mouth over theirs. And none of them dominated her thoughts.

In other words, none of them were Luke.

"I'm sorry, but I can't," said Taycee. "I just can't."

"Yes you can," Jessa argued. "I'm sure this is the reason people aren't voting as much. And if we don't reach our goal . . . Tace, please, think of the farmers. My aunt and uncle. They need you to do this." A pause. "*I* need you to do this."

"Fine," Taycee said, wishing she could fast forward the next few weeks and leave this stupid show behind.

Taycee yanked her apartment door closed with more force than necessary. Broken glass shattered across the hardwood floor as the framed picture of a bright red tulip hit the ground next to her feet.

"Perfect," she muttered, dropping to her knees. "Just perfect."

A low whistle sounded from across the room, making Taycee jump. Caleb's head poked out from the arched opening of the kitchen as he tilted one of the chairs back. When did he get here? And how did he get in?

"Methinks someone's mad," Caleb said.

"Shut it."

Laughter followed—laughter that wasn't Caleb's. Taycee groaned. Of course Luke would be in her apartment right now. As if her horrible day couldn't be complete without a visit from him—a major source of Taycee's current problems.

"So, uh, Sterling's still in it, huh?" Caleb said. "I thought for sure he'd be gone after the horse incident."

Taycee glared. "Don't you have anything better to do than watch some lame bachelorette show on the internet? And why didn't you tell me you were coming again? I would have sprinkled itching powder all over the guest bed."

"Exactly why I didn't tell you. I value my sleep and health too much."

"Ha. Ha." Taycee could almost see him grinning from her place on the floor. She picked up the broken frame and larger glass pieces, and then stalked to the kitchen where she tossed them in the garbage can.

"Want to join us?" Luke asked, waving a handful of cards at her.

"No." She grabbed a small vacuum from the closet.

"She had a bad day," Caleb said, as if it wasn't obvious.

Taycee rolled her eyes and returned to the front room with a hand vacuum, where she sucked up the remaining pieces of glass. This was twice she'd broken something when Luke was around. Wasn't that a bad sign? The equivalent to breaking a mirror or walking under a ladder? Or maybe just knowing Luke had destined her to a lifetime of bad luck—at least whenever he was around.

Taycee returned to the kitchen and jerked open the fridge, pulling out a can of Squirt. She popped it open and let the carbonation burn her throat as she drank. Then she glared at Luke. "It's all your fault, you know."

Luke leaned back in his chair and fanned out his cards. "Your bad day is my fault? How so?"

"Greg was the winner, not Sterling. But because of your little stunt, he decided he couldn't date anyone with a police record."

"Really?" Luke chuckled. "If you ask me, I did you a favor."

Taycee dropped down beside him and plopped her drink on the counter. "Remind me to send you a bouquet of flowers to say thanks for finding a way to keep Sterling in the running." Especially now that she had to "up" the romance factor.

Her head hurt.

"Look on the bright side. At least Sterling doesn't seem to care that you have a shady past," Luke said, resting an arm on the table as he leaned toward her. "Speaking of which, do you have a copy of those mug shots? I'd give anything to see them."

Taycee's eyes narrowed. "You've got problems." But in reality, she was the one with problems. Lots and lots and lots of problems.

"Just think." Luke taunted her with his eyes. "If you hadn't sicced Missy on me, you might have been stuck with me instead. Isn't Sterling the lesser of two evils?"

A rude reminder that Taycee really only had herself to blame for all of this. If she'd just stayed out of it and let things play out on their own, Luke and Greg would most likely still be in the running, and Alec and Sterling would not. "Let's just say that I'd rather go out with Greg any day over Sterling."

"But not me?" Luke teased with a raise of his eyebrow.

"I'd even take you." Over everyone else. In fact, Taycee would love for Luke to swoop in and rescue her from all this.

Luke grinned. "Wow, you must really be dreading your

date with him."

Taycee relaxed against the back of her chair. "He's a nice guy, he really is. We just have nothing in common. And I'm really sick of getting spit on."

Caleb's hand covered hers. "Sounds like what you need is a good game of Rummy to get your mind off stuff." He wiggled his cards. "Sure you don't want in?"

Taycee bit her lip. She had two choices: Go hide in her room and try to work up the courage to let Sterling kiss her. Or hang out with Caleb and Luke.

"Deal me in."

"Ahhh, see Luke? Told you," Caleb said as he tossed some cards her way. "All you have to do is mention cards and Tace can't resist. She's predictable like that."

Taycee picked up her cards and sorted them. "How many nights are you crashing here this time?" Her eyes flickered to her brother, who looked at his cards and not her. "I saw a listing for what sounds like a nice little office space in Colorado Springs. We could check it out if you want."

"Sorry, sis," Caleb said. "I'm only here to do a couple depositions and then it's back to Phoenix."

Taycee frowned—both at the news and at her lousy cards. "I'm starting to think that you're putting me off." She shot him a worried look. "You still want to move back here someday, right?"

Caleb looked meaningfully at Luke before glancing at Taycee. "Sure," he said. "But unless we can settle, there's no telling how long this case will drag on for. I'll be back again in a few weeks though—after this whole bachelorette thing is over. Hopefully then we'll have some more time to hang out. And to . . . you know . . . talk . . . about stuff."

"What kind of stuff?"

Caleb shrugged. "Nothing in particular. You know, just . . . stuff. Life. That sort of thing."

Life? Since when did Caleb want to talk about life? A

sinking pit settled in her stomach. Especially when Caleb went back to examining his cards without looking at her. Luke, too, avoided her gaze.

Something was up. Something Caleb wasn't ready or willing to talk about yet, which probably meant that Taycee didn't want to hear it. But why did Luke seem to know and not her? That bothered her more than she cared to admit. Even though she was younger, she'd always thought of them as a trio—like the three musketeers. But now, sitting here, Taycee felt something she'd never felt with them before.

She felt like an outsider.

Twenty-five

It didn't take long for Taycee to discover that Jessa had also chatted with the bachelors about upping the romance.

On Monday, Sterling took her miniature golfing in Colorado Springs and felt the need to hold her hand after every hole and during the entire ten steps it took to get to the next one. The doorstep scene was even more awkward. He went in for a kiss, and she turned her head just in time to get a wet peck on the cheek.

Gross.

But if Taycee had thought Sterling was bad, Alec was ten times worse. He found every excuse to hug her or hold her hand, and against her better judgment she let him. She even let him kiss her. But when he tried to turn it into a full on make-out session, Taycee broke free and left him standing on the doorstep.

Miles, thankfully, had been better. He held her hand during appropriate times, and then left her with a light peck on the lips. She could handle light pecks.

Now she was down to only one date left: Jake.

He picked her up from her apartment, his eyes a deeper blue than ever as he grinned at her from beneath the rim of a blue baseball cap. He had a natural way about him that made everyone feel like they were someone worth listening to and spending time with—as though he looked beyond people's outside appearance and into their heart. And what he found, he liked. It was his gift.

"So, I was thinking you could give me a tour of your town." His fingers laced through hers as they walked to his car.

A tour of Shelter? Hadn't he already seen all there was to see? "Okaaayy," Taycee said as he shut her inside the car, where Megan was already waiting in the back. Taycee waved before searching Jake's face for any indication that he'd been joking. "Are you serious? You really want a tour of Shelter?"

He nodded. "Believe it or not, I'd love to check out some of the farms and land around here. It's a beautiful place."

"It *is* a beautiful place," she agreed. "But honestly, if you've seen one farm you've seen them all."

"So show me one."

Taycee was glad that a city boy like Jake could appreciate her small town, but she didn't quite know where to take him. Which farm? One of the few still in operation? Or one of the tired, dilapidated ones that had given up the ghost years ago?

As Jake backed out of the driveway, she made a quick decision and directed him to the old Meyer place. Ten miles outside of town, it had once been the home of a good friend of hers. Now it was bank-owned with a tattered "For Sale" sign planted out front.

They pulled up the drive, and a pit formed in Taycee's stomach. Twenty acres that had once thrived with so much life now sat dormant. Well, not dormant, exactly. The weeds sure flourished. But the house and barn had an unkempt, unlived in appearance, making Taycee long for the old days when they used to play tag in and around the corn stalks and eat sugar snap peas straight from the vine.

She swallowed the bittersweet nostalgia and reminded herself that she'd chosen this farm for a reason. Before the show officially started, Jessa had included some footage of the existing farms, along with interviews from a few of the farmers and her aunt and uncle, but she hadn't shown the already damaged parts, like this farm. Whether it made a difference to the viewers or not, Taycee wanted people to see what Shelter Springs would become if something didn't change. She wanted them to understand why she played this part. This was so much more than a silly dating competition to her.

Megan followed them around as Jake examined the property and the land that had once been used for farming. After their previous two dates, where everything had been planned to the last detail, today was different. More relaxed. Nice. Her life had been so packed full of structure lately that it felt good taking each minute as it came.

Jake led her through the weed infested fields, and then bent to examine the plants. He pulled a few from the ground, fisting a handful of dirt before letting it strain through his fingers.

What was he doing? He couldn't possibly be this interested in weeds and dirt—or farming for that matter. Why were they even here? Maybe this was Jessa's idea, a way to generate more sympathy for the town. Or maybe Jake wanted to see for himself the state of Shelter Springs, Colorado.

"Exactly what kind of business is your family involved in?" Taycee asked.

"Agriculture." Jake stood and brushed the dirt from his hands. "About forty years ago, my grandfather started what is now called NWOPO. The Northwestern Organic

177

Production Organization. Basically, it's a long title for organic farming."

During all of her dates, Taycee had tried to keep things lighter and less personal. No one could get attached to someone he didn't really know. But this news caught her off guard, and she couldn't help asking, "You're an organic farmer?"

Jake reached for her hand again, and they started wandering through the field, mashing weeds under their shoes. "Not really, although I feel like I know everything there is to know about it. I'm actually on the corporate side of things and oversee distribution for a network of farms."

"And here I thought you just wanted to play in the dirt for our date," Taycee said with a smile.

He gestured toward the field. "I'm wondering if some of the producing farms might be interested in switching over to organic farming."

Organic farming? Although Taycee didn't know much about the process, she knew that organic produce cost more at the grocery store, which meant that there was a lot more involved in the farming process. She also knew the local farmers were pretty set in their ways. "But isn't that more labor intensive and expensive?"

"Yeah, but it also pays much better. The farming market is becoming so competitive these days that most of the smaller farms, like the ones here, are finding that the only way to stay in business is for them to make the switch."

"What do you mean?"

"Only that organic farming is mostly done by the independent farms. It's a market with an increasing demand, creating a situation where the independents are able to work together, rather than compete against the bigger commercial farming organizations."

Jake made it sound so simple. So easy. Like a minor change could solve a very real problem in Shelter. But it couldn't be that easy. "What would it take to make the switch?"

Jake stopped, looked around one last time, and then pulled her back in the direction of the car. "It's more of a training and educational process. NWOPO operates sort of like a franchise. Farms from all over the country buy into it via an annual membership fee. Then we teach them how to make the switch to organic farming, get them certified, and when it's time to sell we have a distribution channel already in place. It's a pretty smooth system actually."

"It sounds too good to be true," Taycee said.

Jake smiled. "Don't get me wrong, it will take some money, work, and time to get the farms pesticide and chemical free—usually in the neighborhood of three years. But if the farms can survive the transitional period, ultimately the returns are much greater. In addition, they'll live in healthier conditions, have better soil, and better tasting produce that needs less water to grow."

Three years sounded like a century to Taycee, especially with the way things were going now. Very few of the existing farms could survive one more year—let alone three. But maybe the farmers market co-op could help them get through those years. The farmers would be a lot more willing to consider something like this if it meant they could one day sell through regular distribution channels again. That was their biggest concern with the co-op. No one was excited about taking on the responsibility of selling their own produce.

"Hey," Taycee said. "Would you be willing to put together a presentation for the farmers in the area? Talk to them about organic farming and how your company works?"

"If you think it's something they might be interested in, I'd be happy to." Jake stopped and turned to face Taycee. "But please don't think that's why I'm here. I didn't come to drum up more business for my company."

Taycee grinned. "No, you came because your sister roped you into it."

"That may be true, but when I saw your face and read about the girl who owned her own flower shop and liked making people happy, she didn't have to twist my arm too hard. That's why I'm here—not for any other reason. But if I can help at all with your town's situation, maybe there's a chance this can end up being a win-win," he said with a smile.

Taycee forced herself to return his smile, even though she knew it could never be a win-win—not if one of those wins included her and Jake getting together. It made Taycee wish that he *had* come with ulterior motives so he wouldn't care if she walked away at the end of it all.

"I honestly don't care what brought you here," Taycee finally said. "Not if your company really can help the town. In fact, if it's all right with you, I'll see if Jessa can get something set up soon. Maybe Saturday night? Would that work?"

Jake tugged her closer, and his hands circled her waist. "Sure, as long as you'll come with me."

"I'm not sure Jessa would approve of that," Taycee joked. "You know, no preferential treatment and all that." She hadn't been to a town meeting since the whole bachelorette fiasco, and she had no intention of going again anytime soon—especially not as the date to one of the bachelors. There would be whispers and pointed fingers. Maybe Luke would even be there.

No thanks.

Taycee backed out of Jake's hold and led him toward the car. "Okay, so now that that's settled, do you really want to keep looking at farmland, or can we do something else?"

Jake chuckled. "I have some reservations at a restaurant in Colorado Springs, and then I was thinking we could do some window shopping afterwards. Or do you have a better idea?"

A hearty breeze whipped some of Taycee's hair into her

face, giving her a much better idea. She cocked her head to the side. "How do you feel about kite wars?"

"Kite what?" The bewildered look on his face made Taycee laugh.

"Wars," she said as she climbed into his car. "You'll love it, I promise."

"If you say so."

Megan climbed in back with her camera, and Taycee directed Jake to Nicky's Novelties where they purchased a couple of kites. Ten minutes later, he pulled to the side of the road, next to a wide open grassy meadow.

The wind lifted Taycee's hair from her shoulders and whipped stray tendrils across her face. She closed her eyes, enjoying the fresh country air and how comfortable it was being with Jake. He didn't make her nervous. Her stomach didn't knot and twist whenever he was around. Her thoughts didn't scatter. It was nice. Easy.

"So how does this war thing work, exactly?" Jake asked as he assembled his kite.

"Well . . ." Taycee snapped the plastic rods into the connector, making the bright pink and black checked kite go taut. "Basically the first kite to get knocked out of the sky loses."

Jake waited a second before his mouth lifted in a half-smile. "That's it?"

"Welcome to Shelter Springs." She grinned at him. "We like to keep things simple 'round here."

Jake chuckled. "I can live with that. In fact"—His fingers brushed some hair behind her ear—"I'm starting to really like simple." His words, combined with the way he looked at her made Taycee's stomach knot. Not good. *Don't look at me like that. Don't!*

Before she could step away, Jake dipped his head, and his lips brushed across hers. It wasn't a bad sensation. It felt good—his touch, his apparent admiration. She didn't feel chills or fireworks or the all-consuming desire to wrap her arms around him and return the kiss, but she didn't necessarily want to stop it either. Besides, it would make Jessa happy which was always a good thing.

Jake pulled back, and Taycee studied his eyes. So open. So honest. *Do I like you? Could I like you?* He really was the complete package. Why wasn't she throwing her arms around him and kissing him back? Feeling giddy? Twitterpated? At the very least excited?

Probably because when she looked into Jake's blue eyes, what she really wanted to see was deep brown.

Taycee dropped her gaze and picked up her kite. Holding it up, she forced a smile. "Ready?"

"As ready as I'll ever be," Jake said. "But just so you know, if your kite dies first, you owe me another kiss."

Taycee watched him as he backed away. Was he being sincere or was it all an act for the camera—him doing his duty like Jessa had asked?

If they were all alone, completely alone, with no camera, no future viewers, no expectations or pressure, what would this date really be like? Would Jake still look at her that way? Would he still want to hold her hand and kiss her? Or would he relax, let things be as easy and uncomplicated as they had been before?

Because it suddenly seemed like easy just got complicated.

"What's the matter?" Jake taunted, holding his kite high to catch the wind. "Afraid you're going to lose?"

"I never lose at kite wars." Which was a complete lie. Taycee had only ever played with Luke and Caleb, and Luke had always won. Every. Single. Time. Him and his pathetic little cheap kites that always refused to die.

"Until today," Jake said.

Taycee pointed a finger at him. "Pride goeth before the fall."

It didn't take long before both kites sailed high in the sky, beating against the wind and soaring.

182

"Okay," Jake said as he let out more string. "Here's the stakes: If I win, you owe *me* a kiss, and if you win, I owe *you* a kiss. How's that?"

Taycee laughed. "Sounds like a win-win to me."

"Exactly."

"You're on." Letting out more string, Taycee let her kite sail even higher, until it looked like a tiny pink and black diamond diving this way and that as it floated high above the ground.

"The trick of it all is to get the distance right," Taycee explained. "If one's higher than the other, all we're going to end up with is twisted string and two kites stuck together."

"Gotcha. No twisted string." Jake grinned. "So much for simple." He pulled his kite towards Taycee's and missed, hooking his string under hers. Taycee stepped around him to untangle them, wound her string around her handle to lower her kite, and then steered it toward Jake's once again. They bumped against each other and separated.

"Perfect," Taycee said. "Game on." Without missing a beat, she yanked hard on the string and rammed Jake's kite again, making it drop dive before soaring up again.

"You don't play nice, do you?" Jake said.

"Not if I can help it."

"For that, you're going down."

"In your dreams."

Jake sailed his kite into hers, crashing into it and making Taycee laugh. After a few more minutes of battling it out, Jake's arm locked around her shoulders, keeping her prisoner.

"Cheater!" Taycee called, giggling. The strings tangled and the kites wrapped around and around each other. "Stop it! You're going to make us both crash!"

"You said there are no rules. I can do whatever I want."

Taycee's laughter rang out as she struggled to free herself and the kite. Soon, both kites nose-dived toward the ground, with Jake's landing a second before her own.

"I won, I won!" Taycee hopped up and down beneath Jake's arm. "I can't believe I actually won!"

Jake's sandy blond eyebrow raised as he studied her. "You sound pretty excited for a girl who always wins."

"Okay, so maybe I never win," Taycee admitted. "Until now, that is." She threw her arms around him and kissed his cheek. "Thank you, thank you. Seriously, you have no idea how happy this makes me."

"I guess if you're happy, I should be happy," Jake joked. "But seriously, how bad does that make me if I just lost to a loser?"

Taycee grinned. "Only by a second or two."

"True." Jake's arms circled her waist. "But it still means that I owe you, right?"

Before Taycee could remember the bet, his lips were on hers, warm and soft. His arms tightened around her as he tried to deepen the kiss. But she'd finally won her first ever kite war and what she really wanted to do was run and dance and scream into the open sky, "I won!"

Maybe Luke would even hear.

Jake finally drew back with a sigh. "Wow, this really does mean a lot to you, doesn't it?"

"I'm sorry," Taycee said, laughter threatening to burst. "Really, it's just so . . ."

"Funny?"

"No. So great."

Jake shook his head. "Is this some sort of sanctioned sport around here or something? I mean, do you now get a medal for beating me?"

"No, only bragging rights. But believe me, I *will* brag."

"I believe it."

Together, they wound up their kites, and Jake's arm came around her again as he led her back to the car. "Note to self: Don't play any more games with Taycee."

Her shoulder nudged his side. "You're just bugged you lost to a girl."

"It's true. First Speed and now Kite Wars. My pride can't take anymore."

Taycee gave him a side-hug as they walked the rest of the way to the car. "Thanks, Jake," she said. "You have no idea how much I needed that."

Twenty-six

A loud pounding on the door awoke Taycee.

With a yawn, she rolled to her side and squinted at the clock. Seven o'clock. Who would be waking her up at seven on a Sunday morning? Someone with no compassion, that's who.

Jessa.

More pounding.

"I'm coming, I'm coming." Taycee rolled from her bed and raked her fingers through her hair as she padded toward the door. The banging came again before she finally opened it. Sure enough, Jessa stood on her doorstep.

"Do you know what time it is?" Taycee groaned.

"I brought breakfast." Jessa handed Taycee a muffin then waltzed past. "Did you see the show yesterday? Holy cow, girl, you've got the message boards hopping. How many times did you kiss Jake anyway? I lost count."

Taycee suddenly felt very awake. "Three. How could you lose count with only three? And small ones at that. They shouldn't even count."

Jessa laughed. "Burt and Megan must have done some creative editing because it looked like a whole lot more than three. And a good thing, too, because the site is flooded with traffic. With the footage of the farm—which was quite brilliant of you—we scored several more donations. Oh, and *Wake Up Denver* wants to have you on their show in a couple weeks." She said this last part in a rush of words that Taycee almost didn't catch them.

"Whoa—what?" Taycee nearly dropped her muffin as she stumbled after Jessa. "You said no, I hope."

"Of course not," Jessa said. "They want to interview you and the two remaining bachelors right before the final vote. It will be great—the perfect time to remind everyone how much we need their vote one last time."

"Jessa! You told me those two news interviews would be it. Please don't make me do this."

Jessa leaned across the bar. "I knew you'd feel this way, but this isn't a bad thing. It's actually a very good thing. We're so close, Tace, but we really need all the votes we can get. You'll be awesome."

"And if I'm not?"

"The show will be practically over by then so it really won't matter."

"Jessa!"

"Oh please. You've got nothing to worry about. You have those viewers wrapped around your pretty manicured fingers."

Taycee held up her hands, wanting to remove the nail polish and file them down. "They're fake. Just like me."

Jessa rolled her eyes. "You're not a fake. The person I saw on TV last night was the same person I'm standing in front of right now. Taycee Lynne Emerson. My beautiful, talented best friend, who has three bachelors half in love with her right now—and for good reason."

"You're wrong." Taycee sank down on one of the barstools and rested her head on the counter. "It's all a show.

Don't you see that? Those guys *act* like they like me because they want to win, and I *act* like I'm into them because I don't want to screw things up for Shelter. I feel like such a fraud. Please don't make it worse by making me go on some talk show."

"But it's turning into the best story ever." Jessa's hand came to rest on Taycee's. "Small town girl falls for big-city, rich guy—potential savior of our town. Shelter couldn't have asked for better publicity. Besides, I don't know what you're talking about. You and Jake seemed to really hit it off this past week."

"That's just it." Taycee sighed. "He's a great guy, but . . . I just don't know if it's real. I want the people, the cameras, and the pressure to all go away so I can see what's real and what's not because right now it all feels too fake to be real. You know?"

"That makes no sense."

"It's seven in the morning."

Jessa opened the fridge and pulled out a quart of orange juice. "You know what they say, early to bed, early to rise—"

"Shut up."

Jessa smiled as she poured herself a drink. "How about this: By the end of the show, if your feelings toward Jake are still fake, then I'll happily take him off your hands." Something about the way Jessa said it made it sound like she actually would.

Taycee's arms folded on the counter and she leaned forward, resting her chin on her arms. "Wait a sec, you like Jake?"

"I think he's cute, that's all," she said with a nonchalant wave of her hand. "Maybe even good for a kiss or two."

"He's rich too," Taycee taunted.

"Okay, so maybe he'd be good for more than a kiss."

"You're terrible." Taycee picked up the muffin and removed the paper wrapping, shoving a piece into her mouth. "I take it Burt and Megan included the part about organic farming in the footage?"

"Yes, and I spent most of the night researching everything I could about it. From what I've read, it's a brilliant solution—something I can't believe we haven't looked into before. They say that the transitional period is the hardest, but the co-op could be the solution for that." Jessa's smile had never been so big. "It's all so perfect how this is panning out. I couldn't have planned it better myself."

"So you're fine with Jake presenting it to the town on Saturday?"

"More than fine," Jessa said. "I've already shot off an email to the mayor's secretary, who will spread the word."

"Of course you have."

"Smart, wealthy, handsome, and could help save our town." Jessa shook her head. "And you don't know if you like him. Seriously, girl, what's wrong with you?"

Taycee wondered the same thing herself.

"Is it because of the Tin Man?" Jessa asked.

"Who?"

"The Tin man. You know, Luke."

It took a minute for Taycee to get the reference. The one without a heart. It was sort of like a slap in the face, the way the words lodged painfully in her chest. Her initial instinct was to defend Luke and tell her that he had a heart. A really good heart, capable of loving harder and stronger than most people, because that's what Taycee wanted to believe, more than anything. But the truth was, she really didn't know if he did—at least not when it came to finding true love and making a commitment. He'd been engaged at least once before, and he'd admitted that he hadn't loved his fiancée enough.

Maybe Jessa was right. Maybe Luke was the Tin Man.

The thought made her heart hurt.

Jessa moved toward Taycee with a clack of her sandaled shoes on the tile. She leaned against the counter. "You've got to get over that guy. I refuse to watch you get your heart broken over him again—not when someone like Jake is around to take you away from all this."

"All what?"

"This town. The people here. The memories. It's like you're caught in a net and can't get out. What you need is to get away from Luke and leave him behind once and for all."

That had to be the worst advice Jessa had ever come up with. "But you were the one who said you could see sparks between us. I thought you liked Luke."

"And I thought those so-called sparks I saw weren't real?" Jessa countered. "Isn't that what you told me? That he only pretended interest to goad you?"

Taycee's finger scraped at a nonexistent spot on her counter, avoiding the question and Jessa's eyes. Deep down, Taycee wanted to believe that it had been real, that there was a chance Luke could be interested in her. But no matter how much she wished it, that didn't mean it would come true. Because that was how life worked. Sometimes you win, sometimes you lose. And when you lose, you have to get over it and move on.

Which was exactly what Jessa was telling her to do now.

Jessa's hand squeezed Taycee's. "I thought his coming back would be a good thing. If things worked out between you, great. If not, you could finally move on. But since he's returned, all I've seen him do is hurt you more, and frankly, I'm sick of it. In my mind, he never has been, nor will he ever be, good enough for you. You deserve someone who looks at you the way Jake does."

In Jessa's roundabout way, she'd just given Taycee a compliment. But for some reason it felt more like a solid punch to the stomach, knocking the wind out of all her wishes and dreams. Which was completely stupid, considering Taycee had tried time and time again to convince herself of that exact same thing. Yet deep down, that hope refused to die.

Taycee walked into the diner, fighting the fatigue of yet another late and stressful night. One more round of dating was now over and only three bachelors remained: Jake, Alec, and Miles. Which meant only two weeks and five dates left.

Whew. She could do this. She *had* to do this.

Early on, Taycee had pictured herself going on date after date after date and being filmed in the process. That was it. But now there were things like upping the romance, keeping viewers happy, doing interviews, and going on talk shows. Every day, the pressure mounted, making her feel like one of those pressure cookers her mother once used to can grape juice, looking ready to blow at any second.

Did Taycee have it in her to keep this up? With each new date, each new vote, and each new donation to the town, the guilt grew. People gave so freely to the little town of Shelter, expecting what in return? A good romance? A happy ending for her and some chosen bachelor?

Well, it didn't feel happy. Not when a pit formed in Taycee's stomach before each date, making her feel like what she was doing was deceptive and wrong. Was it right that Shelter was benefitting from something that wasn't real?

Jessa didn't think so. She seemed to think that Taycee could turn on and off her feelings like a faucet. Off to Luke. On to Jake. Everyone wins. The bachelorette show gets a happy ending, the money raised forms a much needed co-op, and Shelter Springs gets another chance to keep on keeping on.

But Taycee had doubts. Lots of doubts.

"Taycee, your order's up," Liza's voice called out.

Already? She glanced at the clock in surprise. It had only been fifteen minutes. Was Liza actually being nice now? Wouldn't that be something.

"Thanks, Liza. That was fast." The smell of the curly fries wafted into Taycee's nose, making her mouth water.

"Oh, I'm off early today for a date, so I wanted to make sure you got it before I left," Liza said in her sugary sweet way as she removed her apron.

"That was nice of you." Taycee examined her food. Maybe Liza had spit on it or added salt instead of sugar to the chicken salad. "A date this early in the day? Sounds promising."

"I hope so," said Liza. "Luke's taking me into Denver for a show and dinner. Should be fun."

Wait—what? Liza was going out with Luke? The curly fries suddenly looked and smelled like wooden springs. "Oh, that's great," Taycee managed to say. "I'm sure you'll have a fun time."

"I plan to." Liza's white teeth sparkled through too-pink lips before she disappeared into the back room.

With slow steps, Taycee carried her plate to the far corner of her booth and slid all the way to the end, trying to hide from the eyes of everyone else in the room. She felt transparent, as though a visible cloud of jealousy and patheticness surrounded her, announcing to the world that Luke had just shaved off another chunk of her heart.

Because if he was interested in someone like Liza, there was no way he'd ever be interested in Taycee.

The sting of tears came. She immediately blinked them back, despising them almost as much as she despised herself.

The door opened and Luke stepped inside, looking so good it tore at Taycee's heart even more. Liza came out of the back room and gave him a winning smile.

"Ready?" he asked.

"As if I'd ever keep you waiting." She turned and called out, "I'm off, Maris. See you tomorrow."

"Have a good time, hon."

"I will." Liza looked Taycee's way and waved a smug goodbye, which made Luke look her way as well.

For a moment his brown eyes met hers and Taycee's heart thwacked in her chest, feeling like it would burst from her body any second. The room suddenly seemed devoid of everyone but her and Luke—locked into a staring contest that crackled with an underlying tension and awkwardness. Under normal circumstances, Luke would have grinned and waved, even come over and chatted with her for a few minutes. But not today.

Maybe he didn't know what to do or how to act either.

Liza's head came between them, breaking the connection, and Taycee returned her attention to her food, trying not to feel the deep-rooted pain that came with the chiming of the bells.

She let out a breath as she shoved her curly fries away. Maybe Jessa was right. Maybe it was time for Taycee to move on with her life.

Jake was handsome, kind, funny, rich—the perfect bachelor. It was beyond ridiculous to think that Taycee couldn't develop feelings for someone like him. What she needed to do was try a little harder and really go for it. If not, she might end up spending the rest of her life pining away for a guy who never pined back.

Twenty-seven

Taycee closed her apartment door behind her and leaned against it. Her date with Miles had been horrible. Not horrible in the she-couldn't-stand-him sense. More in the she-was-a-scatter-brained-idiot sense. How many times had he repeated something he'd said because she wasn't paying attention? How many times had the words "Earth to Taycee" forged their way through her fogged mind?

Too many. Way too many.

And when he'd kissed her goodnight, all Taycee could think about was Luke and how he was on a date with someone else. No matter how hard Taycee tried, she still couldn't concentrate or regroup. Even now that she was home, her thoughts still strayed to Luke and Liza and how cute their names sounded together. Were they hitting it off? Was he holding her hand? Making her laugh? Kissing her?

Taycee wanted to cup her hands over her ears and tell the screaming voices to take a hike. She breathed in deeply, trying to organize her thoughts, but they continued to explode inside her head like a finale to a fireworks show. She needed to get out of her apartment, calm down, and find a way to regain some equanimity.

As soon as the sound of Miles's engine faded into the distance, Taycee yanked open her door and escaped to the darkness of the night.

✱

"Thanks for the fun night, Luke," Liza said, leaning against the door of her duplex. "Maybe we can do it again sometime."

"Yeah, that would be great." It was the polite response, but Luke didn't really mean it. Liza could be nice and even funny at times, but he'd really only asked her out as a distraction—a way to keep his mind from going somewhere else.

Liza gave him a flirtatious smile, expectation written all over her face.

Luke cleared his throat and took a step back. "I guess I'll see you around."

"What, no promise of a phone call?" she teased, only there was too much hope in her voice for it to really be teasing.

Normally, Luke wouldn't have any qualms about making such a promise and not following through. Polite, but insincere promises were how you played the dating game. But now he knew better than to do that. Taycee had taught him better. So he gave Liza a half-smile instead. "I like to surprise people."

"Oh." Liza's smile faded a bit, looking more forced. "I do love surprises."

Luke gave her one last wave, and then turned and jogged to his truck. Moments later he drove away, regret tapping on the door of his conscience. He shouldn't have asked her out. It was a dumb move. But after watching all

195

those kissing scenes with Taycee and the bachelors this past week—especially her date with Jake—Luke had made a rash decision to ask out the one girl in town Taycee liked the least. Why? Because he was completely immature.

He'd basically used Liza—something he never set out to do. But looking back, that was exactly what he'd done.

Shame on him.

Turning the corner, Luke hit the brakes when he saw a slim figure cross the street in front of him. Taycee. Wasn't she supposed to be on a date with one of her bachelors tonight? Luke tapped the horn.

Her head twisted around, and she squinted into his headlights. Then she nodded and continued to cross the street, picking up her pace.

Luke unrolled his window. "Hey, you're on my road."

"Forgive me for getting in your way," Taycee called over her shoulder, sounding less than happy.

"What's the matter? Bad date tonight?"

Taycee didn't answer, just kept on walking, so Luke drove to the wrong side of the road and drove next to her slowly, hanging his elbow out of the open window. "If it's any consolation, my date didn't go that well either."

She stopped and hesitated before turning to face him. "Too bad, because you and Liza seem so perfect for each other." Wincing, she clamped a hand over her mouth and stomped her foot. With a shake of her head, her hand fell back to her side, revealing an apologetic look. "I'm sorry. I really didn't mean that. You're just . . . just . . ."

"In the wrong place at the wrong time?"

"Something like that." She glanced down as her foot scuffed against the sidewalk.

Luke had never seen her look so vulnerable before. So . . . down. He didn't like it. "Want to go for a drive with me?" he asked casually, hoping she'd say yes. All of a sudden it didn't matter that she kissed four different guys this past

196

week. Nothing mattered if she would just climb into his truck and take a drive with him.

Her eyes flickered to his. "It's late. I really should head back."

"No, what you should do is come and check out some stars with me. It's a perfect night. Not a cloud in the sky."

Taycee let out a breath and gazed up the road to where his headlights highlighted the street. "Star gazing, huh?"

"That's what they call it."

She hesitated a moment longer before shrugging. "Okay. Sure, why not?"

Luke couldn't hide his smile as he leaned over and opened the passenger door for her. When she hopped inside, he resisted the urge to pull her next to him and kiss that sad vulnerability away.

Luke's hands clutched the wheel as he drove out of town and up a windy mountain road. Thirty minutes later, he pulled into an open meadow and stopped near the middle of the clearing. From behind the seat, he lifted a heavy blanket. "Ready?"

Taycee eyed the blanket with a raised eyebrow. "Is this the second time you've star-gazed tonight, or do you always keep that in your truck?"

"Third time, actually."

Both eyebrows shot up.

"Joking," Luke said. "One of my clients gave me this as a gift the other day, and I keep forgetting to take it inside. So, no, this isn't a repeat."

She reached for the handle. "Okay then."

Luke followed her to an area away from the truck and spread the blanket across the grassy meadow. Taycee laid down first and folded her arms across her stomach as she gazed toward the starry sky above. The moonlight made her skin glow and her eyes look dark and mysterious. Beautiful.

"Coming?" she asked.

Luke didn't need to be asked twice. He dropped down next to her and scooted close enough that their shoulders touched. Then, to distract her from his fairly obvious move, he lifted his finger and pointed at the stars. "Look, there's me."

"Where?"

He maneuvered even closer, bending his head toward hers. "See those four stars that make up a trapezoid and all those stars coming away from it, sort of like the legs of a spider?"

"You mean Hercules?"

"Exactly," Luke said. "Me."

Taycee's quiet laugh seemed to fill the night with something better than happiness. "Aren't you cocky."

"Hey, sometimes you just have to brag—especially when there's someone around you want to impress."

A pause. "I'm sorry. Did I hear that you're trying to impress me?"

Luke's heartbeat quickened as she turned her head to glance at him. He'd arrived at a crossroads that could go one of two ways: He could brush aside her question with a "Now why would I want to impress you?" or answer honestly and risk breaking whatever connection they'd managed to form lately.

Luke swallowed, picking at the blanket between them. "Well, I did compare myself to Hercules." It was as honest as he could get at the moment.

Taycee let out a breath. "I never liked Hercules. Way too conceited."

"Oh." So much for her seeing the honesty in that. Strike one for him. Luke pointed toward the sky once more. "What about Draco then? It symbolizes a dragon that once guarded the pole star. No one could attribute that to conceit."

"Sorry, but no," Taycee said. "The name makes me think of the evil kid in Harry Potter."

Strike two. "Forget Draco and think dragon then."

"As in 'Puff, the Magic Dragon?'"

Strike three and Luke was out. This wasn't going very well at all. He gave up. "Whoever came up with the name Puff, anyway?" he grumbled. "Talk about a sissy name."

"Unlike Luke, right?"

Now they were getting somewhere. "My point exactly. I'm as far from sissy as you can get."

"So it should be Luke, the Magic Dragon?"

"Even you have to admit it's better than Puff."

A moment of silence until Taycee finally conceded. "True. Luke is definitely not a sissy name."

Luke grinned at the night sky, feeling like he'd won something—whatever it was. "Thanks, Taycee Lynne. That only took about ten minutes to get you to say."

She laughed, and once again the sound filled something inside Luke, making him feel better somehow.

"Thanks for convincing me to come," Taycee said. "I needed this."

"It didn't take much convincing."

"True," she said. "Were you on your way here when you saw me?"

"No. I was headed home."

"Well, thanks for changing your plans."

Luke hesitated, feeling like he'd stumbled upon another chance at coming clean. Who knew how many more chances he'd have? He cleared his throat, his heart hammering. "Anything to get some time with you."

The silence that followed made him feel exposed, as if he'd put his heart on a platter for her to take or wave away. A few more seconds came and went without a word. Not good. Was she trying to think of a nice way of letting him down, or was she scared too—like Luke? Hopefully the latter. He should reach for her hand, touch her, something. Only a few inches and his hand would brush against hers. Still, Luke hesitated.

Coward. Hold her hand already, you pathetic excuse for someone named Luke.

Before he could talk himself out of it, Luke's fingers laced through hers. At first her hand hung limply in his, but then her fingers tightened. Luke let out a breath he didn't realize he'd been holding. Her fingers were soft and cold, but her hand fit perfectly in his. Probably the same way she'd feel in his arms or the same way her lips would feel against his.

Luke stared at the starlit sky, feeling that his world had suddenly aligned. As though all the dots had been connected, creating an awesome picture, way better than Hercules or Draco or any of the other constellations out there. He felt something good. Something real. Something he'd never expected to find with his old friend from Shelter Springs, Colorado.

"So Liza? Really?" Taycee blurted. "You had to go and ask out the one person in town who hates me the most, didn't you? I blame you for my ruined date, you know."

A smile came to Luke's face. He could ruin her night. He liked that. Really liked that. "Jealous?" he asked, not daring to hope that she actually was.

"Maybe."

He chuckled, loving the slightly snide way she'd admitted to it. He brought her hand to his face and smoothed it over his cheek before letting it rest against his lips for a moment. Who would have thought that such a bad day could end so well? Not him. It almost felt undeserved. Like doing something as petty as asking a girl out to make another girl jealous shouldn't have paid off. But it had.

"It never hurts to date the diner girl," he said. "You know, free food and all that."

Taycee pulled her hand from his and slugged Luke in the arm. "Not funny."

Luke rolled on his side, facing her. His entire body pulsed with a kind of need he'd never felt before—not even with his former fiancée, a girl he thought he'd once loved. It took every ounce of willpower Luke had not to lean in and kiss her.

He swallowed as he stared into her hazel eyes that were as expressive as they were beautiful. He smoothed her brown hair away and ran his fingers down her neck. He didn't think he could take watching her date or kiss one more guy. He wanted to be the only one in her life. The only one she touched. The only one she looked at the way she looked at him now. He didn't want to share that look. He didn't want to share her.

"What's happening?" Taycee whispered.

"I don't know, but I like it."

Taycee scooted over and snuggled into him, laying her head against his chest. "Me too."

He held her close, locking her against him as if it would keep her from ever slipping away, from going out with Jake or Miles or the scumbag Alec ever again. But the reality was he couldn't.

They stayed that way for what seemed like hours, until the air turned chilly and she shivered in his arms. Only then did Luke reluctantly let her go. He helped her up and drove back as slowly as he could, wanting to extend their time together as long as possible. All too soon he was at her apartment, walking her to the door.

He gave her one last lingering hug, wishing it could last forever. Everything felt too new, too fragile. As if the dawning of a new day could somehow ruin it all. His lips lingered near her ear, brushing against it as he whispered, "Why did you have to go and get me voted off?"

Taycee chuckled as her arms tightened around him. "Not the smartest thing I've ever done, was it?"

"You said it." Luke drew back, and his eyes met hers in a look that made the air crackle between them. All he could do was stare and think about how badly he wanted to kiss her. But that's what all the other bachelors did at the end of their dates. Luke wanted to be different somehow. Stand out.

He took a step back and let his hands trail down her arms. "I'll call you."

"Promise?" Although she tried to make it sound teasing, there was an underlying hint of concern. A distrust. Luke hated that he'd been the cause of it.

"Promise." It was easy to say. The second she walked through that door, Luke knew he'd want to do just that. Call. Text. Be back bright and early in the morning so he could see her wild morning hair and somehow convince her to spend the rest of the day with him.

If only he didn't have animals to see and she didn't have flowers to arrange. If only he didn't have mountains of paperwork to deal with and she didn't have another date with another guy who wasn't him.

Life really sucked sometimes.

Twenty-eight

Taycee's mouth watered from the smells wafting through the expansive room. She hadn't eaten since breakfast and everything smelled good—even seafood.

Jake had brought her to Denver, and they now sat in a beautiful high-rise seafood restaurant overlooking the city. Under normal circumstances, Taycee would have taken in the view and the experience, but every time her gaze traveled that direction, a slight reflection in the glass reminded her that both Burt and Megan were there, filming.

She should have been used to it by now, and she was, for the most part, but here in this quiet, more intimate and romantic setting, Taycee wanted to crawl under the table and hide from all the eyes sneaking glances their way.

Jake leaned across the table and slid his hand under hers. He looked so comfortable, unphased by the fact that they were the center of attention. How did he do it? How did he forget about everything and everyone else?

"So, it looks like I'm scheduled to present to the town tomorrow night," Jake said.

"I know."

His fingers played with hers, tracing each finger up and down. The gesture should have caused goose bumps to emerge up and down her arms, but it only added to her discomfort. After last night with Luke, so much had changed. It made everything even more wrong. She shouldn't be here with Jake, nor should she have gone out with Miles yesterday or go with Alec tomorrow.

"Jessa wants to air some of the footage from it. You know, to get more publicity."

"That should be good for your business too, I would think."

He nodded. "That's pretty much what Jessa said. She called it a win-win, but the jury's still out on whether or not any of the farmers will be interested."

"I think they'll be more receptive than you think. They've never fully embraced the farmers market idea, but they went along with it because it was either that or give up. You'll be giving them the option that it doesn't have to be forever if they don't want it to be."

"True. But it's still going to take some major work on their part if they choose to go that route."

Taycee shrugged. "That's their choice to make. All you can do is give them enough information to make it."

The waiter interrupted them to refill their glasses. Taycee's gaze wandered to a table not far from them, where a guy with broad shoulders and dark hair sat with his back to her. He looked so much like Luke that she couldn't help but stare and wish that the situation could be different. That it could be Luke sitting across from her instead of Jake.

"You seem kind of distracted today."

Taycee's eyes snapped back to Jake's. "Sorry," she said. "I was just thinking about work. I should have phoned in an order today but ran out of time."

Jake frowned. "You should have said something. We could have pushed back our date a little."

"Oh, it's not that." Taycee waved off his concern. "The warehouse closes at four, and I let time slip away."

"Too busy thinking of me?" Jake teased.

Taycee nodded because it was the truth. She had been thinking of Jake. And Alec. And Miles. But not in a good way. More like a stressful, only-four-dates-left I-can-do-this sort of way. She sighed. "It's hard to believe this bachelorette thing is almost over, isn't it?" Especially since it seemed like it had been going on for years, rather than weeks.

Jake lifted her fingers and kissed them lightly. "The show might be almost over, but win or lose, I plan to stick around for a while after."

Taycee's plush chair suddenly felt like concrete. She shifted. "For business reasons?" *Please say yes.*

He chuckled, his blue eyes crinkling at the corners. "That's not what I meant—not that I wouldn't be happy sticking around to answer anyone's questions. I was referring to you. Win or lose, I'd like the chance to spend some more time with you."

Taycee blinked across the table at him. Whoa. Where did all of this come from? One second they talked about a missed flower order and the next Jake said he wanted to stick around for her? She felt blindsided. Suddenly "only four dates left" got a whole lot longer.

"I have to be honest," Jake continued, still caressing her hand. "I never expected to like you this much."

No, no, no. Taycee's fingers quelled in his. She tried to swallow the lump in her throat. "What are you saying, Jake?"

"I'm saying I want to keep seeing you, even after this is all over. Under normal circumstances—without all the cameras and publicity. I'd like to give us a chance."

Taycee couldn't look at him any longer, so she pretended to stare out the window. But what she really stared at was the reflection of Burt and Megan, filming everything. Jake's words. Her reactions. A pit formed in her stomach. She couldn't handle hurting someone as great as

Jake. It wasn't right. Or fair. Why did love have to be so complicated and hard anyway?

"Who ordered the chicken?"

Taycee could have hugged the waiter for his perfect timing. She'd never been more relieved to see anyone. If only he'd pull up a chair and hang out for the rest of the night.

If only.

"That would be me," she said.

The waiter set a plate in front of her and another in front of Jake, and then left. An awkward silence descended, but Taycee had no idea what to say or how to right this horrible wrong. She wanted to open up and tell Jake that she was a fraud, that her heart belonged to someone else. The desire weighted her down with its desire to be let out. But what would happen if she did that? How would Jake react? Would he get up and leave? Walk away from the show like Greg had done? Would Miles?

Two voting opportunities remained. If they didn't get those votes, what then? What would happen to the farmers, to Jessa's aunt and uncle? Would they be able to find another way to make up the difference in only a few weeks? Or would they end up losing everything? All because of Taycee.

Thankfully, Jake switched to a different topic during the rest of their dinner. It wasn't until later, when they meandered around the walkways of a dimly lit park that he brought it up again.

"So, about our conversation from earlier," he said, swinging her around to face him.

"Which one would that be?" Taycee frantically tried to think of a way to change the subject. "The one about organic farming or the one about all the scientific names of my favorite flowers?"

"The one about us." Jake's hands travelled up her arms. "The one that got interrupted by the waiter."

"Bringing us the most amazing meal," Taycee interjected. "Speaking of which, have I thanked you for that yet?"

"Yes." Jake grinned as his hands arrived at her chin and framed her face. "You're avoiding the subject."

Taycee's gaze flickered toward the cameras that were undoubtedly zooming in on them with the expectation of a romantic moment. "Please don't ask me this right now," she pleaded.

"Forget about the cameras," he whispered.

"I can't."

His eyes probed hers, searching, seeking. "Just answer one question for me: Do you like me?"

"Of course I do." *Just not in the way you want me to.*

"Do you want me to stick around after?"

"That's two questions."

"Taycee," he warned.

A battle waged in her mind. Jake's heart versus the lives of a whole lot of farmers. Was this one of those situations where it was okay to hurt one person for the greater good? Because it didn't feel okay. Not by a long shot.

Jake searched her face, waiting for an answer.

"Yes," she breathed finally, even as the pounding in her head screamed "no."

Warmth and hope sparkled in Jake's eyes right before his lips found hers. Taycee kissed him back, putting all of her apologies into it. But when two brown eyes appeared in the back of her mind, she broke away and hugged him instead.

Taycee's date with Alec went better in some ways, worse in others. Although the fear of breaking his heart wasn't a concern since she really didn't think Alec had a heart, he couldn't keep his hands off her the entire night, making Taycee want to throw him into the nearest river to cool him off. She played along as best she could, even let him steal a kiss or two, but she detested every second of it.

By the end of the date when she could finally close the door on Alec, all Taycee cared about was that she had another week behind her and three days of peace before she'd have to start the act all over again.

Why had she ever agreed to do this?

Taycee wandered toward her bathroom and twisted the knobs on the bathtub. Minutes later, she soaked in a much needed hot bath that wafted smells of vanilla. She breathed it in, letting it soothe her. When her phone buzzed with a text message, she picked it up. Her heart raced the way it always did when she saw Luke's name. Which was a lot lately. Although she hadn't seen him since the night they'd gone star-gazing, every day since, sometimes even twice a day, he called or texted. Sometimes both.

Have plans tomorrow? he asked.
No, she quickly answered.
Want to?
Depends.
On what?
Who? When? Where? What? Why?
His response came fast. *Me. 7. Denver. Surprise. Miss you.*

A smile spread across her face as happy flutters raced inside her. Her fingers shook so much she nearly dropped the phone.

Miss you too. What should I wear?
Whatever you want.
So . . . sweats?
You'll look beautiful regardless.

Her stomach flip-flopped as she set down the phone. It all felt so surreal, so unbelievable. She'd dreamed about this happening for more than a decade and suddenly it was here, at her doorstep. An un-coerced, voluntary, real date with Luke Carney.

Giddy—that was the word for it—only it still didn't do it justice. Times giddy by a few hundred million and it might be close.

Her phone buzzed again.

7AM not PM.

You're kidding.

See you bright and early. Don't eat breakfast.

Taycee let out a happy sigh as she settled against the back of the tub. Only seven more hours and she'd get to see him. No cameras. No pressure. No expectations. And no acting. Only her and Luke.

She couldn't wait.

Twenty-nine

aycee's stomach grumbled as Luke drove past the diner. She looked back longingly, and then frowned when Luke turned on the highway and headed toward Denver. "You did say not to eat anything, right?"

"Patience, Taycee Lynne." His hand found hers, and he lifted it to his smiling lips, kissing it, before placing it on his lap and covering it with his own. Taycee didn't think she'd ever get used to how it felt to hold his hand. The initial touch made her stomach drop every time.

"Will you at least tell me where we're going?" she asked.

"I already told you, it's a surprise."

"You won't even give me a hint?"

"Nope."

"Meanie."

He chuckled, rubbing slow circles over her hand. Was this really happening? Her? Luke? Out on their very first *real* date? The whole idea seemed too-good-to-be-true. As though she were cocooned in a beautiful dream that she'd be nudged awake from any second.

"Do you have to be back by a certain time?" Luke asked.

"Nope."

"Good."

Taycee eyed his profile. His near perfect nose with the slight bump on it from when he'd broken it after getting thrown from a horse. The lines at the corner of his eye that crinkled when he smiled. His thick, dark eyelashes that most girls would kill for. And his lips—the ones she'd fantasized about kissing so many times. She swallowed and dropped her gaze to his hand covering hers. They'd spent plenty of time together when they were younger, but now she was no longer his best friend's little sister tagging along. Now he *wanted* to ask her out. Wanted to be with her. Even wanted to hold her hand.

True to Luke's word, they stopped at a small, out-of-the-way restaurant just outside of Denver for breakfast. Taycee had never tasted such fluffy pancakes. With juicy blueberries and rich syrup, they melted the moment they touched her tongue.

"How did you find this place?" she asked. "These are incredible."

"By accident," said Luke. "The owners have a horse they needed me to look at, so they googled veterinarians near Denver and randomly called me. They didn't realize that I lived so far away."

"But you still came." Of course he had. Luke never turned down someone who needed him. Like the time he'd missed going to the swimming hole because a neighbor asked him to watch her kids. Or the summer he mowed the lawn of a recently widowed woman without pay. It was one of the many reasons she fell for him way back when.

"I would have never found this place if I hadn't." He leaned across the counter and lowered his voice. "They even have the most amazing curly fries—not to mention very fast service—and I know how much you hate to be kept waiting on curly fries."

"Yeah, well, Liza did serve me pretty fast the day she went out with you." Taycee paused. "Come to think of it, maybe it wouldn't be such a bad thing if you kept dating her."

Luke picked up the maraschino cherry off the top of her pancakes and dropped it in his mouth.

Taycee's mouth fell open. "Hey, those are my favorite!"

"I know." His eyes glinted at her. "Serves you right."

She shook her head, and then finished her breakfast. Luke left a hefty tip, chatted with the owners for several minutes, and returned with a small bowl full of maraschino cherries. She laughed, nodded her thanks to the couple, and before long, they were back in Luke's truck, driving toward Denver once again.

"How's business going?" she asked.

"Pretty slow, which is actually a good thing because I'm still trying to figure out an effective billing and filing system, as well as a decent way to advertise. And then there's the whole tax issue. What stuff do I need to save? What can I pitch? I have stacks of receipts and copies of invoices sitting around that I have no idea what to do with." He sounded a little lost and worn out.

"Sounds like you could use an office manager," Taycee said.

"Someday that would be great, but I can't afford to pay one right now."

"If you want, I could help," Taycee said. "I've learned a little about how to run a business over the years."

Luke shot her a look. "You'd do that for me?"

"Of course." As if she'd ever turn down any excuse to spend time with Luke. Or to help him. "In fact, I don't have anything going on Monday night. I could come over after work."

"That would be great, thanks." His hand squeezed hers. "Just promise not to think I'm a disorganized slob when you see the mess that is my office."

"I make no promises."

He chuckled.

Thirty minutes later, they pulled into a parking lot of a large convention center. A sign above the door read, "Rocky Mountain Bridal Show."

Taycee blinked. Did Luke know where he'd taken them? Was he lost? "Um . . . you brought me to a wedding expo? Are you planning to propose or something?"

"Well, it's never too early to start picking stuff out, right?" The words were loaded with teasing insinuation.

Taycee refused to let him make her blush. "Right. But just so we're clear, I get to pick the cake flavors."

"What's wrong with the flavors I would choose?"

As if this needed an explanation. "Funfetti and weddings don't go together."

Luke gave her a lopsided smile. "Believe it or not, my tastes have matured a little since high school. For all you know, dark chocolate ganache with raspberry filling is now my favorite flavor."

"Please. You asked for a Funfetti cake for your eighteenth birthday—with sprinkles no less. There's no way your tastes have risen to the level of dark chocolate ganache in only ten years." She pointed a finger at him. "Admit it, Funfetti is still your favorite."

He took her hand and raised it to his lips. "Maybe," he murmured against her fingers.

Taycee suddenly wanted to blurt out that Funfetti was the perfect choice for a wedding cake. In fact, if he was the groom and she the bride, Taycee wouldn't care about anything else. Not even the flowers. He could insist on red roses, orange sunflowers, and purple pansies and she'd happily comply. Standing next to him and saying "I do" would be all that mattered.

Luke gave her hand one last squeeze, and then jumped from the truck. Taycee breathed in deeply, trying to slow her racing heart—not that it obeyed. Probably because she couldn't keep her eyes off Luke as he walked around to open her door. Normally, she was a jump-from-the-truck-on-her-own type of girl, but she couldn't get her brain to tell her hand to pull the handle.

Luke opened her door, and she slid out, somehow managing to land on her feet.

"Seriously, what are we doing here?" Taycee asked as he pulled her toward the building.

Luke stopped and waited for a car to pass, and then moved forward once again. "Turns out that people in the wedding business from all around come here every year. DJ's, caterers, wedding planners, cake decorators—oh, and *florists.*" He shot her a sideways look. "You did say you wanted to start doing flowers for weddings, right? When you're ready, this is a great place to drum up some business. I figured we could check it out."

Taycee stared at him. She had mentioned that once—weeks ago—and he'd remembered. He even planned a date just for her, because coming to a wedding expo was the last place Luke would ever willingly go.

She swallowed the lump in her throat and stopped just outside the doors. "Wow. Thanks, Luke. This is really . . . sweet."

"You sound surprised." The way he said it made it sound like he didn't want her to be surprised.

In that moment, when Luke watched her with a half-teasing, half-hurt expression on his face, Taycee realized something. She hadn't been fair to him. It wasn't that Luke didn't remember the past. It's just that his memories were fewer and far between and perhaps different than hers—the kind of memories a guy would have of his best friend's kid sister.

"No," she said. "I'm not surprised at all."

Thirty

nside the expo, hordes of excited girls buzzed around with bored fiancés in tow, collecting brochures, tasting samples, talking to florists, designers, caterers, DJs, and representatives from other companies.

An energy and excitement filled the building and bubbled over onto Taycee. There was something about weddings, about the idea of love and two people wanting to spend the rest of their lives together. It was a blissful, wonderful time, and Taycee couldn't imagine anything better than creating beautiful floral arrangements to accent such a life-altering day.

They milled through the booths, stopping at some, breezing by others. A florist booth with the most amazing display of bridal bouquets drew Taycee's attention. Everything from clusters of deep red roses to simpler, equally beautiful, bouquets of wildflowers tied with a satin ribbon. Her fingers itched to touch the soft petals and breathe in their sweet fragrance.

"These are gorgeous," Taycee told the woman seated behind the counter.

"Thank you." The woman handed Taycee a brochure, and her eyes flickered to Luke. "You two make a handsome couple." The comment made Taycee's day. If only they really were an engaged couple picking out flowers for their wedding.

Luke's arm came around her shoulders. "That's exactly what I keep telling her," he deadpanned. "But it still took years to convince her to marry me. Can you believe it?"

Taycee fought the urge to roll her eyes. As if any woman would ever believe she could be that brainless.

"Really?" the woman said. "Not many guys would be that patient."

It was comical, the lovesick way Luke peered into Taycee's eyes. "Yeah, well, she was worth the wait."

"So sweet." The woman smiled. "When's the happy day?"

He didn't miss a beat. "January first. I'm planning to start the new year off right with my new bride."

Taycee almost choked on the laughter bubbling up inside her. Could he sound any cheesier? She patted his chest in an indulgent way. "Actually, there's a curse in his family. Everyone has to get married on the first day of a new year or else their marriage is doomed to end in a tragic way." Her voice lowered. "His uncle made the mistake of marrying on January second and lost his new wife only two months later in a roller derby accident."

The woman's smile now looked forced. Her eyes darted past them, as if searching for normal people to talk to. "I'm so sorry. That's uh . . . interesting."

"It is. Very interesting," said Luke. "Have a good day." He shot Taycee a look, and then grasped her hand, pulling her toward the next booth. "Superstitious? Really? That's the best you could come up with for me? I told her I loved you

216

enough to wait years, and you had to go and turn me into some irrational psycho. Thanks a lot."

"No. *You* told her that I was the irrational one for stringing you along for so long."

Luke stopped her with a hand on her arm, guiding her around to face him. "Wait a sec. Did you just say that you would have to be crazy to not want to marry me?"

Taycee's cheeks burned. She might as well get down on one knee and declare her love for him right now. Why did he have this effect on her? Why?

"No," she said, and then pulled her arm free and headed toward the next kiosk, ignoring the low laughter following her. She picked up a catalog and pretended to browse various place settings.

Luke leaned casually against the counter next to her. "Next year I think your booth should go right there." He pointed across the room from them, toward a table near the front. It was a good spot—one of the best, actually. Taycee tried to picture it. What would her booth even look like? What floral arrangements would she bring as samples? What sort of brochure and information would she hand out to people? A nervous pit formed in her stomach. Every kiosk looked so nice, so professional. It suddenly made her feel like an amateur. "I'm not sure I'm ready for something like this."

"Sure you are."

"Luke, I . . ." She searched for the right words. "Believe it or not, I like my life. The slowness of it all. The easiness of it. With the exception of the past couple of weeks, I've been comfortable and happy. I really don't need any more than I already have." But as she looked around, Taycee knew she wanted more. She wanted this. But was she even capable of competing at this level?

When Luke didn't say anything right away, she turned and found him watching her with an unreadable expression.

"I don't believe you, Taycee Lynne. And neither do you. I saw the look in your eyes when you first told me you were interested in doing weddings. And I saw your mind working with ideas while you looked at those arrangements back there." He paused. "I get that you like the slowness of your life—it's one of the reasons I decided to move back. But you should never stop setting goals and trying to achieve them regardless of where you live. You'll only be hurting yourself if you do."

Taycee glanced down at the catalog in her hands. It suddenly felt heavy so she dropped it on the table with a thunk. Was Luke right? Had her life in Shelter become too comfortable and easy? Had she been holding herself back in a way? Would she be standing behind one of these booths right now if it wasn't for her fear of change and the unknown?

Taycee looked around once again, feeling claustrophobic. There were too many people. Too much noise. The excitement and energy from earlier faded instantly, leaving behind a feeling of dissatisfaction. As though she didn't deserve to be in a room with people who didn't shy away from change the way she did.

"I think I've seen enough," Taycee said. "Ready to go?"

"You sure?" Luke craned his neck, looking over the heads of the people milling through the aisles. "There's another florist over that way."

"I'm sure."

Luke followed her out. He slid the key into the ignition, started the engine, and then glanced at Taycee.

"Did I say something wrong in there?" he asked.

"No. But sometimes the truth hurts, and you were right. In a way, I've been a bit of a coward."

His eyebrows drew together in confusion. "I never said that."

A small laugh escaped from Taycee's mouth as she shook her head. "You didn't have to. It was more of a revelation for me. My entire life I've resisted change, and any time something happened to threaten my happy little comfort zone—like this bachelorette thing or you moving back to town—I balked, just like I balked when you and Caleb and my parents moved away. Instead of embracing change and seeing how far it could help me fly, I let fear keep me grounded. The only reason I've grown at all over the past few years is because of circumstances I had no control over."

"For what it's worth, I'm actually really glad you stayed in Shelter." Luke's warm fingers closed over hers. "And you are not a coward, Taycee Lynne. Not even close. You did what you wanted with your life, including moving back to a place you loved, despite the fact that all your family left. You even opened your own business—a successful one at that."

He nodded toward the building. "I brought you here because I know you have a goal of doing more with your business, and I wanted to help with that goal. I honestly didn't mean to make you feel like you were anything less than the amazing person you are."

Taycee gnawed on her lower lip as she stared straight ahead. It was funny how two people could look at the exact same thing and see two very different perspectives. Was this the half-full, half-empty metaphor where Luke was the optimist and she the pessimist? Maybe. Or maybe Luke didn't really know her as well as he thought he did.

Regardless, his words made Taycee want to become what he thought of her. To crawl out of her cozy little hole and make some actual plans. Goals. Really see what she could achieve with her life. She leaned over and kissed his clean-shaven cheek. "Thanks for seeing me that way, Luke."

His hand cupped the back of her neck, keeping her close, while his thumb traced a line down her neck. "What I don't get is how I didn't see you before."

Taycee's heartbeat throbbed like a subwoofer, vibrating through the cab. Luke brought his other hand to her face, caressing her cheek and sending the most amazing sensations through her body. His eyes rested on her lips as he inched forward, closing the gap between them until his lips brushed across hers. The kiss was light and tentative, as if he didn't know whether he should be doing it or not.

Taycee sat, almost frozen. She wanted to throw her arms around him and deepen the kiss, but something held her back. Fear. Shock. Whatever it was, it kept her rigid, as if any movement on her part would make him come to his senses.

His forehead rested against hers while his lips lingered, feathery light against her own. They remained that way for a moment, their breaths colliding together and warming the air between them until Luke slowly backed away. The usual teasing glint was gone, and in its place was an intensity Taycee completely understood. Something was happening between them. Something real and scary and . . . incredible.

Without a word, Luke turned his attention to the road and threw his truck into gear. He drove to a nearby strip mall and pulled to a stop at the curb.

"Be right back," he said. And then he was gone. Out of the truck and through the doors of a small little eatery with a blinking pink neon "Open" sign affixed to the door.

Taycee stared at the sign, watching it blink on and off. On and off. Her thoughts were muddled and obscure. People walked by on the sidewalk, their shoes clopping by with dull thuds. But still Taycee stared at the sign, letting the people pass between them like a blurred image.

Luke had kissed her.

Really kissed her.

Her lips still burned, aching for more. She touched them with a hesitant fingertip, not wanting to disturb the tingling, but needing to feel it. Nothing would ever be the same now. How could it? If Luke had ruined other guys for her before, now they were destroyed. Obliterated.

Just like her heart would be if he decided to walk out of her life again.

Thirty-one

"I think this is a very bad idea," Taycee said as she tried to stand. The afternoon sun beat down on her as the wheels of her rented rollerblades spun. Her arms jerked frantically in the air before she lost her balance and landed with a jolt on the hard concrete. She peered up at Luke. "Told you."

Luke braced one roller blade against the other to keep from rolling. He held out a hand. "The Taycee Lynne I know isn't a quitter. Up you go."

She eyed his outstretched hand, and then grudgingly rested her fingers on his. "Okay, but if I break something, I'm holding you responsible. I haven't tried rollerblading since you and Caleb left." Which wasn't one hundred percent true. She'd gone with a group of friends in high school once. They'd taken her to a skate park, where she'd promptly fallen and sprained her wrist. After that, Taycee had never been invited along again—not that she would have gone. Wheeled shoes didn't belong on her feet.

In a fluid movement, Luke pulled her to her feet, keeping a firm grasp on her hand. "Seriously, who doesn't know how to rollerblade?"

He'd pretty much said that same thing ten years earlier, the summer before he left for college when he offered to teach her. They fit in three lessons before he left, which obviously hadn't done much good.

"No one else had the patience to teach me," Taycee said. Her skates started to move again, and her other hand latched on to Luke's solid bicep.

He steadied her. "Good thing I came back then. No way can you go through life not knowing how to rollerblade. That's so . . . un-American."

Her feet started to roll backwards again, so she gripped Luke with both hands. "So that's what's been missing in my life all these years."

"Yeah," he said. "And me."

"I never said anything about you."

His finger tapped her nose as he grinned. "But you were thinking it."

If she wasn't before, she was now. The feel of his strong arm beneath her fingers and the smell of his spicy cologne served to remind her even more. Suddenly, hugging his arm wasn't close enough, so she took a step closer. Stupid move, because once again her feet rolled out from beneath her and she fell toward the ground again. Luke's arms caught her around her waist. He pulled her up against him, holding her steady.

Okay, so maybe not such a stupid move.

His voice was husky and his breath warm and minty as he murmured in her ear. "I'm glad no one else wanted to teach you. I'm kind of liking this."

"Only kind of?"

He laughed. Gently, the pressure of his hands at her waist eased up as he slowly spun her around. "Just put one foot in front of the other," he said. "It's that easy."

"Maybe for you," she muttered, although he was making it difficult for her to *want* to learn to rollerblade. She liked holding on to him for support way too much.

His hands slipped from her waist as he moved to her side, grabbing her hand. "Glide for a second like this, and then turn the other foot at an angle and give yourself a push to keep going."

Not wanting another sprained wrist, Taycee gripped his hand hard as she pushed her feet forward, trying to copy his movements. She managed it for a few strokes, but when Luke tried to pick up the speed, Taycee pitched forward.

"Easy there, killer," Luke said, raising his arm to steady her. "I guess we'll just take it slow."

"Or I can take them off and jog along beside you."

"Not a chance. You are going to learn to rollerblade whether you want to or not."

"Fine."

An hour later, Taycee was finally able to skate slowly on her own, but her legs burned from the strain of constantly tightened muscles. As she came around a turn, a large maple tree beckoned her with its shade, so she rolled off the sidewalk and trudged across the grass, sinking down beneath the tree. Minutes later, she tossed the rollerblades aside and wriggled her toes in her socks. It felt good to be free.

Luke chuckled as he dropped down beside her and removed his rollerblades. "Not bad for a rusty beginner."

Her eyebrows raised in an I-don't-believe-you look.

He shrugged. "Okay, so you stink."

Taycee's fingers closed around a fistful of grass, and she yanked it from the ground. Then she leaned over and stuffed it down the back of his shirt before he could stop her.

"You're so going to regret doing that." Luke lunged for her arm, but she rolled to the side and leapt to her feet, sprinting away from him. It didn't take long for him to catch up. She soon found herself locked in his arms as he dragged her toward a drinking fountain.

"But I'm not thirsty," she said through giggles as she fought to break free.

"I wasn't planning on giving you a drink. More like a shower."

"You wouldn't dare."

"Actually, I would."

They arrived at the drinking fountain at the same time as a teenage boy. He had a ring through his nose and carried a skateboard under one arm.

"Hey, you wouldn't mind holding that on for me would you?" Luke asked him.

"Luke! Stop it!" Taycee laughed. The poor kid looked uncomfortable and probably regretted ever coming near them. "Don't let him turn you into the bad guy," she said to the teenager.

"I'll give you five bucks if you do," Luke countered.

The kid shrugged and twisted the knob on the fountain, stepping aside.

Taycee glared. "And you looked like such a nice person."

Another shrug. "I could be nice for ten."

"You're on the path to juvenile detention," Taycee said. "You know that right?"

"Don't listen to her." Luke brought Taycee's face within an inch of the water. "Now, I'll let you stay dry if you repeat after me: I, Taycee Lynne . . ."

She rolled her eyes. "I, Taycee Lynne . . ."

"Love Hercules."

"You've got to be kidding me."

The spray of water hit her forehead. "Say it."

"Okay, okay. I, Taycee Lynne, love Hercules."

Luke grinned and pulled her up, looking at the kid. "Don't ask."

"Wasn't gonna." He took a drink, and then held out his palm expectantly.

Luke withdrew the money from his wallet and handed it over. The kid smirked and stuffed it into his pocket, and then stalked away with a tug on his skinny jeans.

"Wow," Taycee said, watching him leave. "I don't even know what to say to that."

"There's a first." He started laughing.

Taycee stuck out her tongue, and then bit back a smile as she spun on her heel to collect the rollerblades.

The amphitheater at Red Rocks reminded Taycee of some Indian ruins she'd seen once—the kind that had been carved out of the mountain and appeared almost like they'd formed naturally over time. Rows and rows of bench-style seating sloped up and away from a stage centered below, blending into the red rock background of the Rocky Mountains. How did she not know a place like this existed only fifteen minutes east of Denver?

"Pretty cool, isn't it?" Luke said, his hand resting on the small of her back as he guided her to their seats.

"It's amazing. I can't believe I've never been here before."

"I hope you like Bluegrass."

"Love it." It really didn't matter what band performed or what type of music they played. With Luke's arm around her, Taycee would love anything. In fact, her mouth hurt from all the grinning and laughing she'd done that day. That's how happy Luke made her.

When they found their seats, he shook out a blanket he'd been carrying—the same one they'd shared stargazing. The night air began to chill, so he wrapped it around them both and pulled Taycee tight against him as they sat down. It felt so good, so natural, so warm. Here, right now, all that existed was him and her, tucked into a warm cocoon with the beauty of the mountains surrounding them.

The concert was incredible, a perfect accompaniment to cuddling with Luke. The strains of music echoed off the rock walls and seemed to come alive, swirling around everyone in a soothing, relaxing way. People sang, clapped, danced, and swayed along with the music. Taycee stayed snuggled next to Luke, content to feel the vibrations of the music through his body.

All too soon, it ended. Luke continued to hold her close until the worst of the crowds dispersed, and then he led her back to his truck. He drove down a dark windy road, eventually pulling off to the side.

"C'mon, you've got to see this view before we head back." He jumped out and came around, reaching for her hand.

"View?" Taycee squinted through the darkness. All she could make out were rock formations and desert shrubs. Still, she slid from the truck and allowed Luke to lead her to the other side of a large boulder. It felt like they'd walked through a magic door that opened up into a completely new world. Denver's lights glowed in the distance, beneath a canopy of sparkling stars.

"Oh. *That* view," Taycee breathed.

Luke's arms circled her from behind, and his chin rested on her head. "The owners of the restaurant we ate at this morning told me about this place. Said if we were coming to the amphitheater, we couldn't leave until we stopped here."

"I'm glad you listened." Taycee inhaled the cool night air, feeling like her heart had never felt so whole, so complete, so alive.

Before Luke came back, she'd been comfortable. Even happy. But standing with him now, it were as if all of her hopes and dreams collided and erupted into something bigger and scarier than she'd ever thought possible. A feeling of rightness mixed with a very real fear that this could all be taken away.

The fear won out and a sudden chill shot through her, making her body stiffen.

"Cold?" Luke asked, tightening his hold on her.

Taycee twisted around, her arms circling his waist as she looked up at him. "Today has been . . ." She searched for the right description.

"Fun?"

"Perfect."

"Hmm . . . even better than I'd hoped." His words came out low and hushed, melting into the night.

Taycee swallowed, her gaze dropping to his chest. Her fingers smoothed over the soft fabric of his shirt, feeling his muscles beneath it. "As perfect as today has been, I have to know what it means—to you, I mean." Taycee clamped her mouth shut, hating herself for sounding so insecure.

"What today means to me," Luke said slowly. His hands rubbed circles up and down her back before he finally said, "When I first decided to move back here, I hoped you and Caleb would still be around because I wanted a taste of my old life back. But in my mind you were still that little fourteen-year-old kid with braces. So it caught me off guard when I first saw you at the diner—all grown up and gorgeous."

His hand moved to her jaw, and his thumb caressed her cheekbone. "When I found out you were the bachelorette, I tried to tell myself that I wanted to stay on the show just to make you uncomfortable, but the real reason was that I wanted to get to know the grown up version of Taycee Lynne. But then I got voted off, which sucked. So I figured I'd lay low until it was all over." He grinned. "I guess I'm not a very patient person."

Luke lifted Taycee's chin, forcing her to look at him. "As far as what that means, I'm not one hundred percent sure yet. You're stubborn, crazy, and more confusing than any girl I've ever met, but I can't get you out of my mind."

Taycee's heartbeat surged, feeling ready to burst. "So, this isn't another one of your practical jokes? You know, make me fall for you, and then walk away laughing?"

Luke stiffened. "Is that what you think this is?"

"No." Her finger rubbed a slow circle on his shirt before she peeked up at him. "But you said it yourself once. You're an eye for an eye kind of a guy, so I had to ask."

Luke dipped his head until their lips were inches apart, with his breath sending shivers down her spine. "Does this feel like a practical joke to you?" he murmured before covering her mouth in a kiss that devoured any lingering doubt. He crushed her to him, searching, seeking, and tasting. Something ignited deep inside her, jolting her into a whole new awareness. Her hands slid up his back and to the base of his neck, clinging to him as she responded to his kiss in a way she'd never responded to anyone's.

This was the reason Taycee had never gotten over Luke. He was it. The one person who could make her feel this alive, this happy, this complete. She belonged right here, in his arms.

Gradually, Luke's lips eased off hers, and she found herself wrapped in a fierce embrace. The throbbing vibration of his heartbeat pounded against her ear with a beautiful, untamed melody. More beautiful than any music any band could ever make.

Thirty-two

Taycee had to tell Jake and Miles about Luke. After yesterday, she couldn't keep pretending that she was into them—at least not unless they were okay with it. Which they would be. They wouldn't be like Greg and leave town before the final vote. They'd understand why Taycee did what she did, and they'd stay to help her finish.

Right?

She shoved the worry aside and pulled open her fridge, rummaging around for something edible. Nothing called out to her. She tried the pantry next. Chips, cereal, and a box of crackers. Hmm . . . no thanks.

Her cell rang with Jessa's ringtone, and Taycee snatched it up.

"Hey, girl, missed you last night," Jessa said.

"What was last night?"

"Jake's presentation, duh. I can't believe you forgot."

"Oh, that's right." Taycee leaned against the counter and pressed the phone closer to her ear. "How'd it go? Was anyone interested?"

"Jake did awesome, of course," Jessa said. "He fielded millions of questions and I think piqued a lot of interest. No one committed to anything last night, but they loved the idea that the farmers market might not have to be a long-term solution. Assuming, of course, it can still be the short-term solution." Worry tinged her words.

"What's wrong? I thought things were going well," said Taycee. "We got more votes last round than ever before, didn't we?"

"Yeah," said Jessa. "But we still have fifteen grand to go and only two voting opportunities left. If we get within a few thousand, I think the farmers could pool together whatever savings they have left to make up the difference, but I'm getting worried we might not make it. I'm really wishing I would have scheduled the voting to go one more round because we could really use an extra week."

One more round. Taycee didn't think she could handle the one week they had left, and yet here was Jessa, wishing for more. Taycee's heart sank. With that much money on the line, Jessa would never agree to risk telling Jake and Miles the truth. And Taycee wasn't sure it was worth the risk either. "We'll make it, Jess. I still have that morning show interview to do before the final vote. I'm sure that will help drive up the numbers."

"Let's hope so." But Jessa sounded anything but assured. "I think this organic farming thing is a good fit, I really do. My uncle was up all night reading about it. I just got off the phone with him, and I've never heard him sound this hopeful before. But what if we can't earn enough for the co-op? They'll be ready to start selling in only a few weeks."

"We'll earn enough, Jess, I promise," said Taycee. "Even if I have to get down on my knees during that interview and beg for people's votes."

"I'm going to hold you to that, you know."

"I wouldn't expect anything different."

"Where were you last night, anyway?" Jessa asked. "I figured you'd at least pop in for a second, just to see how everything was going."

Taycee hesitated. With the way Jessa had been trying to push Jake on her lately, how would she react to the news that Taycee had spent the entire day with Luke? Not good.

"Oh, I knew you'd have everything under control," Taycee said.

"You didn't answer my question."

"Probably because I didn't want to answer your question."

Silence. Followed by more silence. Just when Taycee thought the connection had failed, Jessa gasped. "You went out with the Tin Man, didn't you?" It sounded accusatory—not the typical gushing, overly-excited way most best friends would phrase a question like that. Not that Taycee had expected anything different. Still, it would have been nice if Jessa at least pretended to be happy for her.

"Yes," Taycee finally said. "I spent the entire day with *Luke*—who, believe it or not, does have a heart, and a pretty big one at that—and had the most incredible day of my life. Now go ahead and ruin it for me because I know that's what you're going to do." Maybe Jessa would take the hint and back off.

"What were you thinking?" Jessa said. "Did anyone see you?"

What kind of question was that? It made Taycee feel like a scolded child who'd snuck off and done something she wasn't supposed to, which was ridiculous. "Of course not," Taycee said. "I mean, how could they when he picked me up in a dark tinted car and drove to a hidden cave where we spent the day reducing the mosquito population one by one. I won, by the way."

Jessa didn't laugh, not that Taycee expected her to.

"How could you?" Jessa said. "Luke got voted off weeks ago, which means you shouldn't be dating him, at least not until the show is over. If word got out, we might as well post a banner declaring ourselves fraudulent."

"Aren't you being a tad melodramatic?"

"No! The viewers think you're in love with one of the remaining bachelors. They *want* you to be in love with one of them because they're the ones who picked them. If they find out you're off gallivanting around with someone they already voted off—especially the one from Shelter Springs—what do you think they're going to say? You go, girl? Wahoo? No! They're going to be ticked!"

Which was exactly how Taycee felt at the moment. She took a calming breath and struggled for a level tone. "Look, Jessa. You practically forced me into doing this show, and for the sake of your aunt and uncle and the rest of the farmers, I agreed. I let you push a new wardrobe on me and get manicures, and then I endured weeks of dating with guys I never wanted to go out with in the first place. I understand this show is important, and I would never want to do anything to jeopardize that, but you're the producer of the show—not my life."

"You're not getting it," said Jessa. "What if someone who watches the show saw you with Luke last night? What if they decided to comment about it online and speculate what you were doing out with a bachelor who they voted off when you're supposed to be falling for someone else? How do you think that would go over? Do you think people would still be willing to vote or give to our cause after something like that? I don't think so. Nobody likes to be made to feel like a fool, Tace. Which is exactly how they would feel. A fool who's been taken in by yet another fraudulent charity case."

Taycee frowned. Why had she answered the phone? She should have kept today all to herself as the day to relive the most perfect day ever. Instead, in two minutes flat, Jessa had tainted it. Granted, her friend had a point, but that didn't mean Taycee had to like it.

"Okay, so I never thought about it like that," Taycee said grudgingly. "But he picked me up early, we spent the day in Denver, and he dropped me off late. No one saw us."

"Maybe not in Shelter, but did someone recognize you while you were in Denver?"

"I seriously doubt it. I'm not that famous."

Jessa let out a breath. "Just promise me you won't see him again until after this is all over, okay?"

"Fine," said Taycee, hating how bossy Jessa sounded. "Try to remember, though, that you put me here. As far as I'm concerned, I've been a fraud from the beginning. In fact, I've about made up my mind to tell Miles and Jake exactly that."

"You wouldn't dare."

"It's the right thing to do, Jess."

"And what if they walk?" Jessa's voice escalated. "Is it also the right thing to tell my aunt and uncle—two people I consider my parents—that they'll have to hand their farm over to the bank in a few months because you can't get over your obsession with Luke Carney?"

"That's not fair and you know it," Taycee snapped.

"You know what your problem is?" Jessa sounded angry.

"No, but I'm sure you're going to tell me."

"You're stubborn, that's what. You've made Luke out to be this perfect guy who no one can compare with, and because of that, you've missed out on some great relationships in your life. Now you're letting a guy like Jake slip through your fingers as well. Is Luke really worth this?"

"Yes." Taycee had never been more sure about anything.

"I hope so, because Jake is pretty amazing."

"For crying out loud, Jessa! Enough about Jake!" Taycee practically yelled. "Yes, he's amazing, but do you know what? Luke's amazing too—and a way better fit for me. Again, this is *my* life. *My* choice. Back off."

"Fine," Jessa snapped. "As long as you promise you won't say anything to Jake and Miles."

"Fine." Taycee drove her thumb into the "end call" button and resisted the urge to throw her phone across the room. For the millionth time, she cursed Jessa for turning her into Shelter's bachelorette. Not only had it put her in this horrible position, it had driven a solid wedge into their friendship, distancing them. Yes, Jessa had always been blunt and domineering, but she'd also been someone Taycee could joke around with, talk to, and turn to in both good times and bad.

Not so much anymore.

Taycee's phone rang, and she nearly auto-rejected the call until Luke's handsome face appeared on the screen.

"Hey," she answered, hoping she didn't sound too upset.

"Hey yourself." His voice instantly became a soothing melody to her throbbing mind. "I was wondering if you'd had dinner yet."

Her gaze flickered back to the kitchen. "I was about to open a can of soup."

"Seriously? Canned soup for Sunday dinner?"

"I didn't make it to the store yesterday. It's all I've got."

"Want to come over? I've got some steaks marinating."

The thought of spending the evening with Luke made Taycee want to bolt to her car and drive as fast as she could. But she'd promised Jessa she wouldn't, and a promise was a promise. "I'd love nothing more than to come over, but I can't."

"Got other plans?"

"If I did, I'd break them."

Silence. "That makes about as much sense as . . . well, you usually do, I guess."

Taycee smiled. "It's Jessa. She thinks that if someone saw us together it would be bad for the show's reputation.

Which is probably true. And since we need all the votes we can possibly get, I've promised not to see you again until after it's all over. So I guess this means I can't come over tomorrow night to help you out either. Sorry, Luke."

"I guess I can wait another week."

"Thanks," said Taycee. "Although it will be more like a week and a half since they pushed back the final vote until after that morning show interview."

"What?" The way Luke said it sounded like he'd have to wait years, not weeks. It made Taycee smile.

"After that, I'm all yours." She barely stopped herself from adding "forever." That might come across as a bit much at this point.

He let out a breath. "All right then. I guess I should be grateful I got to spend yesterday with you. But that doesn't mean I can't call, right?"

"Right."

"Every night?"

"And morning," Taycee added. "If you want. During the day would be fine too."

Luke chuckled. "Well, I'd hate to give you the chance to forget about me."

"As if I could." Taycee hesitated, wanting to add something but not sure how to put it. "Luke, I . . ." her voice drifted off.

"You?"

"I'd quit this bachelorette thing right now if there wasn't so much on the line. You know that, right?"

"Yeah."

She swallowed. "I still have two more dates to get through. Which means that even though I don't want to, I still have to act like I'm into both Jake and Miles. And well . . ." This was awkward. And embarrassing. Something Taycee would rather not talk about, but she needed him to understand.

"Then I won't watch," said Luke. "What I don't see won't hurt me, right?"

Relief flooded through Taycee as she heard those words. Pure relief. As much as she'd dreaded getting through the last two dates, she was more concerned about Luke's reaction to seeing her with two other guys. But now she didn't have to worry because he trusted her enough not to watch. Or judge. Or demand that she drop out.

"Thank you," she breathed. For whatever reason, tears stung the back of her eyes. Whether it was because she was already emotional from her chat with Jessa or because of Luke's willingness to understand, she didn't know. What she did know what that she now loved him more than ever.

"Just so you know," Taycee said, holding the phone closer to her ear as if it would somehow bring him nearer. "It's always been you for me."

Thirty-three

Taycee applied some lip gloss and stared at her reflection in the mirror. Alec had finally been voted off, much to her relief, and Miles would be here any minute to pick her up. If it had been up to her, Jake and Miles were the two she would have chosen from the beginning. The two she liked the best. Still, she couldn't wait to get the date over with. Although she liked Miles and had fun with him, the sooner he dropped her off, the sooner she could talk to Luke and get her mind off the fact that she was a horrible person for deceiving two great guys.

Then after tonight, there would be only Jake's date left.

Knock, knock-ety, knock, knock. Knock, knock.

Taycee smiled at the now familiar rhythm of Miles's unique knock. She would definitely miss him when he left town in another week. His smile alone could brighten any day. And his energy—he was like a kid at Disneyland.

Taycee smile as she opened the door. "Hey you."

"Don't you look prettier than a glob of butter melting on a stack of wheat cakes." Only Miles could pull off a line like that and make it sound like a compliment. He stepped forward and kissed Taycee's cheek before his hand caught hers as he pulled her out the door. "Ready for a hick night out?"

"Did you just say 'hick?'" Miles was always full of surprises.

He nodded as an easy smile split his face. "I thought I'd show you some of my world."

"So we're flying to Oklahoma, and I get to watch you ride in a rodeo?"

"Nah." He grinned. "I decided to bring Oklahoma to you."

Normally, Taycee would be intrigued and excited by such a description. But all she could think about was how uncomfortable this "hick night out" would be. Which was sad, because Miles was obviously thrilled. "Sounds like my kind of night," she said with a smile.

"One you'll never forget."

And it was that. Miles drove her to Denver where they ate dinner at some over-the-top Denver version of a barbeque joint where troughs served as sinks and peanut shells dotted the stained concrete floor. Their food came to them on tin plates, and slow, twangy country music played in the background.

"Wow, when you said hick, you meant hick, didn't you?" Taycee teased.

"I've always been a man of my word." Miles paused. "Well, most of the time, anyway."

Taycee leaned forward over her plate. "I'm sensing a story here. Do tell."

"Okay, but don't forget you asked for it." He leaned closer. "Back in high school, there was this sheriff who liked to pull my friends over every chance he got. He used to hang out at a gas station in town, ready and waitin' for one of us to drive by. So one day, me and my buddy decided to do something about it."

Taycee's hand covered his, stopping the story. "This isn't something that's going to get you carted off to prison, is it? If so, I need to remind you that you're on camera right now."

"Nah." Miles waved away her concern. "Like I was saying, one day we waited for the sheriff to take a break and go inside the gas station. Then we snuck up and chained the rear axle of his car to a light pole."

"You did not." If Taycee ever thought of doing something like that to Ralph, he would definitely update her mug shots.

"Sure did." Miles's grin broadened. "Then we hustled to my cousin's truck and waited for him to come back out. When he did, we sped down main street as fast as we could."

"What happened?"

"His siren sounded, and he took off like an inchworm stuck to hot concrete. His tires screeched and gravel spewed everywhere." Miles's laughter rang out as his hand slapped the table. "He was madder than a mosquito in a mannequin factory. We spent a night in jail for that one."

Taycee laughed so hard her sides ached, especially when Miles added, "It didn't solve our problem though. For some reason, that darn sheriff started pulling us over even more after that."

The story was exactly what Taycee needed. Miles soothed her stress, making her forget about the cameras, the viewers, Shelter. She'd miss him when he left, the way she missed Caleb or any other really good friend. He was fun— the kind of guy she would have loved to hang out with in high school.

After dinner, they watched the first half of a demolition derby, and then blitzed across town to catch the second half of a rodeo—just in time to see some crazy lunatic on the back of a motorcycle barrel up a ramp, through a ring of fire, and over a line of cars. Miles yeehawed the entire time, and with his hilarious asides, the date was over almost as soon as it had begun.

He drove her home and walked her to her front porch.

"Well," he said, "this is it, I guess."

"Thank you for a truly unforgettable date, Miles. You are one of a kind." Taycee meant every word.

"Kinda like you." His arms circled Taycee, and he pulled her close. Before she could say anything, his mouth covered hers in slow and thorough kiss. It felt wrong, like she was kissing a good friend, but she let it happen even as the guilt plucked away at her insides. She had to picture the sweet, hard-working faces of the McCrays in order to keep from blurting out the truth.

"Even if I don't get chosen, I'd sure like to keep seein' you," Miles breathed in her ear.

The words echoed through Taycee's head like a pounding hammer. She resisted the urge to run inside and close the door firmly between her and a guy who wanted more than she could ever give.

Taycee swallowed. She had to say something. No way could she leave him hanging like that, especially with the camera filming their every move, their every word. But what could she say that wouldn't give him false hope, while still keeping the viewers hopeful?

"Uh . . ." The words wouldn't come. There was nothing she could say.

"Speechless," Miles teased. "I've been known to have that effect on girls."

"Overcome is a better word." Taycee pasted on a smile and forced herself to answer his question. "And yes, I'd like that too."

Miles grinned, kissed her one last time, and left her with a wink on her doorstep. Taycee shoved her key in the lock and disappeared inside, barely refraining from slamming the door behind her in an effort to block out the world, the stress, the knowledge that she'd just given a genuinely nice guy a reason to falsely hope.

Thirty-four

On Wednesday evening, Taycee closed her shop and walked the short distance to her apartment. There was a time back in high school when she wanted guys to notice her, when she craved being asked out on a date, and when the idea of more than one guy liking her at the same time filled her teenage, girlish fantasies.

But now that it had actually happened, it wasn't nearly as romantic as she once supposed. At the time, it had all been about her. About popularity. About being the kind of girl that guys flocked around. Never had she thought about the feelings of anyone but herself, or that dating more than one guy would lead to having to choose one and hurt the other. Or worse, hurt them both, which was the case now.

Jake and Miles were two good guys who didn't deserve to fall for a girl who was never really available.

Opening the door to her apartment, Taycee slung her purse over a hook and walked toward the kitchen.

"About time you got home," Caleb's voice boomed, making her jump and cover her pounding heart with her hand.

"Caleb! You have got to start calling first."

He was lying on the couch with his ankles crossed and his arms tucked behind the back of his head. "Sorry, sis. Couldn't resist."

Despite the scare, it was really good to see him. His presence made her feel less alone, her apartment not so empty. Taycee plopped down on the armrest next to him. "When did you get back?"

"A few hours ago."

"Why don't you ever let me know you're coming? I would have left some dinner for you in the fridge or something."

Caleb sighed and sat up, resting his elbows on his knees and raking his fingers through his already mussed hair. "Then I wouldn't get to surprise you. It's kind of fun seeing you jump." He yawned. "I have to be in Denver in the morning, but I should be finished by the end of the week. I thought we could hang out this weekend."

"I'd love that." Taycee could really use some Caleb-time and the distraction he'd undoubtedly bring, especially since she couldn't spend the time with Luke. Besides, If anyone could help her get beyond the guilt from her dating deception, it was her brother.

"In fact," Taycee said. "What about taking a few hours on Saturday to check out some potential office spaces? I know you're not ready to make the move, but it never hurts to keep your eyes open, right?"

Caleb's fingers scratched his head in a rapid, nervous way—something he always did when he had something to say that she probably wouldn't want to hear. Her heart sank before he even started talking.

"Yeah, uh . . . well, that's just it, Tace. I won't need any office space. I was planning to tell you before, but the truth is, I've been offered an associate position at the firm I'm with, and I've decided to take it."

A hollow emptiness settled in Taycee's stomach. Deep

down, she'd known something like this was coming, but that didn't make it easy to hear. An associate position. Permanent. Caleb wasn't coming back. Like her parents, he would never come back.

Her brother had been gone for years now. This shouldn't be a big deal. And yet the permanence of it *was* a big deal for her. For the past few years, the hope that Caleb would one day move back—that something would return to the way it used to be—had given Taycee the strength to get by on her own. And now, all of a sudden, that strength felt depleted. As though she was somehow more alone than she had been a minute before.

Why did everyone want to leave? Why did things have to keep changing? Taycee wanted to rewind the clock back to a time when life was simple. When the only worry was finding something to do to stave off boredom.

"How long have you known?" she asked, trying not to sound as broken-hearted as she felt. The question hung in the air between them, like dark gray clouds threatening rain.

"They made me an associate a few months ago."

A lump lodged in her throat. A few months? Caleb had already become an associate? "Why didn't you tell me before?"

The nervous scratching came back. "I planned to. But every time I started to tell you, you'd go off about when I'd be moving back and how excited you were at the prospect. I just . . . didn't have the heart."

No matter how many times she swallowed, the lump remained. "So instead you let me go on and on like some stupid moron."

"That's redundant."

Taycee glared. "Not the time for jokes, Caleb."

"Sorry." He rubbed his fingers together, avoiding eye contact.

"Does Luke know?" She took his silence to mean yes. "Of course he knows." Taycee stood and started pacing the room. "Your former best friend. The guy who left after high school without a backward glance. Who forgot us both. Of course you told him before me—your own sister."

"That's exactly why I told him," Caleb said, his voice growing louder. "Because I knew he'd understand. You, on the other hand would make me feel guilty. Like I'm deserting you."

"I would not!"

"You are, Tace. Right now!" Caleb said. "It's no wonder Luke didn't stay in touch. If he did, every time he contacted you he would have gotten some sob story about how everyone wanted to leave and how things were changing. He would have gotten the same guilt trip you're giving me right now."

"That's not true," Taycee snapped. "I'm not giving you a guilt trip over leaving. I'm giving you a guilt trip over not telling me sooner. How could you!"

Caleb's jaw clenched as he stood, making his way toward the door. "For the same reason I never told you I'm also engaged." He left the apartment with a slam of the door, sounding almost like a crack of thunder.

Taycee felt like he'd just slugged her in the stomach. Caleb was engaged? To who? There was no way he'd ever joke about something like that, especially not in anger. Yet during all their conversations over the past several months, not once had he ever mentioned a girl, let alone the fact that he was thinking of marrying her. How long had they been engaged? Was a date already set? A florist hired?

Caleb. Her only sibling. They'd been so close once upon a time, telling each other everything. They used to stay up late into the night talking, laughing, teasing. What happened? When had a chasm formed between them and how had Taycee not noticed it until now? Had she really been so opposed to change that her only brother didn't feel like he could confide in her anymore? Tell her that he was getting married?

Taycee had missed out on something special. Something important. Something she'd never be able to get back. She'd always looked forward to the time when Caleb started dating someone serious. She'd pictured him calling her, telling her how excited he was and how much Taycee would love her. They'd talk about how he would propose, how he needed to make it as unique and special as possible. In fact, she had hundreds of possibilities stored in her head for just such a conversation.

But none of those conversations would happen now. Taycee had no idea how Caleb proposed, when he proposed, if he'd asked her father's permission and how that conversation went. She had no idea when they'd be getting married or what her future sister-in-law was even like, let alone her name.

The walls seemed to close in and around her. She couldn't stay here. Taycee's hand shook as she fiddled with the door handle, finally throwing it open. She charged into the warm summer air, hugging her arms against her chest.

Her eyes stung as she headed down Main Street in the direction of the park. The smells coming from the diner turned her stomach sour, so Taycee darted across the street, ignoring the hellos of people she passed. She jogged the rest of the way to the park and came to a stop beneath the large oak tree that she and Luke and Caleb once spent hours climbing.

Her fingers dug into the crusty old bark as she pulled herself up to the lowest branch, not caring about the scratches the rough branches left on her legs. She climbed higher and higher, until all she could see were patches of the town here and there through the dense foliage. There, in that natural haven, Taycee let the sobs come.

She cried for all those lost moments, all the memories she could have had but never would get. She cried until her eyes burned and the sky glowed with the promise of a beautiful sunset. She cried until all her tears were dried up.

"Is it safe to come up yet?" a voice came from below.

Taycee started, nearly losing her precarious hold on a branch. She peered down through the leaves to where Luke stood almost directly below her, his arm resting on a branch. The back of her hands wiped desperately at her eyes as she sniffed. "How long have you been standing there?"

"Long enough." With an easy grace, Luke swung up into the tree and slowly made his way to her, finally perching his body across from her. His thumb grazed her cheek in a soft caress. "What happened?"

She sniffed again, wiping her nose with the back of her hand. "Tell me the truth. Was I the reason you didn't keep in touch?"

His eyebrows drew together in confusion. "Why would you be the reason?"

"Because you didn't want me to make you feel guilty for leaving."

Luke chuckled, resting his hands on a tree branch above his head. "Well, you did lay on the guilt a little thick before I left, but no, that wasn't the reason. I already told you why."

"I know." Taycee sniffed again. "I just needed to make sure."

Luke nudged her foot with his. "What's going on? I was in the diner when you blew past earlier."

"Caleb's back."

The leaves rustled in the silence. "I take it he finally told you," Luke said after a moment. "About time."

"You should have told me." Taycee felt more miserable than ever. "I can't believe my own brother couldn't bring himself to tell me that he was engaged or that he wanted to remain in Phoenix. I didn't even know he was dating anyone or that he wanted to stay with his firm. How could he think that I'd make him feel guilty for choosing happiness over me? I don't understand."

Luke's sneaker nudged hers once again. "Are you looking for an answer or are you just venting?"

"Both."

"Well," he said. "I didn't tell you because it wasn't my news to tell. And yes, he mistakenly did believe you'd lay on the guilt."

Taycee sniffed yet again, wishing she'd brought some tissue. "Just because I don't like change doesn't mean I'm incapable of dealing with it when it comes. Yes, it was hard to hear that he's getting married and planning to stay in Phoenix, but that doesn't mean I'm not happy for him." Taycee paused, blinking back the tears. "Caleb's finally getting married. I should have been one of the first to know, not the last. It just . . . hurts."

Luke shifted to a closer branch and reached for her hand, rubbing circles on her palm. "Hurting you was the last thing he wanted to do. That's why he had a hard time telling you."

Taycee frowned at the fading light peeking through the leaves. In a way, she could understand that. She'd created expectations in her mind about Caleb. About life. About the way things should be. But she'd also learned a long time ago that change was inevitable, and, like the wind, Taycee had no control over which direction people went. It was a hard lesson, and one she continued to struggle with, but she would have been happy for Caleb.

She *was* happy for Caleb.

"Maybe it's me who needs to get out of Shelter," she mumbled, more to herself.

"Oh no you don't," Luke said. "You aren't going anywhere, not if I have anything to say about it." His words, combined with the teasing glint in his eyes, were like a kiss on a bruised knee. It almost produced a smile.

Almost.

"Now who's being controlling?" Taycee said.

"I learned from the best."

This time, a small smile formed. "Not nice."

Luke grabbed a limb and swung down to a lower

branch, holding a hand out to Taycee. "Personally, I think hanging out in a tree is over-rated. There's really no view to speak of and the branches are scratchy."

Taycee simultaneously laughed and sniffed. She placed her hand in his, and together they climbed down the tree. Luke dropped to the ground first, and then held up both hands, slowly easing Taycee to the ground. When her feet hit the grass, his arms went around her, pulling her close until their noses touched. "Want to know something?"

"What?"

"I kind of like you," he whispered.

"Just kind of?"

A smile tugged at the corners of his mouth. "Well, maybe a little more than that." In an instant, his mouth met hers in a healing kiss that eased her pain and infused her body with warmth. Peace. Joy. He was exactly what she needed right now—the reminder that there was still something right in her life.

His lips eased off hers, and he hugged her to him.

"I kind of like you too," Taycee mumbled into his shirt, suddenly remembering the promise she'd made to Jessa to stay away from him. She wanted to push the thought back, keep it hidden for just awhile longer. But it was too late. Her conscience was already prodding her in an annoying way.

"I should go," Taycee finally said. "Jessa would kill me if she saw me here with you."

"Forget Jessa and that stupid show," Luke said. But his hands slid from around her back, rubbing up and down her arms before they finally fell away.

It took all of Taycee's will power not to throw herself back into his arms. She searched his eyes instead. Only one more week. Seven days. That was it.

It seemed like a lifetime.

"Thank you, Luke."

"Anytime."

Thirty-five

"You're a little quiet tonight," Jake said as he and Taycee walked hand-in-hand through a park on the outskirts of Denver.

Taycee sighed. He was right. She was being quiet. Mostly because the park reminded her of rollerblading with Luke, which reminded her of the concert at Red Rocks, which reminded her of everything else she'd done with Luke over the course of her lifetime.

As much as she enjoyed Jake's company, it was Luke she craved. Luke's hand she wanted to hold. Luke's lips she wanted to kiss.

"Sorry," she said. "I guess all the craziness from the past several weeks is finally catching up to me. I'm a little worn out tonight."

"Let's sit then."

"Oh no. Really, I'm fine." If he had any idea where her thoughts really were, he wouldn't be nearly so chivalrous.

"It's okay to be tired, you know." Jake's hand relinquished hers and moved to her back, rubbing up and down. "Happens to everyone."

His words coerced a smile from Taycee. "It doesn't seem to happen to you. What's your secret?"

Jake stopped and pulled her into his arms. "Healthy living and lots of exercise. In fact, did you know kissing is one of the best pick-me-ups?"

Her body stiffened. She'd meant to tease him and lighten the mood, not open the door for an invitation like this. But it seemed everything she said today was the wrong thing because Jake was more affectionate than ever. Or maybe it was because this was their last official date. Either way, it made Taycee increasingly uncomfortable.

"I don't know," she said, trying once more to lighten the mood. "I've always thought curly fries and chocolate shakes were the best pick-me-ups." Next to Luke, of course.

Jake's lips twitched. "Did you really just compare my kiss to a chocolate shake? Because it kind of sounded like you did. And it kind of sounded like I came in second."

"Never," Taycee said.

"Good." A full smile formed as Jake inched closer. "But I still plan to prove that I'm preferable to chocolate."

Taycee felt like throwing her hands up in a gesture of defeat. But then Burt stepped into her peripheral vision, coming in for a close up shot. She held back a sigh. There was no escape, not if she wanted it to look real. So Taycee let Jake kiss her.

At first her lips felt stiff and awkward beneath his, but then her thoughts drifted to Luke. How it felt to be held by him, kissed by him, looked at by him. Suddenly, her lips melted against Jake's.

Her fingers threaded around the base of his neck, and she pulled him close, as if she could turn him into Luke by kissing him long and hard. She poured all of her frustrations into the kiss. Jake not being Luke. Jessa signing up for this to begin with. The viewers need for romance. The pressure of helping the town. And now Caleb and his accusations.

But when her eyes started to sting from unshed tears, Taycee pulled back. She couldn't do this anymore, not to Jake. Blinking rapidly, she turned her head away from the camera and buried her face in his chest. His arms pulled her tight against him.

What was she doing? How could she kiss him like that when it wasn't him she wanted to kiss? Why hadn't she followed her gut and told the truth last week like she'd wanted to do? It would have been the right thing to do, even if it had meant a mad scramble to come up with the rest of the money another way.

Instead, Taycee had caved. She'd even given everyone a finale.

Taycee cut a long stemmed rose and pulled the leaves off the bottom part of the stem. Her date with Jake was officially behind her, and for the first time in weeks, she felt the stirrings of relief. Yes, she still needed to get through the interview and find a way to coax Jake and Miles to move on, but the worst was finally over.

Or so she thought.

Bells jingled, and Jessa's voice screeched through The Bloom Boutique. "You promised, Taycee! How could you?"

Now what? Honestly, this show had been the worst thing for thier friendship. Taycee picked up another rose and snipped the end off. "How could I what?"

Jessa appeared with windblown hair and a look that made the room feel chilly. She slapped a picture down in front of Taycee on the counter. "That!" she shouted. "Do you have any idea what you've done?"

There, on a bed of green leaves, was a low resolution picture of Taycee kissing Luke under the giant oak tree at the park. A sick feeling filled her gut. Someone had seen them and had snapped a picture they had no right to take.

"Where did you get this?"

"Off the gossip blog, along with several others. But that's not the point. The point is, you lied to me."

"I'm so sorry, Jessa. I had it out with Caleb yesterday. Luke saw me walking by the diner and followed and—"

"I don't care how it happened!" Jessa shrieked. "What I care about is that you broke your promise. This looks so bad, Taycee! For me, for you, for Shelter. How could you?"

"I'm so sorry," Taycee repeated, still staring at the picture with a sense of loss. The day they climbed the old oak tree was special—or *had* been special—before someone set out to ruin it. Who would do such a thing and why?

"Sorry?" Jessa spat. "You're sorry? How kind of you to be sorry."

In one swift move, Taycee grabbed the picture, wadded it up and threw it into the trash. But it didn't help. Her body shook with frustration and anger. She'd had enough. Of Jessa. Of *Shelter's Bachelorette*. Of always being watched. Everything. "What else do you want me to say? I can't take those pictures back any more than you can."

Jessa let out a heavy sigh and dropped down on a nearby chair. Her rapidly blinking eyes made Taycee feel even worse. Jessa never cried. And if she was fighting back tears, then things really must be as bad as she said.

"Hey." Taycee placed a hand on Jessa's shoulder. "It's going to be okay."

"Is it?" The words came out so quiet, Taycee could barely hear them. "People are really upset, Tace. They're demanding their money back and threatening to sue. A few reporters have called." Jessa paused and swallowed, staring beyond Taycee with a glazed look. "And the mayor even asked for my resignation."

"What?" Taycee felt sick. She let go of Jessa's shoulder and slumped against the counter. All this because someone got a pathetic little cell phone picture of her kissing Luke—a guy she shouldn't feel guilty kissing.

How did this happen?

Jessa's tear-filled eyes trained on Taycee. "We were so close. So close. I really thought we'd make it and that I'd finally be able to repay my aunt and uncle and all the other farmers who have been so kind to me over the years. But now"—she shook her head—"now I've made it worse. I gave them hope, and then snatched it away." Her head dropped to her hands. "Tace, what am I going to do?"

Taycee wrapped her arms around Jessa. Just when she thought the worst was behind her, this happens. But what could she possibly say or do to make things better?

Jessa sniffed. "I know I shouldn't have manipulated you into being the bachelorette. And I'm sorry I did. But you were great and everything was going so well. But now . . ." Defeat reflected in her eyes, making Taycee's heart sink. It wasn't fair that falling in love should have such a disastrous impact on everyone else.

But as Taycee's mom had always told her, life wasn't fair.

"I'll fix this," Taycee said. "I will. It was my fault. I'll apologize and explain everything, and if people still insist on getting their money back, we'll find another way. I promise." But her words sounded empty and hollow. An impossible promise made out of desperation.

Luke knew something was up the moment he set foot in the diner during the dinner rush. All pairs of eyes looked his way. Some accusing. Some knowing. Some disappointed.

He frowned and stepped up to the counter where Liza stood with angry eyes. "What can I get you?" Her voice was like ice.

"Uh . . . " Did Luke dare ask what was going on? Did he even want to know? "I'll take the special." Hopefully whatever it was it would be quick because he suddenly wanted to get out of there pronto. "To go."

"Sure thing," Liza said, punching numbers on the register the way she'd poke someone's eyes out. She slid Luke's credit card through the reader with an angry slice of her hand before tossing it back to him.

Luke eyed her warily. "Something wrong, Liza?" He shouldn't have asked, but the words were out before he could reconsider.

"Why don't you ask your *girlfriend*?" Liza snipped. "Or is it Jake's girlfriend? Or Miles's? I can't remember anymore. From the looks of it, she's not exactly sure either."

Luke picked up his credit card and shoved it back in his wallet. "What are you talking about?"

"Give me a break." Liza planted a palm on the counter and leaned toward him. "Don't play all innocent with me. I saw the pictures of you kissing her. Was that why you asked me out? To make her jealous?"

Pictures? What pictures? Did someone see them at the park? Luke nearly groaned. Oh the perks of living in a small, nosy town. Liza glared at him, as she had every right to do. But it had only been one date. Nobody could be accused of leading someone on after only one date. Not even Luke.

"I asked you out to get to know you better," Luke said.

With one final glare, Liza turned and walked toward the back room. Luke breathed a sigh of relief and looked around for a seat near the window where he wouldn't have to watch everyone staring at him. But the diner was crowded, more so than usual, so Luke slid into the nearest seat he could find and wondered if the special would be worth the wait.

Probably not.

His fingers drummed on the counter until the sound of Taycee's voice had him looking over his shoulder. Babette, a woman who loved gossip as much as she loved coffee, sat directly behind him with her laptop open. Luke would bet his truck that she was the anonymous keeper of the town's gossip blog. Only it wasn't the blog that appeared on her laptop today, it was *Shelter's Bachelorette*'s website, featuring Taycee's last date with Jake—something that Luke had promised he wouldn't watch.

Taycee was in Jake's arms.

"Did you really just compare my kiss to a chocolate shake?" Jake said. "Because it kind of sounded like you did. It also kind of sounded like I came in second."

"Never," Taycee's tinny voice came through the small computer speakers.

"Good." A full smile formed as Jake inched closer. "But I still plan to prove that I'm preferable to chocolate." And then he kissed her.

At first, Taycee's response was tentative, but then her arms went around him, and she kissed him the way she kissed Luke. Luke's stomach churned, but he couldn't tear his gaze away. This was why he hadn't watched the show the past couple of weeks. Luke didn't want to see her with other guys. Didn't want to see her holding their hands, hugging them, or kissing them. It was bad enough picturing it in his mind.

But not once had he ever pictured Taycee responding like that.

Babette craned her neck to look back at him with her fake eyelashes and blue eye shadow. "That girl sure gets around, doesn't she? That how she kissed you?"

With a barely controlled clench of his jaw, Luke stood and walked out of the diner. He set out on foot, leaving his truck behind in the parking lot.

What Taycee did was all an act, a way to keep people interested in the show, that's all. She needed to make it look real. Luke knew this. But what if her response really had been genuine?

Taycee had always made it sound like the show was nothing more than an annoyance—something she couldn't wait to be through with. But what if she cared more about

Jake than she let on? What if she didn't know who she liked better? What if her feelings for Luke weren't as strong as he thought?

Luke suddenly felt like he didn't know anything anymore.

But Taycee did.

He turned and headed in the direction of her place, his steps purposeful. A few blocks later, he stood in front of her door, his fist lifted to knock. He hesitated. What if he didn't like what she had to say? Did he really want to hear her admit that she didn't know who she liked best?

Luke stood there, hand raised, as varying emotions slammed into him all at once. Jealousy. Betrayal. And now . . . fear. The kind of fear that had him dropping his hand and backing away.

Thirty-six

aycee slipped her feet into her sandals and reached for her purse. Her head pounded from the incessant worry and stress that seemed intent on following around her wherever she went, like Eeyore's little raincloud. But the feeling wouldn't go away. Like a storm that hovered for weeks at a time, trapping out the sun, the feeling enshrouded her.

Taycee started forward, knowing the only way past this storm was to force her way through the clouds and find the sun herself. And she'd start with Jake and Miles. Sure, she could rationalize her actions all she wanted—a greater cause and all that—but what she'd done to them was wrong. They deserved an apology. A big one.

Taycee flung her door open and stepped out into the humid evening air. She paused on her doorstep when she caught sight of Luke's wavy brown hair and broad shoulders—shoulders she'd give anything to bury her head in right now. They would be warm and smell good and feel good. But why was he walking away?

"Luke?" she called.

He spun around, his eyebrows drawn together in wary surprise, as if he'd been caught somewhere he didn't want to be. "Hey."

Taycee stepped toward him, suddenly nervous. "Did you knock?"

He hesitated. "No."

The pounding in her head changed from a rubber mallet to a sledgehammer, striking with strong, hard strokes. The way he looked at her made her want to run back inside and let her door take the brunt of whatever he came here to say—or not say.

But her feet wanted to run *to* him, not away.

"I saw your date with Jake," Luke said. The words sounded accusatory and final, as though he'd already formed his own opinions and challenged her to negate them.

Taycee let out a breath of frustration. Not this. Not now. Not after everything else that was going on. "You said you weren't going to watch that."

A flicker of annoyance passed over his features. "Really?" he said. "That's your response? That I shouldn't have watched it? Well it's too late because I already did."

Taycee sighed. "It wasn't what it looked like, Luke. You should know that better than anyone."

He took a purposeful step toward her, and then stopped and raked his fingers through his hair. "I want to believe you, I do, but this bachelorette thing isn't some fictional Hollywood movie. It's called a reality show for a reason. You can talk all you want about how it wasn't the way it looked and how I should know better, but here's what I do know: On that video clip you *weren't* acting."

If it had been Miles or Jake standing there accusing her, Taycee would have expected something like this—even deserved it—but Luke was a different story. She had no reason to act when she was with him. There were no cameras trained on them. No viewers to please. No expectations to save a bunch of farms. He *knew* that. And yet here he was, questioning her motives just like the rest of the viewers.

Questioning her.

"What did you want me to do, Luke?" Taycee said. "Pretend to drop an earring every time he tried to kiss me? Or maybe I should have downed a spoonful of garlic before our date. That would have gone over really well on the final episode of a reality show about finding love."

"That wasn't just a kiss," said Luke. "It was a full on make-out session—one that you looked more than happy to be part of. What do you expect me to think?"

"I expect you to trust me," Taycee snapped. "Do you think I liked pretending to be into all those guys? Or kissing them? Or parading in front of those cameras like some happy-go-lucky girl who couldn't get enough male attention? Because I didn't! I never wanted any of this. I would have rather been with you during all of those dates.

"But I did it anyway. For six weeks, I went out with guys I didn't care about and let my life become public domain so a lot of good people wouldn't lose their farms. But now that's all in jeopardy, and you know why? Because you decided to follow me to the park one afternoon and kiss me yourself!" The words were out before Taycee could rethink them.

Luke stiffened, saying nothing. He simply stood there, looking at her with a mixture of disbelief, anger, and hurt. Then he took a step back, pivoted, and left. It was the second time tonight she'd watched him walk away. Only this time, she didn't call him back.

Taycee bit her lip hard and let the tears fall. One by one, they dripped down her cheek. Her own little shower. So much for forging her way through the storm.

Luke closed his front door and turned on the light. He should have never gone to the diner. Never watched that video. Never showed up at Taycee's. Then he'd still be in his happy little cocoon, completely oblivious to the fact that the girl he was crazy about wasn't so crazy about him right now. She made no secret of the fact that she would undo their kiss at the park if she could—a kiss he'd never want undone no matter how many problems it caused.

Luke dropped down on his recliner and flipped on the TV. A quick perusal of the stations offered him nothing, so he shut it off and resisted the urge to chuck the remote.

The silence of his house suddenly felt like a foreshadowing of his future. Empty. Alone. Deprived. He felt as if he were six again, when his golden lab ran in front of a moving car. Luke had stood there and watched him get hit, watched his best friend get taken away from him. But it wasn't until that night, when he was lying in bed without his dog at his feet to scare the bad dreams away, that it had really hit him. He'd cried—long and hard. And with that cry came a promise to never own another dog again—not if that's what it felt like to have your heart broken.

Unfortunately, that promise did nothing for him now.

The faint sound of Luke's cell phone filled the house. He reached into his pocket and yanked it out, as if it could somehow stave off the ever increasing pain gnawing away at him. He answered without looking at the number.

"Luke?" a familiar female voice asked—a voice he'd never thought he'd hear again.

"Madi?" He hadn't spoken to his ex-fiancée since he moved back. Hadn't really even thought about her. "What's wrong?"

"It's Dad," she said, her voice breaking. "He had a heart attack last night."

"What!" Luke sat up straight.

"He didn't make it, Luke. He's gone." Sobs practically vibrated through the phone.

Luke blinked, not quite able to believe it. Madi's father had been in perfect health. He was a runner. Lived on a strict diet of healthy foods. How could this happen to someone like him? "Madi, I'm so sorry. What can I do?"

"I need you," was all she had to say.

"On my way."

Thirty-seven

Taycee pulled to a stop in front of the town inn and wiped a finger under each eye, removing any smeared makeup. Three windows glowed in the darkness. Which room was Jake's? Was he even here or had he seen the gossip blog and already left town? Taycee wouldn't blame him if he had.

She sat in her car for several minutes, taking deep breaths and trying not to think about what had just happened with Luke. An engine rumbled behind her as a car pulled into the lot. Jake's Audi. He was still here. Maybe he didn't know anything yet.

Taycee wiped her eyes one more time and stepped from her car. Before she lost her nerve, she walked quickly to Jake's car and tugged on the passenger door handle.

Locked.

She tapped against the dark window. It rolled down, revealing Jessa's face with her hair clipped artfully back and her silver dangling earring shimmering in the lamplight. She looked beautiful and put together—the opposite of how Taycee felt.

"What are you doing here?" Taycee said.

"Probably the same thing you're about to do," Jessa said. "Apologizing."

Leave it to Jessa to say it how it was. Taycee almost smiled. Almost. Until she looked beyond Jessa and caught two wary blue eyes looking back at her. She swallowed. "Finished?"

"You're timing is perfect." The door opened and Jessa got out of the car, turning back to Jake. "Thanks, Jake."

He nodded.

Jessa offered Taycee a sympathetic look before walking across the parking lot to her car. Taycee slid into the passenger seat and closed the door, shutting herself into an almost eerie silence. Jake stared straight ahead, his elbow hanging out an open window. Minutes ticked by, coating the car in discomfort.

He finally broke the silence. "Yes, I read the blog and saw the pictures." A pause. "In case you were wondering."

Taycee closed her eyes. Great. Now he thought she was here to deal with collateral damage, which she was, but it was also more than that. She'd wanted him to hear the truth from her, not some lousy gossip blog that exaggerated everything.

"I'm so sorry," she said, not knowing what else to say.

In front of them, a maple tree moved gently in the wind, sending shadows darting across the sidewalk. She focused on the shadows. "I owe you an explanation," she said, "and I hope you'll hear me out." Then she started at the beginning, telling him everything. How she'd wanted out. How she'd never gotten over her teenage crush. How she'd gotten Luke voted off the show. And how she'd wished she could fall for Jake instead.

"I should have told you sooner," Taycee said. "I wanted

to. I even planned to at some point. But there was too much on the line, and the fear of you walking away held me back. It was so wrong, I am sorry. If I could rewind the past few weeks and do things differently, I would."

Jake shot her a hard look. "Of course you say that now, after everything went down the way it did. But the only reason you're sitting here is because of those pictures. You never would have told me otherwise—or, at least not until after the final vote. Instead, you let me believe that you were into me, that you wanted me to stick around after the show." His head shook slowly as he peered out the windshield. "You played me, and like an idiot, I fell for it."

Taycee reached a hand toward him, and then withdrew it. The last thing Jake probably wanted right now was for her to offer comfort. Not when she'd been the cause of his anger. "You're not an idiot, Jake Sanford. Far from it."

Jake continued to stare out the window, his hands resting low on the steering wheel. "What gets me is that I had no idea. Looking back, I can totally see it—the way you started joking around every time the topic got serious or when I went in for a kiss—but at the time"—he shook his head again—"how could I have been that clueless?" His gaze flickered to her for a second and then back toward the building. "You should have told me, Taycee. I would have told you."

He sounded so sure, so confident, but would he have told her? Really? He made it out to be so easy. So simple. Tell the truth. But life wasn't easy or simple. It was complex and hard and filled with a million questions that had no clear answers. There were no directions or warnings that stated, "This is what you should do" or, "Bad idea. You'll be sorry." Sometimes you just had to make a decision and sometimes that decision was wrong.

Jake twisted his head to look at her. "Was any of it real? At all?"

"Yes," she said quietly. "I do care about you. You're the kind of guy I would have fallen hard for if I hadn't already . . ." She couldn't finish. The last thing he needed to hear right now was a reminder of why they'd never had a chance.

Jake nodded again, his Adam's apple bobbing as he swallowed. "Well, as Jessa put it, what's done is done. And since I can't do anything to change the past, I might as well do something to change the future."

"Yeah," Taycee said. "That sounds like something Jessa would say. Only less dry and more abrupt."

A smile tugged at the corners of his mouth before his expression turned solemn once more. "She was right, though. And since I'm the type of guy who finishes what he starts, I'll show up for the interview. I'll even play the part of the supportive, understanding, second-place bachelor who is still mature enough to be happy for the bachelorette. Those farmers will not lose that money because of me."

Taycee felt a moment of relief before the pain struck—the kind of pain that came from knowing she'd wounded someone who didn't deserve it and couldn't do anything to fix it. There was no antiseptic or Band Aids to slap on him, no words of comfort to offer, and no kiss to make it all better. All she could do was walk away and let it heal on its own.

She wanted to tell him thank you. That he was a good man. That even if things had worked out differently, she wouldn't deserve him anyway. But all of it sounded so trite—words meant to heal but really only made it worse.

With a tug on the handle, she pushed open the door. Stepping out of the car, she gave him one last look that she hoped would convey her apologies and gratitude. Then she left to go find Miles.

✱

Taycee closed her apartment door with a soft click and leaned back against it. Her head still throbbed and her body ached like she was coming down with the flu.

Her conversation with Miles had gone pretty much the same as it had with Jake, although Miles had tried to joke off the hurt and lighten the heady feeling in the room. But Taycee could still see the pain in his eyes.

With a sigh, she kicked one sandal off, and then the other. Forcing her feet forward, she headed for her room.

"Hey, sis."

Taycee started as a dark shadow emerged from the kitchen holding a drink. A Diet Coke. Caleb took a swig before leaning against the doorway in the dim light. "About time you showed up," he said.

Had it only been a few days ago that Caleb had dropped the news of his engagement? It seemed like years. What had been such earth-shattering news at the time was now a tiny weed in a meadow filled with Stinging Nettle.

Taycee walked around the couch and plopped down, too tired to remain standing. Her head fell forward in her hands. "I figured you'd gone back to California."

"Not yet."

"Where'd you stay last night?"

"Luke's."

"Oh." The one person Taycee couldn't stop thinking about. Why couldn't Caleb have stayed at Luke's another night? Why couldn't he have already flown back to Phoenix. She wasn't in the mood for another argument or to hear about yet another one of her many flaws. More than anything, she ached to be alone. To curl up on her bed in her favorite yoga pants and let the silence engulf her. "What do you want, Caleb?"

"To apologize."

Taycee stilled at his words. Caleb was never serious. Even when he messed up, he always found a way to apologize in a teasing way, as though it would somehow speed up the process of things returning to "normal."

She peeked at him, not quite sure how to take the sincerity.

He plopped down next to her. "Don't be too shocked. Jenny told me I needed to say sorry and make it sound like I meant it." He paused, and then quickly added, "Because I do."

A laugh bubbled up inside of Taycee. The kind of frenzied laugh that coupled humor with a desperate need for release. It started off as a snicker and grew into a series of giggles.

"What's so funny?"

"I'm sorry. I'm just loving the fact that there's a girl out there who can say jump and you ask how high."

"As if," he scoffed. "I just thought she happened to be right about this. That's all."

The laughter died, and Taycee stared at her hands. "I can't believe you didn't tell me before. I feel like I missed out on an important chunk of your life."

Caleb leaned against the back of the couch and propped his feet on the coffee table. "It wasn't that big of a chunk actually. I've known her for a while, but we've only been going out a few months."

Taycee twisted her head to study her brother. So much about him was still the same. His care-for-nothing appearance. His dry sense of humor. His laid-back attitude. But there was now a depth to him that she hadn't noticed before. He'd grown up a little—not enough to change the things Taycee loved most about him—but enough to add a level of maturity that complimented him. Whoever this Jenny was, she'd been good for her brother. That much was obvious.

"I want to meet her," Taycee said.

"Why? So you can tell her she's making a big mistake? I don't think so."

A smile found its way to her mouth as she scooted over and laid her head on Caleb's shoulder. "No. So I can thank her."

"Thank her?"

"For being a good influence on you." Taycee paused. "And okay. So maybe I do feel a duty to let her know what she's getting herself into."

Caleb's arm locked around Taycee and a finger jabbed into her armpit, making her squeal. "Stop it!" Taycee cried between painful giggles.

"Take it back."

"Okay, okay, I take it back." There was nothing worse than being tickled by Caleb, especially since he wouldn't stop until she finally did as he asked.

He let her go. "Don't ever forget that I will always be your big brother."

Taycee poked him in the stomach that had softened a little over the years. "Big is right."

"You're asking for it."

"I know, I know." Once again, her head dropped to his shoulder as she fought to keep her eyes open. Her body had never felt so tired. So devoid of energy.

"So how's Shelter's bachelorette?" Caleb asked. It was like he'd read her mind and asked the worst possible question he could have asked.

Taycee groaned. "Let's just say I've made a mess of everything and leave it at that."

"How?"

"Don't you understand what 'leave it at that' means?"

Caleb's arm came around her once more, this time in a side-hug. "Sounds like someone has some splainin' to do."

The last thing Taycee wanted was to relive the night all over again. "No. If I tell you, you're just going to do your best Dad rendition and say, 'Don't you know that honesty's the best policy?' and make me wish I'd never told you. So no, I'm not going to explain anything."

"Hmm . . . Taycee Emerson actually lied?" Caleb grinned. "I don't believe it. What could you have possibly lied about?"

"It's more about what I didn't say than what I did."

Caleb laughed. "And what, exactly, didn't you say?" He made her sound like a drama queen who was freaking out over a little white lie.

Taycee succumbed to the bait. "Only that I fell for a bachelor who got voted off weeks ago while still dating the remaining bachelors, even though I had no intention of ever getting serious with any of them."

A grin spread across Caleb's face as he pumped his fist in a triumphant gesture. "It's Luke, isn't it? I knew it!" When he caught Taycee glaring, the grin left his face and he quickly lowered his hand. Then he shrugged. "So why not tell the truth now? Maybe if you fess up and explain what really happened, people might actually understand. Okay, so maybe not the bachelors that you've been stringing along, but the viewers might."

"Might?" Taycee muttered. "There's some encouragement for you. Sure, I'll just march into that interview and say, 'Hey, sorry I lied to everyone, but the truth is I've actually been in love with my brother's best friend for years, and now that he's back and finally paying attention to me, I really don't care about the show or the rest of the bachelors anymore. But we still need your money, so please vote anyway, even though whoever wins really isn't going to win anything."

"Seriously?" Caleb asked. "You've liked Luke all this time?"

Taycee's eyes closed. Out of all that, Caleb would zero in on that one little bit. She blamed her exhaustion on her slip-up. Why did he have to be such a lawyer anyway—always pressing for answers in a way that made people blurt them out? "What am I going to do, Caleb? Even the truth won't make it okay. People are calling the show a fraud and asking for their money back."

Caleb gave her shoulder a pat. "Stop beating yourself up about it and just explain to everyone what really happened.

That's all they really want anyway. A good, solid reason for your actions. Make them understand why you did what you did and things will work out fine. You'll see."

No, she didn't see—especially not when it came to Luke.

"I messed up with Luke, too," Taycee admitted, knowing that was the biggest reason for her misery. More than anyone else, she needed Luke to listen, to understand, and to forgive.

"I'm beginning to feel like a broken record," Caleb grumbled, "so I'll say this one more time and never again. Explain. And. Things. Will. Be. Fine."

If only it could be that easy.

Thirty-eight

On the set of Wake Up Denver, Michael Roik leaned forward in his comfortable leather armchair. "So, Taycee, what's it like going from the beloved bachelorette saving her town, to someone who manipulated the viewers by pretending to be something she's not?"

Only an hour earlier, Taycee had walked into the studio with some serious trepidation. She'd been interviewed by news stations before, but this was different. It had a much larger audience and felt more intimidating. Now, however, only ten minutes into the interview, her trepidation had been replaced with anger. Michael had done nothing but attack her character and belittle Shelter Springs.

"What did I pretend to be exactly?" she asked, her voice hard.

"Available." The way he said it made it sound like she was an idiot for not knowing that.

"But I *was* available."

Michael settled back in his seat with a seedy smile. "Let me tell you how this looks to the rest of us since you can't seem to grasp the implications."

"Oh, I wouldn't say—"

"Twenty bachelors were initially chosen, but a couple weeks before it began there was a last minute add-on. A bachelor from Shelter Springs, of all places. And, according to several reliable sources, you were the one who made that suggestion. Is that correct?"

Taycee shifted in her seat. Okay, so maybe it did look bad. "Yes, but—"

"Here's what people are saying," Michael said. "That you had feelings for Luke and possibly a relationship going on before the show started, so it made sense to add him as one of the bachelors." He leaned forward. "But when he got voted off, that put a kink in your plans, didn't it?"

Michael knew nothing. All he cared about was showcasing Taycee and Shelter Springs in the worst possible light. He was on a mission to uncover some nasty, manipulative person, and nothing she could say or do would change that, especially since he wouldn't let her get a word in edgewise. "You're wrong. I never—"

Michael held up a hand. With his horrid triumphant smile still in place, he faced the camera. "As you all know, the two remaining bachelors, Jake Sanford and Miles Romney, have agreed to join us today."

Taycee lifted her eyes as Jake and Miles sauntered onto the set. Jake, with his confident air, and Miles, with his black cowboy hat and boyish grin. She hadn't spoken to either of them since the night she and Jessa had attempted to right a wrong. But here they both were, as promised. Would they really be supportive runners-up, or would it now be three against one?

Miles pulled her up into a big bear hug, saying, "Don't worry, we got your back," and then Jake followed suit. He reached for her hand and held it in his as they sat down—Miles on one side, Jake on the other.

Michael cleared his throat, his squinty eyes absorbing the affection. "Welcome, gentlemen. Glad you could make it."

Jake nodded. Miles said nothing.

Michael crossed one leg over the other. "Miles, let's start with you. How do you feel about the recent turn of events regarding Luke Carney and Taycee Emerson?

Miles caught Taycee's eye for a moment before returning his attention to Michael. "I feel about how anyone else would feel if a girl they liked had eyes for someone else. It's a blow, but that's life for you. Feelings aren't always mutual, so when they go south, ya gotta accept it and move on."

Michael turned to Jake. "What about you, Jake? From what I can tell after reading all the comments, you were the clear favorite. Any thoughts?"

Jake shrugged. "I have to agree with Miles on this one. Of course it was a disappointment, but Taycee found a better fit for her with one of the other bachelors, and that's that."

"Yes, but how do you feel knowing you really had no chance to begin with?" Michael prodded. "Especially after all the time and money you sacrificed to be on this show? You've got to be a little miffed by that."

Jake shrugged. "I might be if I actually believed it."

"What do you mean?"

Jake leaned forward and rested his elbows on his knees, relinquishing Taycee's hand. "Taycee may have had feelings for Luke before this all started, but I had a chance to change her mind. Each of us bachelors did. If any of us had been a better fit then those feelings would have changed. Happens all the time, actually. But it didn't with her, which also happens. It's the ups and downs of dating. It's life."

Apparently Michael didn't like that answer because he frowned. "You're telling me that you don't you think it was wrong for Taycee to become the bachelorette when she already had a bias or preference for one of the bachelors?"

"They weren't dating at the time the show began."

"How can you be sure they weren't dating?"

"Call me naïve, but I believe Taycee. Besides, Luke had been gone for a decade and had only just moved back to town."

"You're pretty loyal for a guy who's just been played."

Jake shot Taycee a look before answering. "I'll be honest. I was pretty upset at first. But when I heard her side of the story and gave it some thought, I started to wonder how I would have reacted in the same situation. I mean, this wasn't just a show about finding love, it was about saving farms and homes and people's livelihoods. If there hadn't been so much on the line, I'm positive Taycee would have dropped out the second her relationship with Luke started to get serious."

"I'll second that," Miles agreed.

Taycee's fingers fiddled in her lap. As horrible as the interview had begun, Jake's words soaked into the hole in her heart, repairing it a little. If anyone had a right to be angry or feel duped, it was Jake and Miles. And yet here they were, going to bat for her against the mean-spirited Michael Roik. She didn't deserve it.

Michael shifted in his seat and flashed a meaningful look to a guy standing near a large camera. "It's time for a short commercial break. We'll be back in a moment." When they were off the air, Michael rose and strode away.

As soon as he was gone, Taycee said, "Thank you. Both of you."

"Where's Luke?" Miles asked. "If anyone should be here, it should be him."

Miles's words were a depressing reminder that Luke still hadn't called her back. It had been two days now. Two very long days. He didn't answer her calls, didn't respond to her texts, didn't answer his door when she pounded. Where was he? Was he planning to leave Shelter? Had he already gone? Would he ever give her a chance to fully explain?

Taycee let out a breath. "I haven't heard from him since Saturday night. He saw the final episode of the show and was pretty upset with me."

Jake actually smiled. "I guess I can understand that. That was quite the kiss."

Taycee cringed. She didn't feel up to discussing this right now—especially not with Jake and Miles. "Well, thanks for standing up for me. It means a lot that you're both here."

Jake caught her eyes before turning back to face the empty armchair in front of them. "You know he's only using this time to regroup don't you? In another minute or so it's back to the firing range with a freshly loaded automatic."

Taycee clasped her fingers together and sat up straight. "Suddenly, I don't care anymore. Bring it on, *Wake Up Denver*."

But the truth was, Taycee did care. Too much. When Michael returned and asked if the donated money would be returned, and Jake said, "No, Taycee didn't do anything wrong and the town needs the money," it opened up an entire new slew of questions and accusations. Taycee was able to keep her chin up and her claws to herself, but only because Jake and Miles deflected the majority of the bullets.

Or at least tried to. In reality, the shots found their mark. Each one cut in a little deeper, pierced her soul a little harder. By the time it was finally over, Taycee was more than ready to put it all behind her and get away from the horrible Michael Roik. She'd come to the interview ready to explain and apologize to the viewers, but she never had the chance. What did this mean for the town? Would people still vote, even after all that had happened? Or would they still insist on getting their money back?

After it was all over, Taycee found Miles by the lockers in the back. She gave him a long hug goodbye. "Thank you, Miles. For everything. There are amazing things in store for you, I know it."

Miles's hands trailed down her arms. "It was great seeing you one last time, but I've gotta head back and get myself ready for a rodeo next week."

"I hope you win."

He chuckled. "Yeah, that would sure be awesome."

"Good luck to you."

His finger grazed her chin. "Chin up. Everything is going to work out just fine."

"I hope you're right."

One last hug and Miles walked out the door. Jake was nowhere in sight, so Taycee grabbed her purse from a nearby locker and headed out the back door and into the bright, sunny Denver morning.

"Taycee, wait up," Jake called from behind.

Taycee stopped and turned around. "I thought you'd already gone."

"I had to sneak away to take a quick phone call."

"Oh. Well, good," said Taycee. "I want to thank you again. You didn't have to come here today and take my side, and yet you did."

Jake nodded. "You still look worried."

He was far too perceptive. "Probably because I am worried. I feel like a failure. He didn't even give me a chance to explain, which was the main reason I showed up here today."

Jake leaned against his car. "Oh, I don't think Shelter's going anywhere anytime soon. As warped as it is, people love a good drama, and Miles and I were able to get in enough of an explanation that the viewers will understand. They might surprise you."

Taycee let out a breath and folded her arms. "How can you be so nice to me? If I were you, I'd want to get as far away from me as I could."

"Don't think the idea hasn't crossed my mind," Jake joked. "But I've come to realize that maybe we aren't the best fit after all, so maybe this is a good thing. While you're content to live in the small town of Shelter Springs, I like the bustle of Sacramento and all the travelling I get to do. You like kite wars while I'm more of a symphony and Broadway type of guy. In the end, we'd probably drive each other nuts."

Taycee touched his arm as she studied him. Tall. Smart. Good-looking. Heart of gold. A guy who'd won everyone over with his charm and genuine nature. He'd even given the farmers a bigger reason to hope.

"There's someone way better for you out there, Jake, I know it. Someone who actually deserves you."

"I'm sure there is." Jake smiled, but it started and ended with his lips.

"I'm going to miss you."

"And I'll miss you." He gave her a lingering look, and then dug into his pocket for his keys.

Taycee wanted to throw her arms around him for one last hug, just to show him how much his friendship meant to her. But she clasped her fingers together instead and forced her arms to remain by her side. It was time to let Jake go so that he could move on with his life.

Just like it was time for her to track down Luke so that she could move on with hers.

Thirty-nine

New message from Taycee:

> *Where are you, Luke? Please call me! We need to talk.*

Luke's thumb hovered over the reply button for a second, and then he deleted the message, just like he had the few others she'd sent before it. He wasn't ready to open that door just yet—not while he was still in Ohio. It had been an exhausting few days, and he was emotionally spent. Watching a good friend get buried while his family stood by and sobbed wasn't an experience he ever wanted to repeat.

Everything around him still felt subdued and gray, as though some of the life had been sucked out of the house. A wife was now without a husband, a daughter without a father, and two parents without a son.

Luke tossed his phone on the bed and grabbed his suitcase. He'd done as he promised. He'd given Madi a shoulder to cry on and had even said a few words at the funeral. But now it was time to go home and somehow find a way to shake off the heavy feeling that hung over him.

A light tap sounded at the door.

"Come in."

The door opened. Madi took a few tentative steps inside, her long, curly strawberry blonde hair framing her face. Not many girls could pull off red, puffy eyes and still make it look attractive, especially with that hair color, but right now she looked vulnerable and beautiful. Luke wished he knew how to comfort her, but nothing he could say or do would make it all right. That was the crappy thing about loss.

"Packing?" she said.

Luke tossed a few shirts in his suitcase. "I'm booked on a flight tonight. I need to get back."

She nodded and took another step forward, resting her hand on the bedpost. "You're sure I can't convince you to stay? Dad always wanted you to take over his practice, and we could really use your help."

The words tugged on Luke's conscience, making him feel even heavier. Ever since he'd arrived, Madi had been hinting about him staying around for a while—at least until they could find someone else to take over the practice. But Luke had to say no. He hated doing it, but staying here would only create more problems. Madi obviously wasn't over him yet, and the last thing Luke wanted to do was give her false hope, which was exactly what he would be doing if he agreed to stay. Besides, he had his own problems and practice to worry about.

"I'm sorry, but I can't," Luke said. "I have a life back in Shelter now, and it's time for me to get back to it."

Madi studied him with a solemn expression as her fingers tapped against the bedpost. "Does she deserve you?"

Luke's eyes shot to hers. This wasn't exactly the conversation he wanted to have with his ex-fiancée, especially not after everything she'd been through. "What?"

"That bachelorette girl."

Madi knew about that?

She shrugged and tried for a smile. "I saw the way you looked at her. And if that didn't convince me, those pictures of you two kissing did." Her head cocked to the side. "So, I'll ask it again. Does she deserve you?"

Luke had no idea how to answer the question. What made one person deserve another, anyway? "She deserves to be happy," he said. "Just like you do."

"And you."

Luke chuckled, more at the absurdity of the conversation than actual humor. "Yeah, well, a lot of people do I guess." He gave her a wary look, thinking of her father. "But that doesn't mean we always get to be happy, does it?"

A knowing sadness reflected in her eyes. "Right." She took a step back, and her fingers clasped together. "Well, I'll let you get back to packing. Let me know when you're ready, and I'll give you a ride."

"Thanks."

She turned and walked to the door, her hand resting on the doorknob as she looked back at him. "I hope you find happiness, Luke. Wherever that is." Then she opened the door and left.

Luke tossed a pair of shoes in his bag, and then sat down on the bed. Happiness. His parents had always taught him that he was responsible for his own happiness and to never put that burden on someone else's shoulders. It was good advice, and for the most part, Luke had tried to do that. But now that Taycee had come back into his life, she'd somehow taken that happiness and made it bigger and better than ever before. She'd given him a taste of bliss. Misery, too. But mostly bliss.

It wasn't something he wanted to give up.

Luke stood and shoved the rest of his stuff in the bag, his movements more purposeful. Then he slung it over his shoulder and walked out the door, shutting it and the reminder of his old life firmly behind him.

Taycee's sparkly brown eye shadow fell to the floor with a clack, dusting her ceramic tiled bathroom floor with the fine powder. She frowned and kicked the container, creating an even bigger mess. Whatever. Better on the floor than highlighting her puffy, sleep-deprived eyes—something she blamed on Luke and his refusal to call her back. Where was he anyway?

In twenty minutes, Taycee was supposed to be at The Barn for her final interview. It was a day for celebration, yet her feet still dragged. Jake had been right about giving the viewers more credit. Ever since the interview with Michael Roik aired, the site's traffic increased. Jessa had added Luke's name to the final poll, and more people voted during the last round than any of the others. Why that was, Taycee had no idea, especially when the winner turned out to be Jake. Did it mean that people still hoped that Jake was still in the running? Hopefully not, because if they expected Taycee to proclaim her love for Jake, they'd be disappointed—not a reaction she wanted to deal with again.

Which was exactly why she took her time getting ready. Her cell phone rang at 6:30 on the nose, but she ignored it as she put a couple of eye drops in each eye, hoping it would help get the red out. Then she grabbed her purse and walked to The Barn. She needed fresh air to breathe and time to think.

"Hey," Jessa said when she walked through the door. "Where have you been? I was getting worried."

"Sorry I'm late," said Taycee. "I needed some time to think before I do this."

Jessa studied Taycee from under the rim of a black Colby cap. "You know you have nothing to worry about, right? Miles and Jake stood by your side when you needed it most. While I'm sure the viewers would love for you to say you're falling for Jake rather than Luke, even if you don't, it's going to be fine."

"Is it?" Taycee was thinking more about Luke than the show when she asked the question.

Jessa shrugged. "Think about it this way: The majority of our viewers are female, right? Since most of them are probably half in love with Jake anyway, they'll be more than happy to find out he's still available. So you're really doing them all a favor by choosing Luke instead."

Taycee tried for a smile, but it didn't quite feel real. Yes, she chose Luke. Hands down, she chose Luke. But what if he didn't choose her back? What if she blew her one and only chance with him?

Jessa grabbed Taycee's elbow and pulled her toward the couch. "I'm willing to bet that someday we'll look back on this and have ourselves a good laugh, especially when we tell our kids and grandkids about it."

"That would require you finding a guy first," Taycee said. "Settling down and all that."

"I can settle down."

Taycee laughed. "Just don't try to be too efficient when you start looking. Learn from my mistake—and yours—and take it one guy at a time."

That earned her a grin from Jessa. "See? We're already cracking jokes."

A deep breath in and Taycee took a seat next to a table holding a vase of beautiful white chrysanthemums—a flower arrangement she'd made herself. In the US, chrysanthemums were known as the positive and cheerful flower. In some countries of Europe and Asia, they were symbolic of death or grief. In others, they represented honesty. For Taycee, the bouquet typified her journey these past several weeks and now served as a reminder: To be strong. Honest. Real.

With any luck, maybe Luke would even watch. It would finally give her the chance to explain.

"And we're on in three . . . two . . . one . . ." Burt pointed at them.

Jessa opened her mouth to ask the first question, but Taycee held up a hand. She faced the camera and lifted her chin. "This past week, I have been accused of several things: Dishonesty, deception, manipulation, leading people on, etc." She paused. "In a way, you were right because I was never completely honest with you. But that's going to change right now."

Taycee's fingers played in her lap, clasping, unclasping. Clasping, unclasping. "For me, this show has always been about Shelter Springs, rather than the people it was supposed to be about: me and the bachelors. If I could rewind the past several weeks and do things differently, I would. I would treat the show, you viewers, and the bachelors with the respect that you deserve."

A cream linen envelope lay next to the bouquet on the table by Taycee. She picked it up and ran her finger along the crisp edge. "Many of you have voted for your favorite bachelor tonight, and the winner's name is in this envelope. Throughout this entire contest, you guys have chosen well for me because Jake and Miles are two of the best men I have ever known." Taycee paused. "But so is someone else—someone who you voted off a couple of weeks ago because of something I orchestrated. The truth is, Luke Carney is not a player. Far from it, actually. He's the best kind of person there is.

"I've read some of the less-than-flattering comments people have posted about Luke, and I want you all to know that you couldn't be more wrong about him. I was the one who asked Missy to make him look bad so you'd vote him off. Like so many of my other choices these past several weeks, I let fear drive that decision. I had feelings for Luke and never imagined that he could ever return them, so I wanted him off. In so doing, I kept all of you from getting to know what an amazing person he is. Luke is kind, good, smart, funny, and truly exceptional. Had I stayed out of it and let you get to know him, I'm certain you would have chosen him for me in the end, because there really is no one else for me."

Taycee's hands clamped down over the top of the envelope, trapping it under her fingers. "It doesn't really matter whose name is in this envelope, because tonight I'm doing something I should have done all along. I'm making my own choice—a choice that will always be Luke Carney."

The silence that followed landed like a heavy weight on Taycee's shoulders. Not even Jessa spoke. Taycee had said what she'd come to say, but it still felt so unfinished, as if she hadn't said enough, apologized enough, defended Luke enough, or set things right enough.

But maybe that was the point. No matter how hard a person tried to make things right, sometimes it never was enough. That's what forgiveness was for.

With slow movements, Taycee gave the envelope one last pat. Then she stood and walked out the door, back into the night.

Forty

It was late by the time Taycee made it back to her house. She had no idea how long she walked, only that her feet ached and she still didn't feel any better. Only tired. Which was good, she supposed. Maybe she could at least get some sleep tonight.

"Hey," a voice said, making Taycee jump. Jessa sat under the cover of darkness on the top porch step. Her hand patted the empty concrete next to her.

"Hey yourself." Taycee plopped down and rested her head on Jessa's shoulder.

"You did good tonight," said Jessa. "But you weren't completely honest with everyone."

Taycee lifted her head. "What do you mean?"

"You took all the blame for what happened, when it was mostly my fault. I was the one who coerced you into doing the show, I was the one who told you to up the romance factor, and I was the one who told you to bury your relationship with Luke to finish it."

Taycee's lips lifted into a small smile. That admission was big for Jessa. "I could have told you no."

"I know. But you didn't because you're a better person than me." Jessa's sandal tapped against the concrete step.

Taycee yawned, unable to fight the exhaustion anymore. "I wasn't right for the job, Jess. You can see that now, right?"

"No," Jessa said. "You were perfect for the job. If Luke had won instead of Jake, everything would have ended as it should."

The warm humid night air seemed to mix with Jessa's words and seep into Taycee, easing some of the ache she'd lived with for the past several days. Although things were far from great, it helped that Jessa was still here. Still her friend. "Or," Taycee said. "If you'd been the bachelorette instead, things might have ended as it should, too."

Silence. And then, "What?"

Taycee suppressed a laugh. It wasn't often she surprised Jessa, and she loved it when she did. "I'm saying that maybe you and Jake would be a good fit, that's all. You do think he's handsome, rich, and charming."

"I think that about a lot of guys."

Taycee's eyebrows rose.

"Well, okay," Jessa said. "So maybe there aren't a lot that fit into that category around here. But that doesn't mean I'm going to fall for just anyone—least of all one of the bachelors on *your* dating show. I'm not that idiotic."

"You keep telling yourself that if it makes you feel better."

"I will," said Jessa. "Despite everything, though, things still worked out. We raised enough money, and assuming everything goes smoothly, the farmers market will be open in two weeks. And, if they're able to sell enough to pay off their loans, the majority of them plan to sign up with Jake's company in the fall."

"Glad to hear it." Taycee smiled, nudging Jessa's shoulder with her own. "Hey, mind if I ask you a question?"

"Shoot."

"Why are you still in Shelter Springs instead of out in the real world, making your splash? Because it would be huge. And beautiful. Like one of those cool fountain shows." *Please don't say it's because of me.*

"I think you overestimate me." Jessa's sandal tapped against the concrete again, faster this time. "Honestly? I guess it's because I lack the courage."

"Please. You're the most daring person I know."

"It's all an act." Jessa's hands clasped her knees as she leaned back and examined the sky. She rarely allowed her vulnerability to show, but now, right here, on this warm, clear night it was there in her big blue eyes.

What's more, it looked good on her.

"Maybe you should ask Jake if his company has any openings," Taycee said. It hurt to say the words, to make the suggestion that a life outside of Shelter Springs might be a better fit for her friend. She didn't want to see Jessa go, just like she hadn't wanted to see anyone else go. But go they did, and now they were better for it. Maybe Jessa would be better too.

A quiet chuckle sounded. "Yeah, I'll get right on that. After the whole bachelorette fiasco, he's sure to want to hire me."

"He was actually really impressed with what you did," said Taycee.

Jessa's head shook again, but something shone in her eyes that wasn't there before. Hope maybe. "No, if I'm going to venture out of here, I'm going to do it on my own—not that I wouldn't mind living in Sacramento."

Taycee grinned. "I've heard through the rumor mill that Jake isn't leaving until tomorrow morning. According to Mary, he's planning to grab some breakfast at the diner before heading out of town. You should, you know, drop by and say goodbye."

"Maybe I will." Jessa pursed her lips, and then cocked her head at Taycee. "And speaking of guys, heard anything from Luke?"

The mere mention of his name was all it took to suck the happy, light-heartedness away. "No. I'm worried he left town because I've tried everything. It's like he gave up without a fight." A thought Taycee hated voicing aloud because it sounded even more true. More real. The only possible conclusion.

"In that case, I think it's time I give that boy a piece of my mind. In fact—

"No. You've done enough, thanks."

Jessa's finger poked Taycee's shoulder. "You're making it sound like I'd make it worse."

"Because you would," Taycee said. "You'd track him down, probably punch him, and then yell at him—assuming you can find him, that is. Good luck with that."

"And you're saying punching and yelling wouldn't help?"

Taycee tried for a wry smile, but a yawn came out instead. "Just leave this one alone, okay?"

"Fine," Jessa said. "But if he doesn't show his face in the next day or two and beg you to take him back, I am going to track him down and then strangle him, okay?"

"Okay." Taycee agreed. "I'll even go with you."

Forty-one

Luke tossed overnight bag on the couch, and then flung open his fridge. Nothing. Only sour milk and fuzzy cheese. He would have stopped by the diner on his way home if it hadn't been closed. His flight had been delayed, and it was now after midnight, which meant he'd have to wait until morning before he could talk to Taycee.

He closed the door and sauntered over to the couch, dropping down beside his bag. His fingers raked through his hair as he glanced at his watch yet again.

His phone vibrated with a text, and Luke grabbed it from his pocket, hoping Taycee's name would appear and that she was still awake. But it was only Caleb.

Idiot, where R you? If you don't fix things w/ Tace soon, I might have to kill you. Or sue. So sick of hearing about it.

A second later, another text came.

If you haven't seen her final interview, watch it. NOW. Idiot.

For the first time in days, Luke smiled. Really smiled. Forgetting his hunger pangs, he grabbed his laptop and pried it open. What final interview?

Jake's Audi was still parked in front of the diner. Good. Before Jessa could talk herself out of it, she pulled open the door and walked in, head held high.

She clutched her purse and schooled her face into a surprised smile, but Jake was already talking to someone. Liza. She sat opposite him, leaning across the table with dreamy, flirty eyes.

Jessa made a beeline for the table and stopped beside it. "Hey, Liza. Long time no see."

An annoyed glance darted Jessa's way. "I just saw you the other day."

"Oh, that's right. My bad." Jessa scrunched her face in a look of confusion. "Now, was that before or after you took those pictures of Luke and Taycee and emailed them to Babette?"

A flush crept over Liza's face.

Jessa bit back a smile. "Yeah, probably not the smartest move to email them from your home computer since IP addresses can be traced. Jake, here, actually taught me that."

The flush darkened as Liza quickly stood. Before she could escape, Jessa put a hand on her arm. "Tell you what, if you promise to start being prompt with Taycee's orders from here on out, I'll forget about the whole thing. If not, well, let's just say that you're not the only one who can spin news to the town gossip blog. Oh, and I'd love a Sprite."

With a glare, Liza turned and left.

Problem solved.

Two problems, actually, because the seat opposite Jake was now vacant. Jessa slid right in. Jake looked amazing, as always, in a light blue polo with a navy stripe across his chest. It made his eyes look bluer than usual. "Fancy meeting you here. I figured you'd be long gone by now."

Jake gave a wry smile. "There's just something about Shelter that made me want to stay a little longer. And now I know why. I just got breakfast and a show. Nicely played."

"I have my moments."

"Yes, you do." His fingers fiddled with his drinking straw as he studied her.

"I'm actually glad I ran into you, Jake. I, uh, wanted to apologize. Again."

An eyebrow raised in question.

"And to let you know that I was the one who convinced Taycee to continue with the show after things started to happen with Luke." She paused, searching for the right words. "I've always had this issue with failure. As in, I don't like it. At all."

Jake chuckled. "Somehow, I already knew that. But no worries. We're good."

A glass of Sprite came between them, hitting the counter with a thunk. Jessa glanced up. "Thanks, Liza."

"Don't mention it," Liza huffed before turning away.

Jake pointed at the Sprite. "You going to drink that?"

"It's all yours." Jessa slid the glass forward. "I only ordered it to tick her off."

"I figured." He took a swig of the drink before setting it back on the counter. "So I hear you've been given the ax."

The joys of living in a small town. "Funny you should mention that. I actually got an email from the mayor this morning apologizing and saying the job's still mine—if I want it."

"Do you?"

"I don't know." Jessa rubbed at a sticker on her pink painted fingernail. She was officially at a crossroads in her life. She could either take the easy and predictable route or make a leap into the unknown. Whether it was her talk with Taycee or some deeply rooted need to have an adventure of her own, the latter suddenly didn't seem as scary as it used to. "Shelter's been good for me, but thanks to you and your family's company, I'm not sure they need me anymore. It might be time to spread my wings."

Jake took another long swig of the Sprite before setting it back on the counter. He reached for his wallet and pulled out some cash for a tip, along with a business card, which he tossed across the table. "If you ever think of venturing west—say Sacramento—give me a call. We could use someone like you on our team."

Jessa fingered the card with both fear and excitement. Jake was giving her an opportunity to take a plunge and see if there really was life beyond Shelter Springs. Did she dare take it?

Jessa slid the card into her purse. "Thanks," she said. "I might take you up on that."

"I hope you do." Jake stood, easing his tall frame out of the booth. "It was great meeting you, Jessa McCray." He gave her one last smile before walking out the door.

As Jessa watched him drive away, a happy feeling surrounded her—the kind that comes when life gives you sweet, juicy strawberries rather than lemons. Maybe Taycee was right. Maybe it was time to see how big of a splash she really could make.

Forty-two

Taycee hugged on of her soft, ivory down pillows to her chest and stared at her bedroom ceiling.

It was over. Finally.

No more cameras, no more dating a bunch of guys, and no more pretending. Taycee could finally be herself again, whatever that meant. She didn't really know anymore because it felt like something huge was missing from her life. *Someone.*

Taycee frowned—something she did every time she thought of Luke, which was often. If she kept it up, she'd probably etch permanent sad lines across her face. It had been five days since she'd walked away from him. Five days since she'd talked to him.

Five. Long. Miserable. Days.

No more. It was time to put an end to the misery. If Luke didn't want to see or talk to her, that was his problem. Taycee refused to wallow any longer. It was a new beautiful day outside, and she planned to spend it doing whatever she wanted. Forget work. Forget responsibility. And most importantly, forget Luke. She'd earned a day of freedom.

Taycee rolled out of bed, took her time in the shower, and then slipped on some comfy yoga pants and a lime green T-shirt with the words, "Just how many frogs do I have to kiss?" scrawled across the front—a thank you gift from Jessa. She padded barefoot to her kitchen and rummaged through her pantry. Cornflakes? No. Popcorn? Yes. Taycee stuffed the package into the microwave.

Today was a day for celebrating the demise of *Shelter's Bachelorette*. She would watch her favorite non-romantic movies. She would read her favorite non-romantic book. She would eat whatever she wanted. And she would *not* think of Luke.

The buttery smell of popcorn drifted into her nose, reminding her of a certain drive-in style date. Taycee frowned at the microwave. Okay, so maybe she wouldn't eat *anything* she wanted.

She yanked on the handle and grabbed the steaming popcorn bag, playing Hot Potato with it as she carried it out to the trash. When she came back inside, the smell was still there, taunting her with images of Luke throwing popcorn at her while *Sneakers* played on the wall of the garage in front of them.

Argh.

With purposeful steps, Taycee opened all the windows in her house, even going so far as to place a box fan in the front window to help purge the room of that rich, popcorn smell.

Three raps sounded on the door in quick succession.

Taycee turned her frown on the door, not interested in talking to anyone—not even Jessa. Maybe if she didn't answer, whoever it was would go away. She turned toward the kitchen.

"Taycee Lynne? You in there?" a muffled voice called through the door.

On second thought.

She rushed to the door and flung it open, revealing Luke with one hand planted firmly on her doorjamb as he leaned toward her, looking more delicious than any popcorn. Damp hair and all.

Taycee's heart dropped to her toes, and she felt the crazy urge to beat him and kiss him at the same time. "Where have you been?" she blurted. "I've been trying to get a hold of you for days. Did you lose your phone or something? Because if you've been ignoring my calls on purpose, I'm going to . . . to . . ."

"You're going to what?" His brown eyes smiled at her, making her heart beat double-time. He took a step toward her. "Punch me? Write me out of your will? Or were you planning to sic Missy on me again?"

She cleared her throat and lifted her chin. "All of the above."

"Then you'd better get started because I didn't lose my phone."

"What?" Taycee suddenly felt like she really did want to punch him. Her fingers fisted at her side. "How could you? Do you have any idea what you've put me through?"

He closed the door behind him and leaned against it, nodding toward her front room. "What's with the fan and open windows? You're making your apartment hot and muggy."

"I'm trying to get rid of the popcorn smell." Taycee cringed after she'd said it. Seriously, who eats popcorn for breakfast? Someone who needs help, that's who. "Stop trying to change the subject."

Luke's eyes shifted to the TV, featuring *Men in Black*. Yet another non-morning type thing to be doing. He probably wondered if she'd officially gone insane. "Why get rid of the popcorn smell if you're watching a movie? I thought you loved popcorn."

"I like to eat it, not smell it." She waltzed over to the TV and flipped it off. "Are you going to tell me where you've been now? I don't like being ignored."

"I know." He pushed away from the door and moved toward her.

Taycee held up a hand. "If you think I'm going to come running into your arms after you deliberately avoided me for five days with no explanation, you are one stick short of a bundle."

Luke's lips twitched as the usual teasing glint appeared in his eyes. "What makes you think that's what I want?"

Of all the—Taycee's foot stomped against the floor. "Luke Spencer Carney, you stop it right now! I am so not in the mood for this!"

"What are you in the mood for?" A lop-sided smile joined his teasing eyes as he moved toward her. "More popcorn?"

"No!"

"'*Sneakers*?'"

"No!"

Luke closed the distance between them. "Me?"

Without waiting for an answer, his mouth covered hers with a kiss that curled Taycee's toes—another thing that didn't usually happen at nine-o'clock in the morning. Her fingers somehow found their way to the back of his head, pulling him toward her. It had been too long since she'd kissed him, too long since she'd felt his arms around her.

Something that was all his fault.

The almost unbidden reminder took over, smothering the happy moment. She tried to shove it aside for later, but it pestered and nagged until she finally gave up and pushed him back.

"You can't do that until you explain! And even then, maybe not."

"Okay, okay, fine." His hands travelled down her arms, stopping at her wrists. "If you have to know, I've been in Ohio. With my ex-fiancée."

Taycee didn't realize her jaw had dropped until his finger pushed it back into place. Was he joking? The teasing glint was still there, but she also heard an undercurrent of truth in his words. Which she didn't like. At all. "Say what?"

Luke sighed. "Her father—my former boss and mentor—passed away a few days ago. I went out there for the funeral."

"Oh," Taycee said, feeling a mixture of relief and embarrassment. "I'm so sorry, Luke."

"Me too." His thumb traced along her jaw line. "His family asked me to stay to help out with his practice for a while."

Taycee frowned. Awhile? What did that mean? As in more than a few days? She clamped her mouth shut because she knew whatever she said would be the wrong thing. Sorry, you can't. No way. I forbid it. Better to bite the inside of her cheek instead.

His lips twitched as he watched her, like he knew exactly what she was thinking. "I turned them down. I'm back for good."

Taycee had heard those same words before, several weeks ago. At the time they'd nearly induced a panic attack, but not anymore. Now those words made her heart feel bigger somehow, more powerful and capable than ever before. Now they sounded fabulous.

Luke watched her face. Searching. Seeking. "Just out of curiosity, if I had said yes, would you have come with me?"

Those words, on the other hand, made Taycee's heart stop. "Would you have asked me to go with you?"

"I would have wanted to."

"Then I would have wanted to say yes."

A slow smile stretched across his face. "Really? You who hates change?"

"Really." Here, in Luke's arms, change didn't seem that scary anymore. In fact, it seemed downright exciting. It was a strange phenomenon, and yet not strange at the same time.

Maybe Luke was the reason Taycee had been so attached to Shelter Springs in the first place. Maybe his memory had been what kept her here all these years, along with a deeply buried hope that someday he'd return.

And now that he had, home was no longer Shelter Springs, Colorado. Home was Luke.

Epilogue

Three Months Later

Taycee passed through security at the airport and scanned the throng of people milling about. When she finally spotted Luke, leaning against a pillar and looking around for her, a happy smile broke across her face. It had only been three days, but it felt like an eternity. 70 hours too long. Next time she'd make him come with her.

Luke's eyes connected with hers, and a slow smile spread over his face. He pushed away from the pillar and made his way toward her. She quickened her steps and walked straight into his open arms, breathing in his familiar clean scent as he pulled her close.

"I missed you," she murmured against his chest.

"Likewise." He kissed her forehead, and then took her bag and slung it over his shoulder. His arm rested against the small of her back as he guided her toward the airport parking lot. "So, how does it feel to finally land your first big wedding gig?"

Taycee laughed. "Like nepotism. The only reason Caleb and Jenny want me to do their flowers is because I come with a family discount. I like her though. A lot. She's perfect for my brother and will fit in great."

"So you're saying she's stubborn, ornery when she doesn't get fed, and has a police record?"

"No." Taycee poked him in the ribs. "I'm saying she's pretty awesome."

"Oh, right. That too."

Once inside Luke's truck, Taycee scooted across the faded upholstery to the center, where she leaned against his shoulder and rested her hand on his knee. As they pulled from the parking garage, Luke said, "Since we're already in Denver, I was thinking we could hit a movie tonight. What do you think?"

Not her first choice, since she'd rather snuggle up next to Luke on her comfy couch. "I think we should rent a movie, grab some take-out, and go back to my place."

"But *Doomsday* isn't out on video yet," Luke said as he merged onto the freeway and headed toward downtown Denver. He'd been trying to get her to see that movie for the past month, and every time he asked, she refused. A movie about aliens and mass destruction wasn't her type of thing. Not even close—as he knew full well.

"I told you to go to that stupid movie while I was gone," Taycee complained.

"How do you know it's stupid if you haven't seen it?"

"The movie trailer."

"You might like it, you know."

"I really don't think I will."

"*I* think you will. C'mon, Taycee Lynne. For me? Please?"

Taycee hated it when he used her name against her, making it practically impossible to say no. "Fine," she grumbled.

Luke laughed and squeezed her hand. "Relax, I was only joking. There's actually this really cool little cinema that plays older movies." He cast a quick glance her way and cocked an eyebrow. "Want to guess what's showing tonight?"

"No way. Are you serious?" *Sneakers* hadn't been that popular of a movie, at least not in comparison to shows like *Titanic* or *Star Wars*—movies that might draw a crowd. Seriously, who'd pay to see *Sneakers*?

Taycee and Luke, that's who.

"I'm telling you, it's providence," said Luke. "We have to go."

"Agreed."

In no time at all, Luke pulled up to an old-style cinema. Sure enough, the word *Sneakers* was spelled out across a glowing white board in bold black letters. Taycee's head shook at the sight. How did Luke even find this place?

Inside, the seats were shabby and worn, but the theater was clean—and empty. Were they early? "What time does it start?"

"Any minute now." Luke eyed the dimly lit room. "Seriously, Robert Redford has to have more fans than just us."

Taycee laughed as she led him to the center of the room. "I actually love the thought of having this place to ourselves. It's cool. C'mon, let's sit." She tugged him down beside her, instantly annoyed by the armrest that separated them. Her fingers laced through his, and she laid her head on his shoulder.

A few minutes passed, and Luke's foot began to tap against the carpeted floor. He shifted positions and glanced around, and then shifted and fidgeted yet again. It was almost comical sitting beside him, feeling each and every movement. What was he so anxious about?

When he started biting on a nail, Taycee said, "So . . . how about the weather, huh?'

Luke dropped his hand and eyed her with a look of confusion. "What?"

She grinned. "You're acting like a teenager out on his first date. Is something wrong?"

"No."

"Then relax, would you? You're making me nervous."

His foot stopped beating against the floor, but the second the lights dimmed, it started up again. Taycee bit back a laugh. What was up with him? Maybe he'd had too much caffeine.

The screen lit up and turned green as the opening bars of Taylor Swift's "Love Story" floated through the theater. The words "A True Love Story" appeared.

Was this a preview? Taycee hoped so. She loved this song.

As the opening strains of the song filled the theatre, a picture appeared: Ten-year-old Taycee in pigtails, sitting on the back of a horse and clinging to Luke's waist. Taycee gasped as her hand flew to her mouth. What in the world? Luke's hand suddenly felt clammy in hers.

Another picture accompanied the lyrics, this time of Taycee, Caleb, and Luke hanging out at the swimming hole.

The song continued as picture after picture of young Taycee and Luke appeared on the screen. There she was, posing and pointing to her newly affixed braces. Then came Luke, straddling his old dirt bike. Taycee, sitting atop his shoulders after a big football game and holding his helmet high in the air. It was all there. Every single one of her favorite pictures—pictures she'd kept buried at the bottom of her pajama drawer.

Jessa.

As the song continued, the poster for "Shelter's Bachelorette" appeared with Taycee's glamorized face.

Luke's bachelor picture flew into the bottom corner of the screen, followed by more pictures and short video clips of the opening social and their one official date.

It was their story, Taycee and Luke's. Tears stung her eyes, and she let them come, her hand still clinging to his. It was beautiful. Hands down the best movie she'd ever seen.

Taylor Swift's voice faded out, and one last picture of Taycee and Luke appeared, huddled together at the concert at Red Rocks, along with the words, "It's a love story, Taycee Lynne say yes."

Her heart dropped to her feet as she blinked at the words, not daring to hope they meant what they could mean. The chair next to her squeaked as Luke slid to his knee and held out the most beautiful diamond ring she'd ever seen.

"I love you, Taycee Lynne," Luke's voice trembled slightly. "I want to spend the rest of my life with you in Shelter Springs or anywhere else you want to go. Please say you'll marry me."

More tears came. Not trusting herself to speak, Taycee stood and pulled him to his feet, throwing her arms around him and holding on as tight as she could.

"Is that a yes? Because you haven't said anything," Luke whispered in her ear, his warm breath sending a jolt of shivers down her spine.

"Yes," she whispered back. Of course it was a yes.

"Would you mind saying that a little louder? I didn't quite catch it, and this is kind of an important answer."

"Yes!" Taycee choked out as she laughed and wiped at her eyes. She drew back far enough to see into his beautiful brown eyes—eyes she hoped would reappear in one of their future children.

"That's my girl," Luke said, just before his warm lips met hers. Taycee melted against him. A sensation unlike any she'd ever felt careened through her body. It felt like every moment, every memory, every look, every touch, collided into one massive explosion, erupting over her in waves of happiness.

When the pressure of his lips finally eased off, Luke's forehead dropped to hers. He held the diamond ring between them. "Mind taking this off my hands?" he breathed. "I feel a little silly still holding it."

Taycee nodded, and he slipped it onto her trembling finger while she sniffed and laughed simultaneously. She was officially engaged. To Luke. "I love it," she said, her eyes finding his once more. "I love you."

"I love you, too." A hint of a smile touched his lips. Luke gave her hand a gentle tug, cocking his head toward the exit. "What do you say we get out of here?"

"Sounds good to me."

They trotted down the steps and walked hand-in-hand out the door and back to his beat-up truck. As she sat on the cracked and faded upholstery, she watched as he jiggled his keys and walked around to the other side. His easy, confident stride, his broad shoulders, those rich brown eyes.

All hers.

Five months ago if anyone had predicted this day would come, Taycee would have told them they were bonkers. No way would Luke ever move back. No way would she be the bachelorette and he the bachelor on some silly reality dating show. No way would all of her failed attempts to keep her heart safe culminate into the one thing she never imagined possible: Marrying the guy who'd stolen her heart all those years before and had never given it back.

Turned out he didn't have to.

Acknowledgments

There are so many people who have helped me with this book. A big thanks to Wall-to-Wall Books for giving Shelter Springs its name. Buried in Books, for inspiring Sterling's character. Kraig and Nancy, for your hilarious dating stories. Shauna, for sharing your clever and creative brain. And Rachel, for your keen eye and willingness to proofread this book.

To Valorie, Letha, Shelly, Sarah, Lucy, and Cora—the best sisters in the world—for your listening ears, brilliant imaginations, willingness to read my earlier manuscripts, and encouragement. I love you all.

To Braden and Rebecca, you guys rock. I couldn't ask for better critique partners or friends. Thank you for your honesty, your invaluable help, and for being so willing to share your talents with me.

Lastly, to my sweet kids for allowing me the time to write and for wanting to read my books, and to my husband, Jeff, for your love, support, patience, and for picking up the slack when I fall short. I love you.

About the Author

Rachael Anderson is the author of four published books: *Divinely Designed, Luck of the Draw, Minor Adjustments, and The Reluctant Bachelorette.* She's the mother of four and is pretty good at breaking up fights, or at least sending guilty parties to their rooms. She can't sing, doesn't dance, and despises tragedies. But she recently figured out how yeast works and can now make homemade bread, which she is really good at eating. You can find her online at<u>RachaelReneeAnderson.com</u>.

Made in the USA
San Bernardino, CA
19 July 2014